W9-BPJ-278

SPARKS OF DESIRE

It was oddly relaxing, even comforting, Ray thought, to do this kind of work again. He liked working with his hands, liked fixing things. It gave him a sense of accomplishment, a sense of completion. He also liked Sylvie near him, handing him tools, holding the flashlight steady. Liked the way her arm accidentally brushed his from time to time. He shifted his position slightly so those accidents occurred with greater frequency.

"So that's all there is to it?" she asked, surprise filling her eyes. "You just use that thingy to strip the sheath off the wire—"

"That thingy is called a stripper," he corrected patiently. "The wire covering is called the insulation."

"I like sheath better," she said."The stripper and the sheath. Sounds like a box-office hit. Oh no, that would be The Stripper and The Sheik." She grinned in obvious delight. "Anyway, you strip the wire, and when it's naked you put it in this little hole. And it makes electricity. That's it?"

Had she deliberately softened her voice, made it sound sultry? He hoped she didn't know what that kind of voice did to him. If she continued, it could be embarrassing. He swallowed. "Do you want it to be more complicated than that?" he asked, catching her gaze and squelching down impertinent images of making electricity with her. *Watch out,* he cautioned himself. *Talk about making electricity, buddy, and you're playing with serious fire here. Her house might really burn down.*

Ms Alberta Thomann
31704 290th St
Richland, IA 52585-8540

Other *Love Spell* books by Annie Kimberlin:
STRAY HEARTS

Lonely Hearts

Annie Kimberlin

LOVE SPELL BOOKS NEW YORK CITY

LOVE SPELL®

April 1998

Published by

Dorchester Publishing Co., Inc.
276 Fifth Avenue
New York, NY 10001

If you purchased this book without a cover you should be aware that this book is stolen property. It was reported as "unsold and destroyed" to the publisher and neither the author nor the publisher has received any payment for this "stripped book."

Copyright © 1998 by Ann Bouricius

All rights reserved. No part of this book may be reproduced or transmitted in any form or by any electronic or mechanical means, including photocopying, recording or by any information storage and retrieval system, without the written permission of the Publisher, except where permitted by law.

ISBN 0-505-52256-X

The name "Love Spell" and its logo are trademarks of Dorchester Publishing Co., Inc.

Printed in the United States of America.

In Memory of my mother
Grace Adele Drill Bouricius
b. October 24, 1920 d. September 30, 1972

All my thanks to Ann Taylor, who told me that it's our eccentricities that make us interesting; to Paula Montgomery of RUBBER BABY BUGGY BUMBERS for sharing the deep dark secrets of cooking rubber; to Val and Sue at Art on the Block for nurturing my addiction to stamps; to the staff at the Gahanna Post Office for answering my questions; and to Mark, who cheers me on while I slay my dragons.

And most of all, thanks to Zephan and Justis, with my love.

A portion of the author's royalties supports *THE COMPANY OF ANIMALS,* a nonprofit agency that distributes grants to animal welfare agencies providing emergency and ongoing care to companion animals throughout the United States.

Write to Annie at P.O. Box 30401, Gahanna, OH 43230

All of us have dragons. They come in a variety of colors and shapes and sizes. Some of them become our friends; others we merely learn to tolerate. Some of them stay deep in the caves of our hearts. As for the others—well, sometimes we have no choice but to slay those dragons. And each of us must learn to be our own St. George.

LONELY
HEARTS

Chapter One

Oh no! Not again. Sylvie Taylor slumped against the front fender of her car and gazed morosely through the window to the driver's seat where she could see her keys, still in the ignition, dangling just beyond her reach. On the passenger seat she could see the two new bumper stickers she'd just brought home. One read RUBBER STAMPS: *Making the mail more beautiful one envelope at a time.* The other said STAMP OUT NAKED MAIL.

In her yard, Jean-Luc, her white standard poodle, left off his prancing to pose in front of her. He gazed adoringly at her over his shoulder, as if making sure she knew just how wonderful he was, and wagged his tail.

"I know, Jean-Luc. You love me, even if I have

just locked my keys in the car for the gazillionth time." She reached out over the fence to touch the curls on his head. "Thing is, I can't get into the house either. So, we're just stuck here in the yard. Whaddya think about that?"

Jean-Luc's answer was to dance off after a butterfly for a few steps. Then he stopped abruptly and began sniffing the ground, following an unseen trail. He was probably looking for his ball, she thought. Well, a game of ball would just have to wait till she found a solution to her problem.

She turned her attention to her house. What would Princess Delphine do? Well, first of all, the princess was not a scatterbrained dolt who locked her keys in her car, Sylvie thought sourly, purposely ignoring the obvious fact that the princess didn't have a car. Or keys.

"Jean-Luc, come here and help me figure this out. I know the windows are all locked, because I'm sure I checked them before we left. But"—she snapped her fingers in triumph—"I didn't check the upstairs windows." She started off toward the detached garage. "Let's get a ladder and see." But Jean-Luc, hearing the magic word *ladder*, was already standing up inside the gate wagging his tail mightily.

Several minutes later, after finally convincing her dog that he didn't want to climb up after her, Sylvie was on the roof. Her new sandals slipped on the shingles and she lurched, hand out, to avoid a fall. Well, no use complaining about it now; she'd known the sandals weren't practical when she'd gotten them. But she hadn't expected to climb the roof in them.

She carefully picked her way up and over to the first window. It was closed, and wouldn't budge. She toured the roof, checking the other windows only to come up with the same depressing result. She was thoroughly locked out. However, she did discover all sorts of grime ground into the wooden frames. Someday when she needed to work off some serious energy she'd have to come up here with a scrub brush. Cupping her hand on the glass against the glare of the sun, she stared into her upstairs room. She could see her inks, pens, papers and stamps, but couldn't get to them. A fate worse than death, she decided melodramatically.

She wiped her now-dirty hands on the seat of her shorts, then sank down on the hot roof and made a face. Rats! Now what could she do? Well, she told herself philosophically, it could always be worse.

She heard a crash, and a terrified yelp from Jean-Luc.

It was worse.

Heart pounding, Sylvie scrambled swiftly backward down the slope of the roof, scraping her knees on the rough shingles. "Jean-Luc," she called. "Are you all right?"

Then she saw him. Up on his hind legs, proudly pirouetting in his "I'm so very special" dance.

He was all right. She let out a sigh of relief that turned out to be short-lived. At Jean-Luc's feet was the ladder.

"What did you do?" she demanded.

It was a rhetorical question, for everyone who knew her poodle knew Jean-Luc loved climbing ladders. It didn't take a rocket scientist to figure out that he'd tried to climb the ladder and knocked it over. So now she was stranded on her roof, without any means of escape, and her keys were locked in her car. And for what was probably the first time in her life, she'd actually locked all the doors and windows in her house before she'd left. What a time to be efficient. She sighed. Evidently there was a new dragon in the land, come to pester her. "Dragon, thy name is Car Keys Locked In The Car," she muttered.

"Okay, Jean-Luc, I hope you're pleased with yourself. I'll probably die up here, and you'll have to resort to catching field mice and drinking rainwater to stay alive. Unless you learn how to jump over the fence. And that would take a major miracle."

Jean-Luc, looking quite pleased with himself, balanced on his hind feet again, and this time waved a front paw at her.

"Yes, you're extraordinarily cute and absolutely brilliant. But I should have taught you something useful like how to break into my car. Or my house. Or how to track down one of Princess Delphine's knights in shining armor. I know she usually rescues them, but I'd sure like to borrow one to rescue me. Preferably," she told herself, "one who knows how to break into houses or cars."

But Jean-Luc wasn't listening anymore. He was by the fence, on his hind legs, leaning over as far as he could, quivering and wagging his whole body Then he started to woof in excitement.

The woman, along with all of her friends, was completely, certifiably insane. As soon as there was an opening, he would request a different mail route. He wanted to leave The Crazy Lady and her crazy mail as far behind as possible. Just like a bad dream. The pity of it was, he liked this route. It was interesting, and was tree-lined, which made it pleasant in the summer. He'd made several friends along the way, friends who he'd miss. Like little Joshua Martini with whom he'd shared numerous knock-knock jokes since school had let out. But he wouldn't miss this lady. Oh no he wouldn't. This lady, along with every single one of the wacko people who sent her mail, was totally certifiable.

First it was the plastic baseball bat, without any wrapping. No box. Just the thing itself with the address label and postage stuck to it. It was addressed to this Crazy Lady, from one of her equally mental friends. Then it was a beach sandal, but only one of them. He began mentally ticking off the items that had been sent to this woman, unwrapped, in the mail. A whoopie cushion, a pair of scissors, some rubber vomit, a Barbie doll, a toilet plunger, a dog bone. And that was just the beginning of the list. Today it was a can of SPAM. Granted, the SPAM wasn't as heavy as the cast-iron skillet had been, but that wasn't the point. Pieces of mail delivered by the United States Postal Service should be properly packaged. And properly packaged meant the address was clearly written—*not* in rebus form—and easy to read.

Take that envelope he delivered last week. Some of the female postal workers had thought it was lovely. And he might have thought so, too, if it hadn't been going through the United States mail. Of course, as soon as he'd seen it he should have immediately known its recipient. The envelope was covered with a drawing of a living room, in full color, complete with snoozing dog in front of a fireplace. The address—when he *finally* found it—was written in tiny cursive script inside a drawing of a picture frame that hung on the wall over the fireplace.

And the postage. That was another thing. Postage belonged in the upper-right-hand corner. Not scattered all over the envelope, not on the back of the envelope, or in the lower-left corner, or in the middle of the address. Who did these people think they were to have such fun at the expense of the United States Postal Service? They were probably the same people who always complained that the mail was so slow.

He heard the dog before he saw it. He had known she had a dog—the evidence was in the front yard, but the dog had always before been in the house. That was the only good thing he could say for her—that she kept her dog in the house. Now, he could see the barker—a white standard poodle—hanging over the fence, licking the air at him in greeting.

Wait a minute. He knew that dog. It was Jean-Luc, a regular boarder at the vet clinic.

"Hey, Jean-Luc," he called. Then it hit him. Jean-Luc belonged to The Crazy Lady. How did someone as wacky as she was get such a nice dog? He'd always wondered what kind of a weirdo named a poodle after a bald guy. Well now he knew.

Just over the fence where Jean-Luc was carrying on, she saw the mailman coming down the road. Hah! Knight in shining armor indeed! Annoyed, she started mentally playing with words, mailman, male man—now there was a redundancy for you.

He stopped by the fence to scratch Jean-Luc on the head, in just the right spot. *How did he know where Jean-Luc liked to be scratched?* she said to herself. Then, still scratching the dog, who was showing all the signs of complete and abject adoration, the mailman raised his gaze to where it collided with hers. Collided, stuck, locked, and punched her in the stomach. Even from this distance she felt that pierce of connectedness, that sense that she knew this man in some elemental way, that they were destined to play a part in each other's lives.

There had to be some mistake, he thought, staring up at her, aghast. There on the roof was the woman he'd seen two weeks ago at Melissa's wedding. Just as the music was starting, he'd caught some small movement out of the corner of his eye. He'd turned slightly, seen her, and his world had turned upside down. Her auburn hair, with tiny flowers and ribbons tucked into it here and there, was like a frizzy veil, showering down upon her shoulders. Her pixie's face had the barest sprinkling of freckles across the bridge of her delicate nose, and an expression of absolute delight in her eyes. She'd been wearing a filmy sort of dress, lacy and delicate, adding to the ethereal quality about her. She looked like a fairy, a sprite, a sylph. She was the princess of all the fairy tales in his childhood. Then he'd noticed that her hands were green.

He should have realized he was in for trouble. But never in his wildest moments had he imagined trouble this big. The will-o'-the-wisp who he'd tried repeatedly to exorcise from his mind, who had haunted his dreams, flitted around the corners of his consciousness, teasing him, tantalizing him, was The Crazy Lady.

Her sandal slipped. She suddenly, painfully, and inelegantly found herself sitting on her rump. It was the proverbial bucket of cold water dashed on her soul. *Destiny indeed!* she mentally harrumphed. *Don't be absurd, Sylvie, this is not one of Delphine's adventures. Much as you may despair, this is reality.*

"Hello," he called up to her. "Are you all right?" he added after a second, as if he really didn't want to get involved but his mother had drilled manners into him.

He had a slight accent from somewhere on the East Coast—New Jersey maybe.

"Actually, I'm sort of stranded," she called back.

"Sort of? Or actually?"

She frowned. So he was a comic, was he? "Actually. Jean-Luc knocked the ladder down and the windows are locked, so I'm stuck."

"Did you do such a thing?" he asked Jean-Luc with obvious familiarity.

"You seem to know my dog," she said, then instantly cringed, hearing the challenge in her voice and not liking it.

Once again he raised his face to her, and she had a fleeting image of the rays of the sun creating a nimbus about him.

"I deliver mail to the Hartley Vet Clinic. Jessie and Dr. March introduced me to Jean-Luc last winter when he was boarding there. What a nice dog," he added, more to Jean-Luc than to her.

"Yeah, well, this 'nice dog' has a warped sense of humor. He knocked over my ladder."

"It was probably just an accident." He left off scratching Jean-Luc and straightened, one hand on his hip, the other shading his eyes against the glare of the sun, his feet planted firmly on her sidewalk.

She felt a twinge of annoyance. He could at least offer to put the ladder up for her instead of standing there staring at her as if she were painted green. Or as if he thought she might turn into a witch and fly away. Maybe his mother hadn't taught him any manners. This was a case of simple common courtesy. If she'd been walking down the street and found someone stranded on a roof with their keys locked in their car, she'd offer to put *their* ladder back up for them.

"Would you like me to put the ladder back up for you?" he offered.

About time. She bit back any number of scathing comments. Whether this man was destiny or not—and the whole idea of destiny was absurd she reminded herself, that was something that happened in Delphine's imaginary world, not hers—she needed that ladder. Besides, she wanted to see him up close. "That would be nice," she finally said. "I'd appreciate it."

He undid the gate latch and slipped into her yard, careful not to let Jean-Luc escape, she noticed. He easily slung his mailbag off of his shoulder onto the ground and strode purposefully over to the ladder.

Now that he was closer, she could see his features better. He had an interesting face, full of planes and corners. Two dark slashes for eyebrows, short dark hair in the kind of waves that probably felt springy. When he looked up she saw his eyes were a startling blue, a bright blue, a clear blue, almost, but not quite, turquoise. It was a blue that had the simple elegance and multihued beauty of watercolors rather than the homogeneity of markers. She itched to draw this face, to capture it, to make something of it. A sorcerer perhaps, or a prince . . .

"You need a longer ladder," his voice came to her, breaking into her musings. "This one is barely long enough to reach the roof. That's why Jean-Luc was able to knock it over so easily." He set the ladder against the house, pushing against it firmly a couple of times, to make sure it would stay put.

She stared at him dumbly. What was he talking about? And had she really heard a hint of disapproval in his voice?

"The angle from the ground to the roof is too steep to give you any stability." He looked up. "I'll hold onto it while you climb down."

How silly of her to think that he disapproved of her. He didn't even know her. And she didn't know him, so there.

Carefully, because of her slippery sandals, she swung one leg over the gutter and with her foot tentatively reached out for the ladder. The gutters were full of leaves, she noticed in annoyance. Have to clean them out again. Just one more thing she didn't have time to do. She swung the other leg over, conscious of her bare skin, wishing that she had long pants on, feeling somehow vulnerable in shorts. Then, irritated at herself for feeling that vulnerability, she took charge of herself. She was acting like a ninny. He was just the mailman. She caught sight of him holding the ladder steady, and a rush of awareness swept through her. He was the male man, yes, he was a very male man indeed. Get a grip, girl, she told herself sternly. Male man indeed. As if it were some kind of accomplishment.

He noticed that her hands weren't green anymore, and her legs, oh those legs were long and slender. They were coming down right in front of his face, lovely legs, luscious legs, looking smooth and silky . . . He felt his eyes glaze.

Jean-Luc let out a sudden bark, startling her. Her sandal slipped on the rung of the ladder. She felt herself pitching wildly, straining helplessly to grasp at anything that was stable. She was falling. Knocking into something hard. Landing. On top of the mailman. The male man.

Then he was sprawled on the ground and she was on top of him. And he hurt. Badly. He sucked in a sudden breath. It was difficult for there was something heavy on his chest. The pain was so bad he saw red. It took him a moment to realize the hurt was coming from his ankle.

"Are you all right?" Her face was hovering over him. "I'm so very sorry. I'm such a klutz!" Her face disappeared for a second as she scrambled off his chest, but there she was again, concern in her gray-green eyes. "Can I get you something?" She frowned. "No, I guess I can't. I'm still locked out of my house. Damn!"

He wasn't seeing red anymore, and the pain was receding to the proverbial dull roar. It was still excruciating, but somehow he was able to detach himself from enough of the agony to be able to think and to speak coherently. Maybe.

"My ankle," he muttered.

Instantly her face disappeared again, but he felt her hands on his leg. They were surprisingly gentle. "It looks twisted," she reported. "I think you need to get your shoe off. In case it swells, you know."

He squinted against the brightness of the sky and glanced about to see her framed against the light. She was sitting on her heels, a contemplative look on her face. "It might be easier if you let me do it," she said.

Do what? he wondered fuzzily as he felt a furry muzzle nuzzle his cheek. Jean-Luc, he realized.

"Is that okay?" she asked. "Jean-Luc, go away.

Do you want me to take off your shoe? I'll try not to hurt your ankle."

"Sure," he muttered, closing his eyes.

A new and sudden burst of pain. His eyes flew wide open. The Crazy Lady was killing him. He had to get out of here, before she succeeded.

"Almost through," she said cheerfully.

Almost through killing him. He knew he should have traded routes. First it was SPAM, now it was death. All because of The Crazy Lady.

Chapter Two

It wasn't easy, getting that shoe off. Of course, he was a mailman, Sylvie reminded herself. He walked all day and probably didn't know about rosemary foot baths. She tossed the shoe aside and threw a quick glance at his face. His eyes were squeezed closed. Oh no, she had hurt him after all. "I'm sorry, I didn't mean to hurt you," she said apologetically. "But your ankle is really swelling."

"It's okay." His voice was gritty and tight. "No problem."

"Well, I'm afraid it is a problem. You see, I can't drive you to the hospital because my keys are locked in my car, and I can't get in my house to call the EMS squad because my house is also locked. But if you wait here, I'll trot next door to the Mathesons' and see if I can use their phone."

She heard a sudden barking. But it sounded as if it were from inside her house. Sylvie frowned, looking around. "Jean-Luc?" she called.

Jean-Luc's furry head appeared in the living-room window. His mouth was open in a doggy grin and he appeared to be very pleased with himself.

"Jean-Luc, how did you get inside?" Sylvie demanded.

Jean-Luc woofed.

How could he possibly have gotten in? She sifted the possibilities through her mind. Aha! She came up triumphantly with a gem. The dog door. But wait a minute. She'd locked it. She *knew* she had. She specifically remembered locking it. Didn't she?

"Wait here," she told the mailman, "I'll be right back."

Trotting around to the back of the house she saw Jean-Luc halfway out of the dog door, grinning at her.

"You brilliant creature!" she crowed. "What a good boy you are. The good guy dog saves the day. Whaddya think, can I get through that door?"

Jean-Luc seemed very enthusiastic at the prospect of his mom wriggling through his very own door. "I know, I know," she told him. "You've never seen me do this. Well, there's a first time for everything." She scraped her leg on the metal frame of the dog door. "Ouch!" Quick inspection proved no permanent damage. Then she was in.

Running through the house to the front door, she unlocked it, swung it wide open and pushed out, letting the screen door bang closed. The mailman was right where she'd left him.

"Okay, got to get you into my house so I can—"

"No."

"What?" She couldn't possibly have heard him correctly.

"I said, no. Just please, leave me here," he said in a voice that was tight as a spring. "Call the post office, ask for Harvey Schmedlapp. Tell him what happened. He'll send someone right over."

She put her hands on her hips and gaped at him in amazement. "I can't do that."

"Why not?"

"Well—" she sputtered. "It wouldn't be neighborly. It wouldn't be helpful. It would be despicable, that's why. My house isn't the Bates Motel, you know," she pointed out.

She caught his scowl. Maybe he thought her house really *might* be the Bates Motel. Well, sheesh! She was just trying to help.

"I'll be just fine," he practically growled at her. "And I won't be offended."

A low rumble of thunder muttered overhead. Sylvie glanced up at the sky to see dark gray towering clouds racing toward them. "You'll be very wet."

She watched the emotions shift on his face as he, too, saw the thunderheads. He obviously was not happy about the development. Well, too bad. All she wanted to do was help him. Why was he getting all bent out of shape? Because he's a man, she told herself. Men don't like to be in situations where they're not in control. He was not in control, therefore he didn't like it.

"Okay," he said at last. "But you'll have to get my mailbag and bring it in as well."

"Got it," Sylvie sang out as she trotted dutifully across the lawn. She intended to sweep the mailbag up gracefully and whoosh it to safety. She grabbed the shoulder strap and swung. The bag didn't budge. What was in here? Man, oh, man, what kind of muscles did it take to haul one of these things around all day? Surreptitiously she snuck a peek at him. He was watching her, his eyebrows just slashes over those clear blue eyes.

How could she do this under such intense scrutiny? "You're looking at me like my brothers used to."

"How is that?"

"As if you're waiting for me to fail so you can bully me about it." She faced him squarely, legs apart, hands on hips, her stance just daring him to laugh at her.

He did. Well, actually it was more of a pained chuckle. Surprisingly, it sounded nice, deep, soft, and she wondered what his laugh would sound like if he weren't hurting. For an instant she caught a fleeting sense of intimacy with him.

Big whoops! Hold it, Sylvie! First destiny, now intimacy. Change of subject real fast now.

"How do you haul this thing around? What's in here?"

"Cans of SPAM."

"What? SPAM? Really?" *Other* people sent SPAM in the mail? Ignoring the pound of sarcasm in his voice, she surreptitiously peeked inside the bag, edging the flap wider so she could see better.

"You can't snoop in there. It's illegal," he pointed out.

Instantly her hand jerked back out. "I'm not snooping," she lied. "I just wanted to make sure the mail wouldn't get wet." She felt the first light drops of rain on her cheek. "Oh no. Here it comes. This is not going to be pretty," she warned him, "so don't even bother to watch." She felt her face turn red with exertion as she put all her meager strength into dragging the bag across the lawn. Forget trying to carry it. Forget any semblance of grace. He must be incredibly strong. Of course, Princess Delphine would've been able to carry it, no problemo. She would have cast an itty-bitty spell to make it as light as a feather. Well, Sylvie girl, she told herself, reality rears its ugly head once more.

Finally with one last burst of determination,

she hauled the bag up the step to the shelter of her covered front porch and slumped over for a second to catch her breath. Then she scampered down again and over to the mailman.

"Can you lean on me?"

Since he probably outweighed her by a hundred pounds, the suggestion was patently absurd. But, she noticed gratefully as a drop of rain ran down her cheek, he didn't laugh.

Somehow, the two of them working together got him struggling to his feet, and then in a sort of hobble, over and onto her porch where he sank down on her porch swing, out of the rain.

She was staring at him with wide eyes that were full of concern. It made him uncomfortable, and he shifted on the swing. His ankle was propped up on one of those rattan stool things, with a giant-size bag of frozen peas wrapped around it. Frozen peas of all things! She'd insisted on it. Still, he had to admit, she was only trying to help. Yeah, after she had tried to kill him. He closed his eyes, as much to escape the expression on her face as to make himself relax.

"Who do I need to call?"

He kept his eyes closed. "The post office. Ask for Harvey Schmedlapp. Tell him what happened."

By the banging of the screen door he knew she'd gone into the house and he was alone. For a moment he listened to the whooshing sound of the rain on the roof, and from the distance, a grumble of thunder. A slight breeze wafted the delicate scent of lilacs across the porch. Then the rain came running off the side of the roof in a sheet, making a splashing sound on the ground below. Her gutters were obviously clogged. He concentrated on the sounds of the rain, willing his mind away from his throbbing ankle. There was another, softer door bang, and then he felt a wet nose thrust into his hand. He opened his eyes.

"Hi, Jean-Luc," he muttered. "Yup, I really did myself in. No, you don't need to take care of me. I can take care of myself, thank you." Still, he smoothed down the curls on the dog's head. He'd been taking care of himself for years, he thought somberly, and he always would. There was no one else to do it, and hadn't been for a very long time. Foster families, even the good ones—and he'd had a good one—didn't exactly make for a nurtured life. Helen and Phil were good to him, they treated him like their own children. But they just weren't his own parents. No matter how much they tried, no matter how much he'd wanted to believe otherwise, he knew now that he was alone in the world.

Still, if he allowed himself to peer into the seldom visited deepest part of his mind, he would find memories of his mother reading and singing to him at bedtime. Smelling of lavender and roses, she hugged him close, and whispered that she loved him more than anything in the world. Then, he had known without a doubt that he was cherished. But those memories were kept well guarded, away from the light of day, like precious jewels.

Another bang of the screen door, this one loud, demanding his attention. The Crazy Lady was standing in front of him, an innocent smile on her face, a tall glass in each hand.

"I thought you might like some lemonade while you wait. I talked to Mr. Schmedlapp. He said someone would be here in about fifteen minutes to get you. They'd have to get the mail back to the post office before they took you to the hospital. I told him your ankle was really swelling up, and he said I could take you. To the hospital, I mean."

Oh no! "He asked you to take me to the hospital?" How could Harvey do this to him?

"No." There was impatience in her voice, and she waved her hand as if in explanation. "I told him about the swelling and I *offered* to take you to the hospital so you don't have to wait while they take care of the mail." She looked pleased with herself. "He said it was very kind and thank you," she added pointedly when he didn't respond.

He cleared his throat. "Yes, it is kind of you. But I don't want to put you to this trouble." He wasn't going to tell her that he was sure she'd probably find another way to murder him.

"No trouble," she said breezily.

Oh, it'd be trouble for him, he groaned to himself. He had to find some way out of this.

He'd blame it on the bureaucrats. "I need to go with Harvey. I think there's some kind of policy about it. Something to do with liability." He hoped she'd believe him, though he never had been good at lying.

A frown wrinkled her forehead. "Oh. All right. I guess you have a point. I wonder why Mr. Schmedlapp didn't say anything about it. Well, this glass is sweating and my hand is getting wet, so please take the lemonade."

All at once, he saw not The Crazy Lady, but the wispy sprite who had been haunting his dreams. The fine features, clear almost translucent skin, perfect eyebrows perched over perfect moss-green eyes. And her hair, wild and free, all the existing colors of red, scattered about her shoulders. Hair that screamed out danger. And it was wet. Perfectly formed raindrops scattered all over the frizzy stuff.

He took the lemonade, anything to make her stop hovering over him.

Jean-Luc, sitting prettily at her feet, barked.

"Oh, all right, Jean-Luc, here's one for you." The Crazy Lady stuck two fingers in her glass and pulled out an ice cube. She tossed it to Jean-Luc. He caught it on the fly, then settled down to stare off into the distance while he crunched it delicately.

"Your dog eats ice cubes?"

"Yup. He thinks they're a treat. He also loves frozen peas. That's why I always buy giant bags of them." She settled into the wicker chair next to the swing. Next to him.

To put some distance between them, he shifted his gaze down to the glass in his hand. There was a quartered lemon at the bottom, and something purple floating on the top. "What's that?" he asked, not wanting to sound ungrateful, but afraid he did.

"Violets. I think they're pretty with lemonade, don't you? Here, Jean-Luc, have another ice cube. Now lie down. Good boy."

"They're perfectly edible," she continued over the sound of Jean-Luc's crunching. "I usually freeze them inside ice cubes, but I haven't had the chance to do that yet this year, so I just picked some fresh ones."

Jean-Luc grunted from his spot on the porch. The Crazy Lady nudged him with her foot. It was bare, he noticed. And her toenails were painted bright pink. Then he realized what she'd said. She'd just gone outside in the rain to pick violets to put in lemonade? That explained her wet hair. He looked from the violets in his glass to her. She had raised her glass to her lips, but now she paused.

"What?" she asked.

"I've just never heard of putting flowers in lemonade."

"Oh." She sounded surprised. "I've always done it. But only with violets, because they're the prettiest. The dark purple ones, that is. I have white violets, too, but they don't go well with the yellow. I could always use rose petals, I suppose, or nasturtiums, but I like violets the best."

He was right the first time, he thought as he watched her take a sip. She *was* crazy. A poodle named after a bald guy, cans of SPAM in the mail, and flowers in lemonade. He didn't even want to think what other wacky things she might do.

"I have some elder ointment that would be good to put on your ankle, if you'll let me."

"What?!" He sounded terrified, even to himself. This was ridiculous, he thought. "No thank you," he answered stiffly. "I'll wait for Harvey, and he'll take me back to the post office." Then I'll go home, he thought to himself. I'll surely be able to drive in a short while.

"But," she protested, "elder ointment has been used for sprains since—oh, for hundreds of years."

"Not by me."

"Well, of course not, but by your ancestors."

"Not *my* ancestors." He was sure of it.

"Did your ancestors come from anywhere near England?"

He nodded.

"Then chances are they did use elder ointment. It's probably as old as England."

He decided to stall her, take another tack, until Harvey could get there and he'd be safely out of her way. "Which is why it's called *elder* ointment? Okay, tell me. What is the stuff? Any relation to *younger* ointment?"

She chuckled. "Very good. You're quick, even when you're in pain. It's an ointment made from leaves of the elder bush, and red poppy flowers, and some other stuff. Very soothing."

"Probably because of the poppies," he muttered.

"Very likely," she agreed cheerily. "I have some all made up, I'll just get it." She looked ready to scramble out of her chair. "Really, it helps."

She obviously was not getting the picture. "No, thank you." He said the words very clearly and distinctly, so she couldn't possibly misunderstand. "I'll just wait here for Harvey." He realized that he had to find some way to get rid of the bag of peas before Harvey arrived. Even if they *did* make his ankle feel better he wasn't going to let anyone see him attached to a bag of frozen vegetables.

She made a big production of lifting up the bag of peas and scrutinizing his ankle. He braced himself in readiness, but she didn't touch it. "It looks pretty awful," she offered.

He closed his eyes again and leaned his head against the back of the porch swing. "It feels fine, just a little sore," he lied through his teeth. No way was he going to admit how much he hurt. Anyway, it *would* feel better tomorrow, he promised himself. Tomorrow was Saturday.

He'd have the weekend to rest, then he'd be fine. He had always been a good healer.

She didn't answer. In fact, she was silent. Well, that's a first, he thought sourly. But whoa. Wait a minute. She really seemed to be trying to make him feel better and he was behaving like a heel. The wicker from her chair creaked in annoyance. He opened his eyes just enough for a sidelong glance. She'd huddled up in the chair, feet drawn up on the cushion, ankles crossed, arms wrapped around her knees. All the cheeriness was gone from her expression, the sparkle had left her eyes. Now he *felt* like a heel.

As a peace offering, he took a tentative sip of his lemonade. "Hey, this is really good." He took another, fuller swallow.

"You sound surprised," she said somberly.

"I am. What brand is it?"

"Brand?"

"Yeah, you know. What brand of lemonade?"

She mumbled something.

"I didn't catch that." What was wrong with her now? he wondered.

"It's not a brand. It's fresh. Homemade."

He felt his mouth drop open and closed it. "You just made this?"

She nodded.

So that's why there was a quartered lemon in the bottom of the glass. No one had ever made him fresh lemonade before. And then gone out into the rain to pick violets to put in it, even if he did think it was a dumb thing to do. And he'd been treating her as if she were a blight on the earth. Well, she *was* a blight on the earth, but he didn't have to treat her like one. No one had gone to such trouble, any trouble, for him in a very, very long time. He swallowed the great lump that suddenly sprung up in his throat.

"Thank you," he said gruffly. "It is truly excellent lemonade. The best lemonade I've ever had." No response from her. He tried again. "Life gave me lemons, and you made me lemonade."

There, he thought triumphantly, he saw a grin. A Small one, but it was a start.

"I feel responsible for hurting you," she said in a small voice, shrugging her shoulders up as if in supplication. "If I hadn't fallen off the ladder you wouldn't be hurt. The least I could do is make you lemonade. And I only offered to give you some elder ointment because I know it really does work."

"Tell you what, why don't you let me have some to take home. And I'll try it. I promise. Okay?"

A hint of her previous sparkle returned to her eyes.

"Okay."

Chapter Three

The next morning Sylvie carried her mug of tea upstairs to her rubber room. This was the heart of her house, where she created the designs that had made her company, Some Enchanted Rubber, a household name among rubber stampers.

She absently took a sip of tea as she picked up one of the sketches she'd sweated over until the early hours. It was the mailman. Well, it really wasn't the mailman, it was a sorcerer, but his face was unmistakably the face of the mailman. His stance was proud, robe billowing in an unseen wind, arms upraised as if challenging the powers of the universe to deny him anything. Yes, she thought with great satisfaction.

This was a good one. It would make a terrific rubber stamp.

She picked up another drawing, also of the mailman. This time he was a prince, reclining against a cushion, his eyes closed. He appeared to be asleep, but in the lines around his mouth, in the slash of eyebrows, there was a look of unacknowledged pain. The clothes were travel-worn and stained. His fingers curled protectively around the strap of a leather pouch, on the ground, at his side. This one would go wonderfully with the stamp of the succoring maiden, the one where she was kneeling, holding out a bowl of something or other. Yes. She could see it now. The Prince in Pain and the Succoring Maiden. It was as if the two images were meant to be used together. Perhaps with one of the dogs looking on in concern. Maybe a window in the background; she had several castle windows to choose from. Or maybe the crowd of onlookers.

This was the magic, the power, of rubber stamps. People were free to choose their art, free to combine stamps, in an endless number of possibilities, to create entire worlds of their own. And no two pieces of stamped artwork were ever exactly the same.

So. It was a done deal. These two new designs would go in her next supplement. "The question is, Jean-Luc," she said to her poodle, at her feet, as always. "How can I incorporate them into the Adventures of Princess Delphine? Let's see, Delphine, along with her faithful canine companion, Halcyon, can come across a prince hurt in the woods, so of course they'd have to care for him. After all, the princess has a savior complex. But then, Jean-Luc, my very own faithful companion, how does the wizard come into it? Is he a good wizard or a bad wizard? What's the relationship of the prince and the wizard? They look alike, so they're obviously related. Brothers? And my other new design, the one of that dragon. Where does the dragon come into all this? Perhaps the prince was hurt while trying to slay the dragon."

One of the things that made Sylvie's stamp company unique was the ongoing adventures of the Princess Delphine and her faithful companion, Halcyon, that introduced every new stamp. Sylvie put out a catalog every year, and then every three months she put out a supplement of new stamp designs—and the newest installment of the story. Stampers loved her story. Some of them even wrote to her suggesting possible stamps and story twists. Well, she had her new stamps—the dragon, the wizard, the prince, and a couple of others. But she had to come up with names for these new characters. Names.

Oh my goodness! She had no idea what the mailman's name was.

She'd never even introduced herself. There hadn't been time. Mr. Schmedlapp had driven up as soon as she'd handed the mailman the pot of elder ointment. He'd thrown a hasty thanks over his shoulder as he hobbled out into the rain, to the truck, leaning heavily on the Schmedlapp's arm. That was the last she'd seen of the mailman. The male man.

Suddenly, she had to find out who he was, to find out how he was doing, what the doctor had said. After all, it was really her fault he'd been hurt. She would call the post office. But wait—Jessie! He said he delivered mail to the clinic, and knew Jessie and Melissa.

Letting her drawings flutter to the table, she raced downstairs to the phone. She knew the number by heart.

"Hartley Veterinary Clinic."

"Hi, Suzette, this is Sylvie. Is Jessie free?" She put her hand down on the counter. The sticky counter. It was sticky from the sugar she'd spilled last night while making lemonade, only the sugar wasn't in granular form anymore, it was goo. She poked at it with a finger. It had mixed with dripped lemon juice and was now a dried smear of sticky yuck. She grabbed a dish-rag, got it wet, wrung it out, and slopped it on top of the dried sugar. That would soften it. She'd wipe it up later.

Jessie's voice came on the phone. "Hi, Sylvie. Going away again? Do we get that great guy dog for the weekend while you jet off to some far-away place and hawk your stamps?"

"No, nothing like that. Not until next month.

Say, Jess, you know that person who delivers your mail?"

"Ray?"

"Is that his name?" She tried to sound casual.

"Tall, sort of rangy, dark curly hair, drop-dead gorgeous blue eyes, wonderful sense of humor but sort of shy?"

Shy? He hadn't seemed shy yesterday. He'd been rather grouchy, but then, he was hurt—and besides the rest fit. "Yeah. His name is Ray? Do you know his last name?"

"It's Novino. Ray Novino."

There was silence for a second or two, before Jessie spoke again. "Say, Sylvie, are we . . . ahem . . . interested in Ray?"

"No!" Sylvie protested. "Of course not. And get that sly tone out of your voice right now. Nothing like that at all. He just got hurt in my front yard yesterday, and I want to find out how he's doing."

"Hurt?" Sylvie could almost hear Jessie's ears perk up. "How hurt?"

"He sprained his ankle. At least I hope he only sprained his ankle."

"How'd he do that? I know you don't have any gopher holes in your yard. And Jean-Luc wouldn't trip him, Jean-Luc likes him."

"No, nothing like that. I, um, I sort of fell on top of him."

Another silent pause, then a low whistle. "You fell on top of Ray? Man, oh, man, I'd sure like to fall on top of him. Studly, yes, but I like him, too," she camped in a very faux-Irish, femme-fatale accent.

Sylvie felt her face turn red. Good thing Jessie wasn't here or she'd really never hear the end of it. "It wasn't like that, silly. I was climbing down my ladder, I slipped, and I fell on top of him."

"Okay, spit it out. The whole story this time, not just the good parts version. Believe me, though, falling on top of Ray must've been a great big good part."

"Stop it!" Sylvie pleaded, chuckling in spite of herself. She told Jess the whole story. What there was of it, which wasn't much, she reflected. "Anyway," she ended, "I want to find out how he's doing."

"Yeah. I *really* believe you. Okay. Have it your way. Say, you wanna know where he lives?"

"Sure." She tried to sound as if it didn't really matter one way or another. She didn't think she succeeded.

"You know that corner apartment on the other side from mine? The one with all the roses? The one that faces the park? That's Ray's. And, before you ask," she teased, the grin sounding clearly in her voice, "the answer is yes. He lives alone. Now, Sylvie, go forth and—um . . . make sure you have a very good time. Just don't forget to tell your auntie Jess all about it. Oh, wait'll I tell M'liss that you have the hots for Ray. She'll die! We've wanted him to find someone for just ever."

"Jessie," Sylvie wailed. "I don't have the hots

for him! I just feel responsible for what happened. I just want to make sure he's okay. Nothing else, not at all. No hots. You know how I feel about romantic relationships. They don't work."

"Sure, Sylvie. Anything you say."

Hanging up the phone, Sylvie realized she probably shouldn't have called Jessie at all. Jessie was a dear friend, but had a bizarre sense of the romantic. Oh well, no use fretting. What was done was done. And speaking of things to get done, she had to do some chores and put some more elder ointment in a jar, to take over to Ray.

She turned his name over and over in her mind. Ray. What an evocative name. A slice of sun piercing the darkness, carrying light, like a promise, through the clouds. A ray—the vehicle through which life-giving light came to earth. Shadows and colors and light. She was an artist. Light was very important to artists.

Suddenly she realized she was staring at the phone. Where was her mind today? Let's see. She would take him the ointment, and a loaf of that onion herb dill bread—she had some in the freezer—and she'd make a card. Yes! That was it. She'd make him a one-of-a-kind-rubber-stamped-hope-your-ankle-is-better card. She turned abruptly, called for Jean-Luc to follow, then trotted back upstairs to her rubber room.

Jean-Luc curled up on his bed, his favorite teddy bear between his paws.

"Good boy," Sylvie praised him. "I'm going to make Ray a card. If I need you to help, I'll let you know."

Jean-Luc licked his nose. Sylvie knew it was his way of agreeing.

She quickly surveyed the shallow shelves, filled with the three thousand plus rubber stamps, which lined the walls. She picked out her ladder stamp, and that one of the falling woman. A house that could pass for her house. Hmm, which poodle should she use? She didn't have a mailman stamp, but one of the ordinary men would probably work if she colored his clothes blue, and over here were several tiny stamps of postcards and letters. On to the section of shelves that held weather stamps. She needed some towering clouds in the sky, threatening rain. What color inks would be best? She pulled open the drawer where she kept her ink pads arranged first by type of ink, and then by color. She chose grays, blues, and greens for the grass and trees. Oops! She almost forgot her lilac bush. Grab that stamp and some purple inks.

Purple and blue reminded her of a bruised ankle. Ankle! She waltzed over to her shelves of body parts and picked out a big foot-and-ankle stamp for the inside of the card.

When she had assembled her stamps, inks, pencils, and decided on just the right paper, she gave herself mood music. Sgt. Peppers on the CD player. Singing along loudly and off-key about the Lonely Hearts Club Band, Sylvie started on the card. Intent, excited, full of anticipation. It would be perfect! He would love it.

He took the card that she held out to him. He recognized the scene right away, of course. The ladder, the poodle, the falling woman, the man looking up, even the lilac bush. When he glanced down at her—she barely reached his shoulder—he also couldn't miss the look of expectation in her uptilted face. She evidently expected him to say something.

"Where did this come from?" he asked.

"I made it," she announced.

She made it? "How?"

"Stamps. I'm a rubber stamp artist. Surely you've noticed the envelopes I get, and the ones I send. And it's my business, you know."

"What is?"

"Rubber stamps. I own a rubber stamp company. You know. Some Enchanted Rubber. It's my company."

He shifted his weight on the crutch, hopping a bit, trying not to jar his hurt ankle. She clutched a large paper bag in her arms, she'd shifted it a couple of times since they'd been standing there. It looked like it might be heavy. He should offer to take it from her. After all, he had been drilled with manners when he was growing up. He should invite her inside. As if he were a normal friendly man, and she were a normal friendly woman.

He sighed. He didn't want her in his house. He didn't want anything to do with her. This time he really was going to get her—the sprite he'd seen at Dr. March's wedding—out of his mind. He had to. She was—his thoughts came to a screeching halt. He'd been about to tell himself she was driving him crazy.

Stalling for time, he opened the card. Inside, under the image of a purplish-bluish foot, in lovely handwriting—handwriting that if possessed by the general population and used on all their mail would make his life much easier, thank you—were the words, *Short ladders cometh before a fall. Thank you for rescuing me. Sylvie Taylor. P.S. Jean-Luc also says thanks. You saved him from a dismal future diet of nothing but field mice.* Under the words was a paw print.

"See," she pointed with her chin. "Jean-Luc signed it, too."

He really didn't want to do this, but he had no choice. After all, he owed it to Helen, his foster mother, to do her proud in social situations. "Do you want to come in for a minute?"

"Sure," was her chipper reply. "I brought you some goodies."

"More frozen peas?"

"Is that sarcasm I hear dripping from your tongue?"

She was sure a saucy little thing.

"Jean-Luc and I are friends," he pointed out

reasonably. "I just don't want him thinking he has to guard his treats from me."

When she chuckled, he inexplicably warmed to the sound. He discovered an answering smile coming from somewhere deep inside, a smile that would explode if he didn't let it out.

"Wow!" she said in mock amazement. "You can actually smile. Cool!"

He shrugged. "Not much to smile about in the last twenty-four hours."

Instantly, all amusement vanished from her face. He found himself fascinated by the way her eyes got large and wide. The way her hand flew to her mouth. "Oh, I'm sorry. I forgot to ask. How's your ankle?"

"It's fine," he lied. "I just need to keep off it for a couple of days."

But she didn't go away. She continued to gaze up at him, as if waiting for something, as if expecting something. Then he remembered. He'd invited her in. Into his house.

He was going to regret this. Big-time regret coming up.

He turned clumsily, trying not to trip himself with the crutch, and held open his front door. "Come in."

Chapter Four

She heard the music as soon as she stepped into the hall. She found herself following the sound, as Jean-Luc usually followed the scent of a dog cookie. "The Brandenbergs," she said.

"You like Bach?"

"Don't sound so surprised. Just because I like the Beatles, and Rodgers and Hammerstein, and Puccini—even if he does write totally romantic slop, but it is just so gorgeous—doesn't mean I don't know Bach when I hear him," she teased. "In fact, I can recognize Bach at ten yards."

When he chuckled again, a warm liquid feeling sluiced through her. What was it about him? She had to stop this before it got out of hand. Control this sudden urge to touch him, to feel him, to explore him tactilely. She could see his eyes begin to soften, begin to grow friendly, could feel the first threads of friendship grow and expand, becoming stronger and more resilient, as if it were a palpable thing, shimmery and sparkling, warm and alive.

"How did you learn about music?"

She stood in place, turning slowly to see the room while she answered. "Oh, the usual, you know. I grew up with music in our house. My mother liked Brahms, my father liked Gershwin. My brothers liked Rachmaninoff and Chopin respectively. But I think Gareth, my middle brother, only liked Chopin because no one else in the family did. It was his way of revolting. Wow!" She'd caught sight of his bookshelves and took the shortest distance to them. "You have some good books here. Browning, Byron, Shelley. Hey, don't you like any American poets? Where's your sense of patriotism?" She grinned at him over her shoulder. "And you work for the government. Do they know you read only British poets? And dead ones at that." She waggled her eyebrows at him. "You might be a spy, disguised as a mailman."

"Do you ever take anything seriously?"

"Not on Saturdays. Saturdays are my days to play." Then, seeing that he was still holding the bag that he'd taken from her, awkwardly because of his crutches, she plucked it out of his arms. "Let me show you the goodies I brought." She looked around. His apartment had so much virgin wall space. She could do wonderful things on all these walls! "This is mostly food-type stuff—except for the elder ointment—so can I take it into your kitchen?"

"Make yourself at home," he said dryly.

"Thanks, I will." But she had already peeked through a doorway and discovered the kitchen. "Here it is. Now, look." She took the bag and breezed through the doorway. "Oh, what a nice kitchen. I like the clean counter look. My kitchen always looks like a preschool class just made their own sandwiches in it. And then ate them there."

"What kind of sandwiches?"

"Whatever. You never can tell with preschoolers. My brother Florian—the one that likes Rachmaninoff—has three kids. Five, four, and two. They think food is wearable." She reached in the bag and brought out the elder ointment in a small canister. It was one of her favorites, painted as a Persian miniature. "Now, special herbal tea. You need to drink it twice a day for a couple of days. It'll make your ankle feel better. And this—" Suddenly she popped herself on the forehead. "I completely forgot. What did the doctor say?"

"Is this a joke or something?"

She frowned. "Joke? No. No joke. The doctor. What did he say? I assume it was a he, though I don't really mean to be sexist. Lots of doctors are women, look at Melissa."

"She's a vet."

"That's a doctor. But what did your doctor say?"

"About my ankle?"

She was not going to let him exasperate her. She really wasn't. "Yes," she said with deliberate politeness. "Your ankle. What did the doctor say about your ankle?"

"They gave me a pair of crutches and told me to call back if it wasn't better by the end of the week."

"But that's awful!" she burst out. He sounded so unconcerned about it, so blasé, as if a sprained ankle were on the same level as a hangnail.

"Why?"

"Because it must hurt like the dickens. And here I'm making you stand on it."

The look of genuine concern on her face was like a little poke at his soul. He'd not let anyone care for him in years, since he'd left Helen and Phil's home when he graduated from high school. It was nice, in a strange sort of way, that someone, anyone, was fussing over him. And was taking him by the arm and guiding him, gently but firmly, to the chair. And if he leaned just a speck closer to her he could smell her elusive scent, something with roses in it. He could almost catch it. He leaned toward her. There it was.

His eyes shot open wide. His heart slammed in his chest. He felt himself almost falling into the chair. It was a scent from his childhood, one he'd thought he'd forgotten, one that he'd never thought to encounter again. It was the scent his mother always wore.

He'd read somewhere about some psychologist who said that scents are among the most powerful memory triggers in the world. Well right now memories upon memories of his mother were flooding his senses. And with them came washing over him the most intense sense of loss.

"Gee, it must hurt a lot. You turned absolutely white." Her voice made its way through the mist that seemed to embrace him. "Let me make you some of this tea. Where do you keep your cups? I can nuke some water in your microwave and it'll be done in a jiffy."

He shook his head, trying to clear it, shake the mist down to the bottom. "In the cupboard by the sink," he made himself say. He willed his heart to return to a normal beat, breathing slowly and steadily. There. That was better. As if from a distance he watched her open the cupboard and raise up on her toes to select a mug. He concentrated on her long legs, this morning in worn blue denim, making himself focus on the here and now instead of on the long ago. She left the cupboard door open, moved to the sink, and turned on the tap. She let the water run, testing it with her finger every couple of seconds. Finally it evidently met with her approval.

"You know, you shouldn't drink the water that comes from the tap first thing. It's more likely to contain all sorts of nasties and stuff that it's picked up from the pipes while it's been sitting there. That's why you need to run the water until it gets cold. Because that's the water that hasn't been sitting in the pipes in your house."

"But it's been sitting in the city pipes," he pointed out, feeling as if he'd conquered his emotions, or at least suppressed them. "And that might be worse."

She set the timer on the microwave, punched the start button, then faced him, leaning back against the sink, her eyes sparkling. "Yeah. I know. That's a scary thought, isn't it. I comfort myself by thinking that surely enough people use water every day to keep it moving so it doesn't pick up all sorts of uglies."

When she shrugged expressively, he realized how tiny she was, how he could put his arms around her and actually crush her to him. Wait a minute! Where did that thought come from? Send that thought right out the window. Post-paid.

"But," she continued cheerfully, "if the uglies don't get us that way, they'll find another."

Here was a safe topic. "You think they're out to get us?"

"Not consciously out to get us, I don't think the uglies of the world have consciousness. But it's not nice to fool Stepmother Nature, you know. Too many cancers floating around looking for a home. And cancer is not a nice houseguest."

Her voice had changed. The cheer was gone, replaced by a somber tone, one of regret, and he thought he could barely detect a good bit of well-hidden pain. He had no right to pry, he wasn't even interested, he told himself. But he couldn't leave it there. So he spoke. "Sounds as if you know."

She raised her eyes to meet his, and it was as if he were gazing into a crystal-clear pool, and he could see all the way down to the bottom of her soul. "When I was fifteen my mother died from cancer."

Now why did she tell him that? she asked herself sternly. She didn't go around telling people that. At least, she didn't ever *mean* to tell people. It wasn't a secret or anything, just something she didn't usually mention. But she had. To this man. And now, it was time to change the subject before she started thinking about her mother's death. That would be disastrous.

"So," she forced cheer into her voice. "Have you ever had chamomile tea before?" She busied herself rustling around in the paper bag to find the jar of tea leaves. "It's what Peter Rabbit had after his adventure in Mr. MacGregor's garden. It's not as awful as it sounds, especially with a spoonful of honey in it. I brought you a jar of honey in case you didn't have any." She realized she was babbling, and he probably thought she was a complete ditz, but it kept her mind occupied. And away from thoughts of her mother. "I know the honey is in here somewhere." She rummaged around in the bag so she wouldn't have to look at him.

"No violets?"

She pulled her head out of the bag and found him watching her with an amused expression.

She pulled herself up to her full five-foot-five inches. "Are you teasing me?" she challenged, meeting the twinkle in his eye with one of her own.

"Yes."

It threw her off balance. She found herself chuckling. "I didn't expect you to admit it. My brothers never would've."

"Great ones for teasing?"

She nodded. "Especially Florian. He said it was the responsibility, the patriotic duty, of the eldest brother to unmercifully tease any sister that might be born to the family."

"But you love him," he said pointedly.

She looked quizzically at him.

"Your tone of voice says you love him, and the way you're standing."

A sense of wonder stole through her. For some reason he'd taken off his defensive armor. She nodded to herself. Yup. Now she could see why Jessie was so enthusiastic about him. "You are a very perceptive man. And you're right. I do love him. I adore both of my brothers, and my dad. I know that they love me. I am truly lucky to have them."

The microwave dinged. The water was hot. Time to make tea.

Several hours later, Ray sat again at the kitchen table. Glaring at a mug of the alleged tea. It was the most vile-tasting stuff he'd ever been bullied into drinking. Nothing, not even the promised honey, could mask the sickening sweet taste. The stuff could probably be of some use as a secret weapon. Perhaps a new form of torture. *"If you don't talk ve vill pour zees tea down your zroat. Zen you vill tell us vat ve vant to know."* He could see it now. He hobbled over to the sink and poured the offending liquid down the drain. It would probably wipe out all the nasties lurking in his pipes.

He would never tell her he dumped it, of course. He'd promised to make a fresh cup in the evening, and then again tomorrow morning. But behind his back his fingers had been crossed. Just in case.

The cut-glass jar of tea leaves was still on his table. He reached out to examine the label tied with a bright red ribbon around the top. The label was done with more of what he now knew was her artwork. Vines entwined around the border, delicate, fragile, just as she was. The words *Chamomile Tea* written in her clear handwriting. Should be called *Sylvie's Witch's Brew*, he thought pointedly.

Hefting the jar in his hand, he considered his kitchen. The cupboard door was still open, she'd never closed it. There was a splatter of water on the counter she'd not wiped up. There was a scatter of bread crumbs, and the cutting board—and that bread. Nothing wonderous about that bread. He shuddered. It had *things* in it. Green things. She said it was onion herb dill bread. Still, he had to admit it didn't taste as awful as the tea. In fact, the bread was actually good—as long as he didn't think of it as bread.

He put his kitchen to rights and made his way into his living room where things were also out of place. Some of his CDs were in an unruly stack, not neatly arranged on the rack. Books had been pulled out, looked through, then shoved back in, without evening them up at the edge of the shelf.

How had she managed to create such chaos in just a couple of hours? And, the greater question, why had he let her? It wouldn't do to pursue that line of thought. After all, she was just being helpful. As she said, she felt responsible for his sprained ankle. That was all there was to it.

He gathered the errant CDs, and put them on the rack, by composer. This was why he liked living alone. He could keep his life arranged, orderly, under control. And quiet. He valued his quiet life. She was not quiet. Nothing calm about her, from the riot of her red hair to the cheerful slap her sandals made on his polished wooden floors. Her voice was bright, energetic, and she laughed easily. She hummed to herself while she was cutting the bread, making that awful tea. She sang snatches of songs, looking up at him expectantly, obviously inviting him to join in. But he didn't know the words to her songs. She was noisy all right. But she was gone now, and once more there was peace. Once more there was quiet. Chaos became order.

Then what was this nagging, unfamiliar sense that hovered around the edges of his being? He looked at that sense, turned it over and over in his mind until he knew what it was. It was loneliness.

She hadn't meant to stay that long, she thought as she drove home through the late afternoon. At Ray's apartment. She'd only gone over to take him the card and more elder ointment. After all, it was her fault that he'd sprained his ankle. But somehow they had managed to negotiate an unspoken truce. In fact, she had found him to be surprisingly pleasant company. He was bright, witty, and had a delightfully droll sense of humor—though he'd probably bristle at being described as 'delightful.' Yes, she could see why Jessie and Melissa were so fond of him. She could become fond of him herself. She always welcomed a new friend in her life.

Well, friends needed to be taken care of.

"Let's see," she said out loud to herself. "The tea is good. What else will help his ankle? Rosemary foot baths to soak in? Yes. That sounds right. I can take all the stuff over tomorrow. That'll make his ankle feel better in no time."

But he was going to be nothing more than a friend. Friendship was all she wanted from people. It didn't do to fall in love with one's friends. Because when the romance was over—and the romances were always over eventually, it was only a matter of time—one ended up losing not only one's lover, but one's friend as well. She didn't want to lose anyone. Not ever again.

Sylvie Taylor's First Law of Relationships was simple. Friendships are fine, but no romance allowed.

Chapter Five

"I hear you fell on top of Ray," her friend Karen said.

"Does everyone in the Greater Hartley Metropolitan area already know what a klutz I am?" she asked, exasperated. "Or is there someone Jessie actually missed telling?"

She and Jean-Luc were next door, at what Karen fondly called her farm, enjoying the late-morning sun by the pond. Well, she and Karen were by the water. Jean-Luc and Karen's troop of currently six Newfoundlands, were in the pond, engaging in a variety of doggy water activities. There was a game of what appeared to be Canine Marco Polo going on with a big, brightly colored beach ball, a game of tug, and some general swimming. Brian Boru, Karen's largest Newfie, was in the shallow end of the pond, nosing around under the water for something, anything, that might prove to be interesting.

"I don't think Jessie has told everyone yet," Karen said. "Besides, the Greater Hartley Metropolitan area consists of only about thirty thousand people, and a lot of cats and dogs and cows—at least in the surrounding parts. Now when you compare the human population of Hartley to the population of the United States, I really don't think there's a great number of people who know you're a total klutz."

"Is that supposed to be comforting?" Sylvie asked as a waterlogged Newfoundland slogged his way to them wagging a sopping tail.

"Yup," her friend answered cheerfully. "Good boy, Brian," she praised the dog, patting him on his wet head. "What a good boy to find a stick under the water." The wagging became more enthusiastic. "Yes, it's a lovely stick."

Brian dropped the stick in her lap, then shook his massive, furry, and very wet body, slinging droplets of water and slobber over an area at least the size of Rhode Island.

"Yuck," Karen muttered under her breath. She threw the stick into the pond. "Go get it," she told him in her cheer-the-dog-on voice.

The big dog lumbered off congenially.

From out in the pond Jean-Luc whipped his head around. Jean-Luc loved to play retrieve.

He plowed his way through the water, up the shore and to the women.

"He heard the magic words," Sylvie warned her friend.

"Do you want to play, too, Jean-Luc?" Karen asked the dripping dog. She reached into the bag next to her and pulled out a tennis ball. "Here, go get it," she sang out as she threw the ball into the pond.

Jean-Luc was off like a shot.

"Didja ever notice how they move so differently?" Sylvie asked lazily. "I mean, poodles and Newfoundlands. Different as night and day. Jean-Luc is fast and fleet. The Newfs always look like they're moving in slow motion."

"Didja ever notice how you always bring up my dogs when you want to change the subject?" Karen answered just as lazily.

Sylvie turned to look at her friend. Though Karen's voice may have sounded lazy, her eyes were anything but. She shrugged. "I guess *I am* trying to change the subject," she admitted.

"Why?"

"Don't be so nosy," she said with the privilege of a long friendship.

"It's genetic," was the chipper reply. Brian brought back the stick and she threw it again.

"Yeah, you and Roger just have inquiring minds and you just have to know."

"So tell me."

"Tell you what?"

"I want your version of falling on top of Ray.

I heard Jessie's, but I'm sure the truth isn't nearly as salacious as she made it out to be."

"The truth never is."

"Sad but true."

Sylvie was confused, a not unusual state. "Do you mean the truth is sad, or it's sad that it's not as salacious as Jessie made it out to be?"

"Whichever." Her friend threw her a grin. "Just tell me. I'm a big girl. I can hear the truth and not think less of you for throwing yourself at men. Or on top of men, as the case may be."

"Speaking of throwing, here you go, Jean-Luc," Sylvie said. Her dog flew off after the ball. "Thing is, Karen, I want to talk about it, and at the same time I don't."

"Ah," her friend said wisely. "You mean your feelings are ambivalent."

"Oh no," she groaned in mock despair. "Not the psychological stuff. You're not at work now, you're being my friend."

"Can't help it. It's an occupational hazard. Sort of like you going around with ink all over your hands."

Sylvie examined her hands. Karen was right. There were splotches of green. "I was using some permanent ink this morning," she explained. "Working on my new supplement. Oh, Karen, I have this gorgeous new dragon, and a sorcerer, and a—"

"I'm sure your new stamps will be a big hit, they always are. So let's get back to your feelings of ambivalence. Are you confused about what happened? Or about your feelings about what happened? Tell Dr. Matheson all about it."

"The one thing I'm *not* confused about," Sylvie grumbled good-naturedly, "is that Dr. Matheson should go jump in the pond with all her dogs."

"Feeling a bit aggressive, are we?"

Sylvie chuckled. Her friend was a true idiot. And a true friend. "I like Ray," she finally admitted.

"This is confusing? It's good to like people. We're supposed to like people. It's partly the result of a well-socialized childhood. You introduce the child to a variety of friendly people, in positive situations, and the child grows up feeling comfortable around people."

Sylvie rolled her eyes. "You sound like you're talking about puppies."

"Puppies, children. Very similar. Except puppies are easier to housebreak."

Sylvie snorted.

"Okay," her friend offered. "I'll cut the dog-trainer-person-psychologist routine. I'm just your buddy now. Why are you confused about liking Ray?"

"Because I don't want to like him."

"Now *this* makes sense." Her friend nodded sagely as she threw the stick again for Brian Boru and then wiped her wet hand on her jeans. "Of *course* you don't want to like a man you just fell on top of. I mean, you can't spend your life falling on top of men and then ending up liking them. Why, civilization as we know it would simply collapse."

"I hope you don't treat your patients like this," Sylvie pointed out. "I hope you take them much more seriously than you take me. And I'm your friend. I deserve a little respect here."

"So tell me why you don't want to like him."

"Because I don't believe in romantic relationships. You know that." She again heaved the soggy ball for Jean-Luc. Her dog joyfully hurtled after it.

"Aha. It's becoming clear now. You mean you don't just like him, you mean you *like* him. As in oo-la-la like."

Sylvie nodded her head miserably. "And I don't want to." She pulled up a piece of grass, held it to her lips, and blew. The grass shrilled.

"Because you think he'll leave."

"Yeah."

"I've heard this before you know."

"You have?"

"Yup. From you. You have a fear of people leaving you. Especially men, for some reason. I've never quite figured that part out." Karen plucked a piece of grass and tried to blow through it. "I wish I knew how you did that." She threw the grass down in disgust and turned back to Sylvie. "You seem to think if you never fall in love then you'll never feel the pain of losing someone you love. But think about this. There are several people you love. There's Melissa, and Jessie," Karen ticked them off on her fingers. "And Madeleine, and Sally, and even me."

"Yeah, but you're my friends. It's different with men."

"It's a different kind of love, I'll give you that, but it's love just the same. And Sylvie, if you lost one of us, one of your best friends, you'd feel the same pain you're trying to avoid by not becoming romantically involved with men."

Sylvie abandoned her grass harp and picked a clover. She pulled it apart, all the little thingies, whatever they were called, one by one.

A sopping tennis ball was dropped in her lap. She looked up from the clover to see Jean-Luc prancing on his hind legs enticing her to throw the ball again. She dropped the mutilated clover and obliged him.

"You can't spend your life trying to avoid the pain of living," Karen said. "Take my word for it. Every day I see people who try to do just that. It is not healthy. Speaking of healthy, it's time for lunch." She stood up and scanned the pond.

"C'mon, dogs!" Karen called. "That's enough! Out of the water."

"Let's go, Jean-Luc," Sylvie yelled to her dog, scrambling to her feet.

The Newfoundlands sloshed heavily out of the pond. Jean-Luc, swimming proudly with the ball in his mouth, pointedly ignored Sylvie. He turned around to swim farther into the pond.

"Jean-Luc Picard Taylor, get out of the water now!" Sylvie ordered.

Her dog looked over his shoulder at her. She could see him considering his options. Beside her, Karen chuckled.

"I have a cookie for you," she bribed her recalcitrant dog.

Jean-Luc turned around and swam for shore.

"You better work on 'come' before you start taking him to Tanner's agility classes," her friend advised.

"Yeah, I guess it's back over to see Tanner for a few refresher lessons. I wish he'd obey me without bribes," she said wistfully.

"You've created a Frankenstein there. You should've named him Shelley."

"But Frankenstein was the doctor, not the monster," Sylvie pointed out. Then a thought struck her. "What would you say about someone who only reads poetry written by dead poets?" Jean-Luc finally climbed out of the water, shook himself soundly, and trotted up the slight bank to sit in front of Sylvie. He wanted his cookie.

"Gee," her friend teased. "How'd they write poetry if they were dead?"

Sylvie groaned. "I mean," she said carefully, "they wrote their poetry when they were alive, but were now dead. What would you think if someone only read poetry by people who were now dead?"

"That they had good taste in poetry."

"I'm serious," she protested, scrounging in her pocket for a piece of dry cat food, Jean-Luc's version of a cookie.

"So am I. Leave it, Hetch!" Karen called. The elderly dog named Hetch Heckety left off his nosing and trudged drippingly toward them.

Sylvie sighed deeply. Would she ever be taken seriously by her friends? One of the Newfoundlands, a young male named Dinny Burns, stuck a very soggy head under her hand. She scratched obligingly. "Six wet Newfs. Six wet Newfs," Sylvie sang to the tune of "Three Blind Mice" as they, surrounded by the wiggling herd of sopping dogs, headed up to the farmhouse.

"So what would happen," Karen asked as she leaned against the counter in her sun-splashed kitchen. She spread out several pieces of homemade bread on a plate as she spoke. "What would happen if you and Ray were to become friends?"

Sylvie stepped over a still wet, snoring and snoozing Newfoundland—it was Andalucia, who Karen had rescued from a neglectful home. Brian Boru was stretched out in the doorway, breathing noisily in his sleep. After a handful of frozen peas from the stash in Karen's freezer, Jean-Luc had commandeered the couch in the living room, while the rest of the dogs were scattered throughout the house sleeping off their water adventure. Sylvie set two spoons decisively on the handwoven place mats. "I told you, I don't want to be friends with him."

"You said you didn't want a romantic involvement with him. That's different from becoming friends. What if you left out the romance and became friends?"

"We'd end up romantically involved. He's that kind of guy. And it would be spectacularly marvelous for a while." She noticed more than a hint of wistfulness in her voice. She didn't like it. "And then," she finished briskly, "he'd leave."

"You seem so sure about that."

"Sure as spit."

"So you're not even going to give him a chance to prove you wrong?"

"Don't need to," Sylvie said, pouring the mint tea. "It's certain as taxes." There was silence. She looked up to see her friend gazing at her shrewdly. It made her squirm. "Why are you looking at me like that?"

Karen set the plate of bread down on the table, then opened the refrigerator. "I want to know what has convinced you that he'd leave."

"I saw his house."

"Well, what was wrong with it? Did it have dirt floors or something?" Head in the refrigerator, she handed Sylvie a bowl of egg salad.

"It was impeccable," Sylvie said mournfully, picking a long silky black dog hair out of the egg salad, a not uncommon occurrence at Karen's house.

"Aha." Karen closed the refrigerator and triumphantly held up a bowl of cut strawberries. "Katie tried to hide them from me, the wretched teenager. For this, I ought to sentence her to cleaning the whole house."

"But Katie would think of that as a reward," Sylvie said as Karen shoved a chair toward her. "Your kid has a clean house fetish."

"But wait, what light through yonder window begins to dawn." Karen sat down and leaned forward, her elbows on the table. "Now I understand your dilemma. You haven't done dishes for a week; your clean laundry, which you did on Wednesday, is still in the basket in the middle of the living room—your dirty laundry is, of course, in a heap in your bedroom—and you can't see the kitchen table for the papers and hodgepodge of *impedimenta* heaped on top of it. You have to wash dishes before you can eat, and you actually get around to scrubbing the kitchen floor once a year, whether it needs it or not."

Sylvie nodded miserably. "Only I did the laundry on Tuesday. And then I have to fall on top of this guy whose house could pass the queen's white glove test." She spooned egg salad onto her bread and mashed it down to turn it into a sandwich.

"Maybe he has a maid," Karen suggested.

Sylvie shook her head. "I don't think single guys go around getting maids."

Karen forked a strawberry into her mouth and chewed thoughtfully. "So you think that even if you got to know him, and the two of you hit if off, that he'd leave you because you're a slob and he's anal retentive?"

"Yup. That's about it."

"All men aren't like that, Sylvie."

"Then what's your excuse for still being single?"

Karen sighed deeply. "That's not my excuse."

"Then what is?"

"How many men do you know who want to share a house with a thundering herd of drooling, shedding Newfoundlands? Not to mention Katie. Although," the older woman said thoughtfully, "she's past the drooling stage, and she doesn't shed."

"And you," Sylvie said softly reaching out to cover her friend's hand with her own. "You're terrific."

"Yeah," Karen agreed, staring into her glass of iced tea. "So are you. We're two terrific women who are more than worth the trouble we'd be."

Chapter Six

A knock on the door interrupted Ray from his appraisal of the postage stamps spread out on the dining-room table. Was it Sylvie? He was afraid to let himself wish it were, afraid of what that might mean. He wasn't sure he was up to a tornado ripping through his apartment again. *C'mon, Ray,* he chided himself. *Admit it. You actually enjoyed her company.*

Well, maybe a little bit, he conceded. He set down the postage stamp he was examining, pulled himself to his good foot, and crutched his way to the front door. He opened it.

"Hi, Jessie." He didn't know whether to be disappointed or not. Still, he liked Jessie. She was relaxed and comfortable to be around.

"Sylvie told me she fell on top of you, so I've

come to see about your foot. How is it?"

Ray opened the door wider to let her in, wondering what else Sylvie had told her. "It still hurts," he admitted.

"It's supposed to. It'll take a couple of days before you feel like running a marathon. Can I look? Call it an interest in all things medical. Even if you're not canine." Her freckles stood out on her friendly face. Without waiting for an answer, she stooped down to examine his ankle. "Lovely shades of purple and black. Very impressive. Sort of like modern art."

He chuckled. "I hope not."

"Sure it is," she said cheerfully. "We could take a casting of it, paint it all up authentically, and call it *Sprained Ankle*. Hang it in some museum somewhere. People'd come from all over to see it. We could probably sell it for a bunch of money. Someone did that once with a mitten their dog chewed up. Called it art and got a gob of money for it."

"You're strange," he told her affectionately.

"Yup. I'm also on my way to the store," she announced. "I figured you might not feel like driving around and doing battle with the lines at the grocery store today. Can I pick something up for you?"

He thought for a moment. It was Sunday, the day he did his cooking for the week. He always did his major grocery shopping on the first Saturday of the month. But this was toward the end of the month. He could use some perishables. Milk and bread, real bread that didn't have any green things in it, he thought, remembering the stuff Sylvie had brought over.

"That would be great," he told her. "Let me write some things down and give you some money."

He hobbled back to the table where he'd been working on his collection. There was a small notepad and pencil. As he wrote, Jessie followed him over to his table to take a look.

"Where are these from?" she asked, referring to the scattering of postage stamps on the table. "Are they new?"

"Just came last week. Most of them are European."

"This one's pretty." She bent down closer. "Of course, it's Irish. Bound to be lovely."

He groaned. Jessie was well known for her fixation on anything Celtic.

"Is it a valuable one?"

"I'm not sure. I haven't had time to look all of them up."

"What?" she sounded overly dramatic. Jessie was good at being overly dramatic. "You mean you don't know every single postage stamp printed by every single post office in the world? You can't just rip 'em off by heart?"

"No. I don't know every single postage stamp. Besides, individual post offices don't print postage stamps. You ought to know that."

Jessie grinned at him. "You know what I mean. You have about a gazillion of these little thingies. You probably have more postage stamps than Sylvie has stamps of a rubber kind. And that's a lot."

At the mention of Sylvie's name, Ray felt his neck muscles tense. "She has a lot of rubber stamps?" How could anyone possibly have that many rubber stamps?

"Yeah. You oughta see her rubber room."

"I think I'll pass."

Suddenly, Jessie's eyes brightened. She clapped her hands like a small child. "I know!" she exclaimed. "You both collect stamps. Isn't it cool?"

He scowled at her. "What's cool?"

"You and Sylvie," Jessie announced irrepressibly. "You collect postage stamps, she collects rubber stamps. They're both art forms."

"I don't think so. Postage stamps are more than just art," Ray pointed out. "They're about history and about culture. They're necessary, useful, not frivolous."

Jessie's eyes grew big. "Warning here, Ray, because we're buddies and because I like you. Don't ever tell Sylvie that her stamps are frivolous. It won't be a pretty sight."

He shook his head in amusement. "You're something else, Jessie."

"I'm not something else. I just don't want two nice people to start a civil war over stamps—postage or otherwise. You don't know Sylvie. She's sort of rabid about her rubber."

"I thought she was your friend."

"She is. She's one of my best friends. But she's still irrational when it comes to her stamps. You just wait. She'll start making you cards and then—" Her eyes got wide again as he glanced up at her. "Did she already start?"

Ray nodded his head toward the bookshelves where he'd propped up The Card.

Jess sauntered over to look at it. "Yup. That's one of hers all right. It's good. The ladder, and Jean-Luc, and you with her falling on top. I like it."

"Open it," he invited her after the fact.

"She got the ankle color the exact shade of bruise," Jessie said in amazement. "I'm impressed. All her school wasn't a waste of time after all."

Against his will, Ray was curious. "What school?"

"Sylvie has a double masters in fine art and medieval history. In fact, she and Madeleine, Melissa's cousin you know, were roommates for their art degrees. Very *useful* things to study, art and medieval history. Very practical. At least, that's what Sylvie's father always says, but I think he's teasing. Anyway, she took the classes, passed the tests, and now she can make bruises like this. And you should see her castles. Wow! She goes to England and places like that and looks at their castles, then she draws pictures of them and turns them into stamps."

He should of known she was educated, he thought ruefully, rubbing the back of his neck.

An aura of education and class and old money surrounded her. He should have noticed it earlier. But he hadn't wanted to notice it. She had probably grown up with a maid who followed her around picking up the carnage.

It's a good thing you don't want her, he insisted to himself. *She's impulsive, and messy, and leaves cupboard doors open. She puts flowers in her food and named her poodle after a bald guy. She sent SPAM through the mail,* he added, trying to summon up appropriate outrage. And failing.

But, he reminded himself, *when she looked at your ankle her hands were gentle. She did everything she could to make you comfortable.*

"Yoo hoo!" He was startled to see Jessie's hand waving in front of him. "Are you in there? You sort of disappeared on me for a moment."

"I'm right here. I was figuring out exactly what I need from the store," he lied.

She would take Karen's advice and be friends with Ray, Sylvie thought resolutely as she backed out of her driveway. After all, bunches of people paid Karen lots of money to help them figure out their lives. Of course, they were crazy, but it kept Karen in dog food.

"So Jean-Luc," Sylvie said confidentially to her still-damp dog ensconced in the backseat of her car—poodles took a long time to air dry. "We're going to go and visit Ray. This is purely a social visit from one person to another. Simple friendship and neighborly concern. No overtones of something else. I will *not* admire his body." She sighed. It was such a nice male body, trim, long, slender limbs, sort of like Michaelangelo's *David*. And that fascinating face, all planes and edges, topped with crisp curls to pat down—like Jean-Luc's. And those eyes . . . "I will *not* try to match his eyes to Marvy markers," she promised her dog. "Marvy doesn't make that particular shade of blue anyway, which is too bad because Ray's eyes are a glorious color. I could use that color for the sky just after the sun has set, or for shadows in mountains." She was caught in the deliciousness of the color and its possibilities. Of course, she could probably blend that color starting with a clear true blue and adding a smidge of black and maybe a whisper of green. She'd have to take a good look at his eyes again. *Just to study the color,* she told herself, not to look into the depths that she just knew were there.

Jean-Luc stuck his head over the back of her seat and nudged her arm, as if reminding her what she was supposed to be promising. "And I won't," she continued, "try to do him in rubber anymore. Two images are enough to make from any man, even if that man does look like Ray." She sighed deeply in regret. A man as gorgeous as Ray should have a whole series of stamps. Or perhaps even a supporting role in the continuing story of the Princess Delphine and her faithful hound companion, Halcyon.

Jean-Luc threw her a single bright woof.

"I do, too, mean it," Sylvie protested. "Honestly, I don't see why you can't believe me. It's the truth. Karen said I should try to be friends with Ray. Nothing more. Of course, I don't think we can." She drew to a stop at a red light and morosely stared out the window while she waited. "The thing is, he's really neat, he's the kind of man I'd choose to fall in love with, except that he obviously has a neatness fetish."

Jean-Luc nudged her arm again.

"Trying to promote a head scratch, are we?"

Jean-Luc wagged his tail in great hope. His hope was fulfilled, until the light turned green.

That was quick, he thought an hour later as another knock on the door interrupted him again. He'd have thought Jessie would take longer at the store.

"Come on in, Jess," he called, before he realized she'd have her arms busy with grocery bags. He got to his feet and was hobbling over to the door when it opened.

Sylvie Taylor's pixie face peeked around the door. "Hi. It's us."

Us?

The door opened a little wider as Jean-Luc proudly pushed his way in, dragging a leash of red webbing.

"Jean-Luc, how are you, boy?" he greeted the dog, holding out his hand.

Jean-Luc loved the attention.

Sylvie, he remembered. He looked up to see her standing in the doorway, uncertainty written over her face, a paper bag in her arms. He wondered what was in this paper bag. He wasn't sure he wanted to know. "Come in."

She came in. "Jean-Luc is slightly damp. We were at Matheson's this morning and he was swimming with the Newfs. I hope you don't mind a wet dog."

He ruffled the poodle's ears. "Nah, I don't mind a wet dog. Especially a wet dog who is as nice as this one is," he added this last to Jean-Luc rather than to Sylvie.

Jean-Luc stood up on his hind legs and toddled a few steps.

"That's his cuteness dance," Sylvie explained. "He wants to make sure you realize how very cute he is."

"Very cute," he agreed.

"Cute and very straggly looking right now. I have to clip him soon. I keep him in a puppy cut because it's easiest to take care of. But it's a bit too long."

"You don't do the fancy frou frous?" It wouldn't surprise him if she did.

"Actually they're not just for decoration, they are useful."

"They are?" What could possibly be useful about that silly haircut most poodles had.

"Poodles were originally used as water-retrieving dogs. The long curly fur made them waterlogged, but if it were all cut off the dogs would get cold. So people cut off most of the coat and left it longer over the chest and the joints, which would keep the important parts of the dogs warmer." She looked at him, her eyebrows raised in question. He felt he could watch her face forever. "Doesn't that make sense?" she asked. "Oh. And you know those colored ribbons? When the dogs were swimming all you could see were their heads and it was difficult to tell them apart. So the hunters put different colored ribbons in their hair to tell them apart."

She beamed at him. "But Jean-Luc does not retrieve dead birds out of the water, just tennis balls and stuff like that, so I cut all his hair the same length. Equal opportunity for all your curls, eh, Jean-Luc?" Jean-Luc wiggled his tail.

"You clip him yourself?"

She nodded. "I decided that if a groomer could learn to clip a poodle, then so could I. So I got a book from the library, and some clippers and I figured it out. It's not difficult once you get used to the idea. Sort of like topiary, actually. Only dogs are easier because topiaries are so ephemeral. You have to keep at them because the wretched plants have this habit of growing. Dog hair grows, too, I guess, but dogs are smaller."

"Do you clip your bushes to look like poodles?" He struggled to keep the sarcasm out of his voice.

"Not anymore. But I did once. In my backyard. I wanted to see what it would be like to wake up and see it. Topiaries were all the rage hundreds of years ago. As far back as ancient Rome, actually."

"Ah, yes. Jessie mentioned you were interested in history."

"Yeah. It's sort of fascinating to learn how people used to live."

"You also think about the future a lot?"

"Future?"

"You named Jean-Luc after a spaceship captain. Didn't you?"

"Oh. Yes, I did." She shifted the paper bag to her other arm. "My brother Florian says it's because I don't like the present. He says I'm fascinated by the past and the future. Anything but the now."

"Is that true?"

She pursed her mouth in thought. "Probably," she admitted. Then her face came alive. "Oh look!"

He looked. He didn't see anything special but she was already at his dining-room table, with his stamps.

He caught himself just before he yelled at her not to touch them. She had the ominous looking paper bag clutched to her chest, and was bending over to see his stamps better. Evidently she knew enough not to touch them.

"Not supposed to touch them, am I? Oil from my fingers and all that."

He swallowed. He was glad he'd caught himself before he yelled. "That's right."

"Looks like you collect them. Jean-Luc, get your feet off the table right now. You can't touch these stamps, they're delicate."

"I do. Here, boy." He held out his hand to Jean-Luc. Jean-Luc, knowing a good thing, came.

"Have you been collecting for a long time?" She cocked her head to peer up at him, inquisitive as a bird.

He nodded, shifting away slightly, just enough to evade her gaze. His mother had given him his first stamps and a notebook to keep them in for Christmas—the Christmas before she died.

There was something on his face, Sylvie thought. Something that said keep out, in big letters. She wondered what it was, what had happened to close that door. She'd only asked him if he'd collected stamps for a long time. Well, it was obviously something he didn't want to talk about. She could accept that. There were some things she didn't want to talk about either. So she merely nodded in return, allowing him his privacy. After all, that's what friends did. Even when it made them crazy wanting to know what it was that their friend didn't want to talk about.

"How's your ankle? I see you're still attached to that crutch."

"I'm becoming very fond of this crutch."

"Ankle still sore? I brought more elder ointment." She patted the paper bag, which rustled cheerfully. "And Jean-Luc and I have something else to make your ankle feel better, and also an invitation for you."

He raised his eyebrows in question. For a moment time quietly ceased to exist, and she was locked in forever, studying his face. The blue of his eyes with their shuttered expression, the planes and angles of his cheeks, the shadows of his curly hair on his forehead, his mouth, wide with nicely chiseled lips. Out of the corner of her eye, she could see his steel strong hands gently caressing Jean-Luc's head. *What a contradiction,* she thought. And for one split second she allowed herself to wonder what it would feel like if those strong hands were to caress her.

Then Jean-Luc shoved his head under her hand.

"So what's this invitation?" Ray asked.

Time began again.

Chapter Seven

She seemed out of breath, he thought. He wondered why.

"Well," she said, "we brought you all the things to make a rosemary foot bath. That's to soak your foot in. It'll make your ankle feel ever so much better. And when you're all better and are doing your mailman thing again I'll bring you more stuff so you can soak your feet when you get home from work."

"Rosemary foot bath?" he asked faintly. What new torture was this? At least he didn't have to drink it. He hoped.

But she was already bustling into the kitchen, Jean-Luc bounding after her.

Ray could hear the paper bag rattle, and then something clunked. He hobbled after her. "I took a shower this morning," he pointed out. "My feet don't need a bath."

She stood at the sink, measuring some sort of dried herby looking thing into a large blue crockery bowl. "This isn't to get you *clean*, it's a medicinal bath for your ankle. Trust me. After a soak in this, your ankle will feel so good you'll want to dance one of Jessie's Irish jigs."

He didn't think so.

She filled the bowl with water and slid it into the microwave. "There," she said beaming at him. "It'll take about two minutes to warm up."

She pulled a small plastic container out of the brown bag. "Cookies, Jean-Luc?"

Jean-Luc sauntered up to her and sat perfectly, as if he hadn't the slightest interest in what she was offering.

"Shake," Sylvie said, holding out her right hand. Jean-Luc raised his paw. She shook it. "Good boy." She tossed him something tiny and reddish brown. Jean-Luc snapped it out of the air.

"What's that?" he asked, not sure he wanted to know. Given her propensity for strange food . . .

"Dried cat food."

"Your dog eats cat food?" That made sense, he thought. She eats flowers, her dog eats cat food.

She chuckled. "No. He eats dog food. This is just a reward."

"What happened to frozen peas?"

"They get all mushy when you put them in your pocket. Here." She held out a few pieces of dried cat food. "Tell him to shake. Some people think teaching a dog to shake is demeaning. But I think it's very sociable."

He glanced at her warily. Then at Jean-Luc. Jean-Luc was sitting politely, and drooling.

"Jean-Luc, shake," he said to the dog.

Jean-Luc obligingly raised a paw, but this time Ray thought he detected a hint of resigned tolerance in the dog's expression. "Here you go, boy," Ray said, trying not to chuckle as he handed the dog a piece of dried cat food.

The microwave dinged and Sylvie flitted over to pull out the bowl of her new witch's brew.

Rats! He'd hoped if he could keep her talking about her dog she'd forget about this foot bath thing. He should have known better. He glanced at Jean-Luc to find the poodle gazing at him. Ray would have bet any amount that the dog was saying, "Better luck next time, pal."

"This is going to feel so good," Sylvie told him. "You'll see." She set the bowl down and tested the temperature with her little finger. "It is just right. Just like Baby Bear's porridge," she announced.

"I really don't need—"

"Now," she added briskly, "where do you want to sit? How about the living room?" She picked up the aromatic bowl and headed for the doorway. Suddenly it occurred to her that he wasn't following. "Come on, don't be shy. This won't hurt." She shifted the bowl and some water sloshed over the side. "Oops!" she muttered.

"Look, you don't have to go to all this trouble."

"Nonsense." She blithely continued into the living room. "It's no trouble at all. Besides, I'm responsible for spraining your ankle, so I'll be responsible for helping it get better." Honestly, why were men such sissies?

"There," she said with great satisfaction as he finally stuck his foot in the bowl. "Doesn't that feel better?"

There was a surprised look on his face. "It really does," he said, amazement evident in his voice. "What's in here?"

She nodded in satisfaction. "Rosemary and oil and some other stuff. I hate to be the kind of person who says they told you so." She grinned at him. "But I told you it would feel better. Now, lean back, and just rest your ankle in the bowl. Give it about fifteen minutes and you'll want to dance that jig."

"No jigs," he said. "I don't dance."

"Too bad. Dancing is fun."

"So what is this invitation?" he asked her a few minutes later. His foot was still in the bowl. Jean-Luc, after one sniff of the bowl, had looked at it in disgust and settled down at Ray's feet. Sylvie was rummaging through his CD collection.

"Jean-Luc and I wanted to invite you out to Kedrick Park for a picnic dinner. Gee, you really like Bach, don't you? I thought I'd bring some things, fried chicken and stuff, nothing big and fancy. It's Sunday, and at six o'clock there's a free concert in the park near my house. You know, high school alumni orchestras and bands, and that sort of thing. Gives them a chance to perform. I forget who's playing tonight, but it's in the paper. So please say you'll come with us. Jean-Luc and I hate to eat alone." She pressed the play button with a flourish and turned to grin at him with utter delight. She'd managed to find the only Tchaikovsky he had. The Sixth Symphony. "I love this," she announced breathlessly. "It's so passionate. So, will you do a picnic with us?"

He didn't want to think of Sylvie and passionate in the same moment. So he thought about a picnic. Tonight was meat loaf night. He made meat loaf every Sunday. The leftovers were his lunch for the next two days. If he went on a picnic with her that would mean no meat loaf—and that meant no leftovers for lunches. He'd have to rearrange his weekly menu.

She was looking at him with that expectant look again, the one that said she was waiting eagerly for him to say yes so she could get all excited. If he refused her he'd feel like a heel. He sighed mentally. Jean-Luc had bounded up and was tottering on his hind legs again, waving his front feet as if imploring him also. He gave in. Meat loaf would have to wait until tomorrow night. But there was Jessie.

"Jessie is getting some things for me at the store, so I'll have to wait for her to get back." He felt that was a test of sorts, to see her reaction.

"And then after that will you come with us?"

He could see his peaceful Sunday afternoon disappearing before his eyes. "Okay," he said, and realized he'd said it without regret.

"What do you think about this table over here?" she asked.

"Good choice. Under the trees for shade, level spot. Not too much evidence of birds on it. Clear across the park from the parking lot."

"Is this sarcasm I hear?" He really should have let her carry the picnic basket, after all, he had his crutches to contend with. But no, he had to do the studly man thing and carry it himself.

He flashed her a grin. She caught it and sent it back.

"This is it, then."

He set her basket on the bench and bowed with a flourish. "Your basket, madam."

She curtsied. "Thank you, kind sir," she answered graciously. "First things first." She whooshed up a tablecloth and shook the folds out, letting it settle like a cloud on the picnic table. Albeit a heavy cloud.

"Did you do this?" Ray asked.

"Do what?" she asked, her attention on the picnic things in the basket.

"The tablecloth. Is it more of your artwork?"

"Yup, more of my rubber habit. Do you like it? Here, sit down and look at it while I unpack the stuff."

"I'm not exactly an invalid you know. Just a sprained ankle."

"I know. You go ahead and look. I'll be interested in what you think of it. Jean-Luc, keep your gorgeous nose out of that basket," she warned.

Jean-Luc sat right down and gave her a haughty stare, as if it were beneath him to nose around in a picnic basket, and how insulting of her to accuse him of it.

"Jean-Luc, why don't you check things out. Okay?" She pulled out a long line and snapped one end on his collar and tied the other end to the leg of the picnic table. When she unsnapped his leash and folded it up, Jean-Luc began a survey of the interesting smells in the surrounding grass.

"What's with the fifty-foot leash?" Ray inquired.

"He doesn't always come when he's called," Sylvie explained ruefully. "I have to take him to more doggy school. Classes start in a couple of weeks."

They stood silently for a few heartbeats watching Jean-Luc explore the world within the radius of his long line. Slowly, an awareness of Ray as a man started to simmer in Sylvie's mind. Her nerve endings started to shimmer. It was the beginning of a long, languorous meltdown.

No, she scolded herself silently. *No meltdowns. Remember you're only going to be friends.* After a small sigh of resignation, Sylvie returned to her task of setting up the picnic, and Ray turned back to the cloth. Out of the corner of her eye, Sylvie saw him study the cloth, touching it here and there.

The cloth was one of her favorites, done with stamps and fabric ink finished with a layer of sealant. Perfect for picnics, and it wiped clean. It was a forest scene with castle windows and turrets peeking out through the trees. There were dragons trying to get into the castle, and princesses and princes trying to keep them out. Fairies congregated here and there to cheer or jeer the hapless humans on. There were several word stamps in opportune places, with appropriate sayings.

She surreptitiously watched Ray examine one particular fierce looking dragon closely. "Do not meddle in the affairs of dragons," he read aloud. "For you are crunchy and taste good with ketchup." He looked up at her, an eyebrow raised. She gave up all pretense of concentration on her task, and their gazes collided.

Once again she was fascinated. She could

watch his face forever. Watch the expressions on it, watch them change as quickly as the weather in spring. Sunshine to thunderstorm. Clear to cloudy. Blues to grays. *Be friends, keep it on the friendship-and-nothing-but-level, and you will be able to watch his face forever,* she warned herself and wrenched her gaze from his. "Yes, ketchup," she answered, not trusting herself to look at him again just now.

Because, she cautioned herself, *it would be so easy to fall in love with that face, with those blue eyes, with those hands.*

Ah yes, but those blue eyes like order, organization. They would most definitely not fall in love with your house.

That's right, go ahead and call me a slob. Sticks and stones and all that.

"Is there any special significance to all these dragons?" his voice interrupted her inner conversation, brought her back to reality.

"Of course." She paused.

"Are you going to enlighten me?" he asked dryly, his lips twitching in an ill-concealed grin.

"We all have dragons," she explained. "There are dragons all over the place, trying to get into our lives, to disrupt things. To make us miss buses, or forget to pay the electric bill, or lock our keys in our cars." She pulled out a covered dish of potato salad and set it down with more of a thump than she'd intended.

"Isn't that why there was a Saint George? To slay the dragons for us?"

She faced him across the table, across her cloth, across miles and miles of painted forest. "We can't let other people slay our dragons for us, we each have to be our own Saint George."

"That doesn't sound like something you'd say."

"I don't mean that other people can't help us, they can. But only *we* can recognize our dragons for what they are. When the battles come, they are between each one of us and our own dragons. The dragons keep coming, and we keep fighting them. And each dragon that we slay makes us stronger, gives us strength."

It was an odd juxtaposition, he thought, for Sylvie to stand across from him talking about strength. She was as delicate as a flower, as a dandelion seed. She looked more like a fairy than a dragon slayer. *What are her dragons?* he wondered before he could stop himself. Whatever they were, he suddenly knew that he'd fight them for her, if she'd let him. And if she wouldn't, if she insisted on fighting them herself, he'd stand on the sidelines and cheer her on.

Jean-Luc butted his head into Ray's arm. "Are you tired of being left out of the conversation?" Ray asked, glad to be interrupted from his thoughts. Jean-Luc wagged his tail and his expression was undeniably human in its agreement.

"Maybe if you ask Sylvie she'll have something that I can throw for you. If you're descended from great retriever dogs you probably still like to chase things and bring them back."

Sylvie chuckled. "He's manic about his b-a-l-l. He's rabid about it. He's totally irrational, possessed, when it comes down to a catch. Are you sure you're up to this?"

"Lady, I schlepp bags of mail around all day. I can certainly play fetch with a dog, even if I'm chained to these crutches."

Sylvie reached into her bag and brought out a tennis ball. As she handed it to him there was a sparkle in her eyes, a suggestion of impishness, as if she knew something that he was going to find out for himself.

"Come on, Jean-Luc, let's show this woman what you and I can do."

Trying to snatch the ball out of his hands, Jean-Luc leaped and pranced in front of him as Sylvie unclipped his long line.

"Now, Jean-Luc, you be good and do not under any circumstances run off with the ball. Do you understand?" Sylvie cautioned him.

Jean-Luc, his attention riveted to the ball, patently ignored her.

The game of b-a-l-l began.

Ray seemed to be having as much fun as Jean-Luc, Sylvie thought. It was nice to see him actually relax. He usually seemed so uptight and controlled. Maybe he needed a good strong dose of Rock Water, the flower essence for people who were rigid and stuck in their own paths. The next time she made him lemonade, she might put in a few drops. He needed more spontaneity in his life, more fun, more flexibility. Well that was something she could give him. She was the Queen of Spontaneity.

She unwrapped a cut-glass bowl of *baba ganoush*. She loved the eggplant dip more than almost anything in the world. She tore pieces of pita bread to accompany it and arranged them on a platter. Food fit for a friend, she thought in satisfaction as she surveyed the table. Next to the *baba ganoush* and pita there was the potato salad garnished with orange nasturtium petals, deviled eggs, sliced tomatoes sprinkled with basil, fresh fruit salad with mint leaves, and cold chicken that had been marinated in lime juice and yogurt, then baked till crispy. Freshly squeezed lemonade sloshed in an ice-filled pitcher. It was lovely.

Oh. She almost forgot. She retrieved a small covered plastic box from the picnic basket and opened it. It was full of newly picked violets, probably the last of the season. She scattered them lightly over the tablecloth and stood back to admire what she'd done. There. A picnic.

"Jean-Luc! Come back here!"

Sylvie whipped her head around to Ray's cry. Jean-Luc was racing off toward the parking lot. The parking lot that was busy with coming-and-going cars. Ray, clumsy with his crutches, hobbled after him.

"Jean-Luc Picard Taylor, come!" Sylvie hollered uselessly as, heart beating wildly, she raced frantically after her dog.

Chapter Eight

Pounding after Jean-Luc as hard as she could, Sylvie felt a rush of adrenaline. Her dog was tearing off straight for the mass of cars moving through the parking lot! Visions of disaster slammed one on top of each other in her mind. Jean-Luc would be hit by a car, and then she'd have to find a phone somewhere and call Melissa, and—oh my—what if Melissa wasn't home, and where would she find a phone, there weren't any pay phones at the park, but maybe someone would have a car phone she could use, but how could she possibly find someone who had a car phone among all the people in the park? And once she'd gotten a hold of Melissa, she'd have to get Jean-Luc into her car to get him to the vet clinic. At least she had an old blanket in her car to wrap him in, but her car was locked so she'd have to go back to the picnic table for her keys and by then Jean-Luc might be—no, don't think about *that!* She panted as she ran after him, ignoring the stitch in her side.

Jessie! And Sally!

There they were, strolling casually toward Jean-Luc, who was making a beeline for them. "Catch him!" she managed to call. "Please catch him!"

Jessie stooped down, opening her arms wide. Jean-Luc threw himself at her with reckless abandon. Jean-Luc loved Jessie.

"Hey, you great guy dog." Jessie's voice came to her across the park. "Have you been terrorizing your mom again? Not coming when you were called? You're going to be in big trouble some day. That's a nasty habit to get into. Yes, I love you, too. Look at this wonderful ball. Yes, it most certainly is a lovely ball, all covered in dog slobber."

Sylvie finally caught up with them, huffing mightily. "Thank you. I'd never have caught him. Hi, Sally."

"That's what you get for having a dog," Sally told her, waving her hand airily. "If you had cats you'd expect them to not come when they're called. Unless they felt like it." She grinned smugly.

"That's okay, Sally," Sylvie panted, chuckling. "I like you. Even if you are a cat person."

Then Ray was there, also, only slightly out of

breath. "I'm sorry, Sylvie. One minute he was racing after the ball, bringing it back for more, the next minute he took off."

"That's okay," she gasped and gulped for air. She was really out of shape. She should start hauling mailbags around, then maybe she'd have Ray's stamina. "He does that, don't you, you monster?"

Jean-Luc looked up at her, grinning with satisfaction.

"Ray, you know Jessie, and this cat person here, the one who pretends she doesn't like dogs, is Sally. Sally teaches kindergarten. Sally, this is Ray. And he does like dogs."

"We can't all be purr-fect now, can we?" Sally teased, as Jessie and Sylvie chorused a "Yuck, yuck."

"Hello, Ray," Sally continued. "You must be the guy Sylvie fell on top of."

Sylvie felt herself turn what was probably a bright and vibrant pink. "Jessie," she groaned.

"Well, I had to tell Sally," Jessie explained reasonably. "This was big news." She turned to Ray. "You know your life is boring when the most exciting thing that happens is when one of your best friends falls on top of the mailman."

Ray, bless him, thought Sylvie, chuckled. He didn't seem overwhelmed by her friends. Of course, he already knew Jessie, but put Sally and Jessie together and they could be totally and embarrassingly obnoxious.

"Jessie said you guys were here on a picnic," Sally explained. "And we decided to join you. We know you always pack enough for the proverbial army, Sylvie, but just in case we brought a watermelon and some dogs to grill."

"Not dogs, Sally," Jessie countered with mock seriousness. "*Weenies*. We brought watermelon and *weenies* to grill. We don't eat dogs. We like dogs."

"People in other countries eat dogs," Sally pointed out. "I read in a book somewhere that there are some places where people will eat anything with four legs except a chair. It said that they especially liked white puppies."

"Sally, that's gross," Jessie admonished her.

"Yeah," Sally agreed. "Just think, they would have loved Jean-Luc."

"If he doesn't start coming when he's called," Sylvie said, still trying not to sound out of breath, and failing, "I might send him to visit those people." She bent down to address her dog nose-to-nose. "What do you think, Jean-Luc? Would you like to end up as main course for some hungry family?"

Jean-Luc gave her his *poor-little-innocent-me?* look.

"So, Sylvie, Ray, are you going to invite us to join you, or what?" Jessie entreated.

The four of them, Sylvie's hand firmly on Jean-Luc's collar, made their way back to the table. Ray found himself amused and delighted by the three of them together. Sylvie kept turning a charming shade of pink. Sally and Jessie certainly knew how to tease her, and were definitely old hands at making Sylvie blush. And when Sylvie blushed, she was even more lovely than before.

They reminded him of his foster sister and her friends, full of laughter and joy and good-natured teasing. As if none of them had a care in the world. There was something naïve about their good spirits, something innocent, untouched, that left him feeling old and jaded.

"Oooh!" Sally squealed when they were close to the table. "The baby goosh stuff. I love it!"

Baby goosh? What in the world . . .

"*Baba ganoush*, and you know how to pronounce it, so don't pretend you don't," Sylvie cautioned. "I can see right through you, like a window."

"Windows can't see through people, Sylvie," Jessie said in a stage whisper. "You're misplacing a modifier or something."

"Nah," Sally corrected her. "She's mixing metaphors. I'm a teacher, I know these things. Hey, Jean-Luc, do you want some baby goosh, too?"

"Don't waste it on him," Jessie said, peering into the bowls of food on the table. "He'll eat anything. Let's give him the nasturtium petals. Ray, have you eaten Sylvie's flowers yet?"

"Well, I—" he began, but was interrupted.

"Isn't it a lovely Sunday, here in the park,"

Sylvie said loudly and deliberately, as if trying to change the subject.

"It's hot up here," Jessie chorused.

"It's hot and it's monotonous!" Sally sang.

What were they doing? he wondered in amazement.

"They're making fun of my love for Sondheim musicals," Sylvie explained, handing him a paper plate and motioning toward the food.

He quickly shuffled through his mind, had he heard any Sondheim? No, he didn't think so.

"Sylvie's family are such elitist snobs," Sally explained, "that they can actually listen to the William Tell Overture and not think of the Lone Ranger."

"Oooh, Sally, that's a good one," Jessie exclaimed. "Is it original?"

"Unfortunately, no. I borrowed it."

"Let's see," Jessie continued. "They can listen to the 1812 Overture without thinking of puffed wheat. There hafta be some others. We'll have to think of them."

"Anyway, Ray, in their infinite wisdom, they, Sylvie's family, think musicals—even Rodgers and Hammerstein—are lowbrow," Sally continued in an overly confidential tone of voice.

"Lowbrow, like cavemen," Jessie added, heaping her plate with potato salad.

"Like low man on the totem pole," Sally added.

"Like limbo—how low can you go?" Jessie camped.

"Don't mind Mutt and Jeff there," Sylvie told him. "They think they're funny."

"I'm Jeff," Sally announced. "I'm no dog."

"The scary thing," Jessie told him, "is that Sally *is* a kindergarten teacher. People actually trust her with their little rug rats." She snapped her fingers. "Maybe that's why so many little kids are monsters. Because they had Sally as a teacher and she warped their minds."

Sally rolled her eyes. "I'm a good teacher. Hey, Jessie, don't take all the chicken. Give some to Ray."

He held out his plate and Jessie deposited a piece of chicken on it, then before he could maneuver to the bench on one foot, Sally spooned some odd looking potato salad on his plate. At least the deviled eggs looked harmless and ordinary.

"Nasturtium petals," she whispered in answer to his unspoken question. "Sylvie thinks they're pretty and we don't want to disillusion her. We just sneak them to Jean-Luc."

"I heard that." Sylvie laughed. "And that's a bald-faced lie. You do too eat them. You even said they were good once."

" 'Once' is the operative word, dear. Please pass the baby goosh."

Ray found himself face to face with a bowl of something that looked like something a sick dog had done, but Sally scooped it onto her plate with gusto.

"If this is baby goosh, what's grown-up

goosh?" he managed to ask, trying to make light of the unappetizing substance. He couldn't bring himself to call it food.

"It's eggplant dip. And it isn't baby goosh, it's called *baba ganoush,*" Sylvie explained cheerfully, apparently oblivious to the fact that normal people didn't eat things that looked like that. "It's Lebanese. Eggplant and tahini mostly, with a little garlic and lemon juice. Try it," she urged. "Just dip some pita bread into it. It's wonderful."

With three pairs of female eyes on him, there was no way he could politely refuse. *Helen*, he said silently to his foster mother, *it's all your fault for drilling manners into us at dinnertime.* He took up a bit of the pita bread—at least this bread didn't have green things in it—and gingerly dipped it into the goosh. Maybe if he closed his eyes it wouldn't be so bad.

She had to give it to him, she thought. He did eat it. He even managed to smile politely as he reached for his glass of lemonade. Well, *baba ganoush* was not for everyone. "It's okay if you don't like it," she told him. "My family doesn't like it either."

"They're complete Philistines," muttered Sally, dipping another piece of pita. "How did they ever end up with a daughter like you? Maybe you were switched at birth."

"Say, Ray," Jessie said, making a big production of slipping Jean-Luc a piece of tomato.

"Stick around and you'll end up immortalized in rubber."

Oh no, Sylvie moaned to herself. *Please, don't let Jessie—*

"What?" Ray asked.

"Yeah. Sylvie will turn you into a rubber stamp for her company and people all over the world will use you in their so-called artwork. I'm an evil sorceress, and also an elf. Sally here is a lovely princess holding a cat, what a surprise. Melissa is a wise woman—very apt. And Karen is a peasant, no hidden message there, it was her suggestion. Sylvie even did a series of flower children—actual flowers with faces, not hippies—using Angie. You know, Melissa's stepdaughter. Maybe she'll turn you into a wizard. Or a prince."

Sylvie buried her face in her hands.

"What's the matter, Syl? You embarrassed or something? I don't see why you should be. It's an honor," her friend continued. "I'm proud of being an evil sorceress and an elf."

Sylvie sighed loudly and peeked at Ray through her fingers. He didn't seem to be alarmed. "Sometimes when I'm drawing designs for stamps I use real people as my inspiration," she tried to explain, sure that her face was a perfect carmine red. She knew any explanation she could give would fall flat. She'd done those drawings of him because she'd been attracted to him, because he had such an interesting face, because she wanted to create an image of him that would last forever. If she'd been a sculptor she'd have put him in stone.

He cleared his throat. "That's nice," he managed.

Oh, he was polite.

From across the park there was the sound of an orchestra tuning up. "The concert is going to start soon," she announced, pasting what she hoped was a smile on her face. It felt more like a grimace. "If we're going to eat the watermelon we better do it now." Once the music started Jessie and Sally would have to be quiet.

"Don't you have some meteor shower to watch tonight, or something?" she later whispered to Jessie as they were gathering up the dishes.

"Nope. Perseids won't be for a few weeks yet," Jessie answered cheerfully. "You'll just have to put up with our lovely company."

"Well, just don't embarrass me, please," Sylvie begged.

"Gee, I'm sorry. I didn't mean to embarrass you, Syl."

"Well, you did. Like that time with the guy with the Irish Wolfhounds."

Jessie squirmed. "I really didn't mean to."

"You didn't mean to embarrass Melissa then, either," retorted Sylvie, knowing she was turning the screws. "There's nothing going on here, just remember that." She caught her friend with a pointed glance.

"Sure thing, Syl," Jessie agreed. "Nothing going on. That's the same thing Melissa said when she already had the hots for Peter. I really believed her, too. By the way, I have this bridge . . ."

Sylvie good-naturedly picked up an empty paper cup, took careful aim, and threw it. Jessie, chuckling, ducked.

The concert was typical of an alumni orchestra, Ray thought. They did some popular tunes he wasn't familiar with, and some classical favorites. Nothing spectacular, but fun. He'd managed to sit next to Sylvie, with Jean-Luc on his leash, between them. It was a lovely evening. His ankle wasn't hurting anymore and he was sitting next to the woman who for the past few weeks had haunted his dreams, inhabited his dreams, been his dreams.

"So what's up for this week?" he heard Jessie ask Sylvie during a break in the performance.

"Same old, same old," Sylvie answered. "Monday I burn the rubber. Tuesday I cut it. Wednesday I index it, Thursday I mount it. Friday I decide what stamps I need to make the next week."

"This is the tale," Sally added solemnly, "of Solomon Grundy."

"You *burn* rubber?" he asked.

"For my stamps. I buy rubber in big rolls, then on Mondays I start turning it into stamps."

"She keeps the raw rubber in its own refrigerator," Jessie put in, leaning around Sylvie to peer at him. "Sometimes she gets confused and opens the wrong fridge and that's why her food tastes strange."

"I do not," Sylvie protested.

"Well when you're burning your rubber it smells like cremated tires. Sometimes when you're cooking and you forget what you're doing and start doing something else—"

"Like the time," Sally broke in, "you were doing beef stew and suddenly remembered that you hadn't watered your garden. So you got the hose all set up and found there was something wrong with it." She frowned. "Why did it have holes in it? I forget."

"There were holes in it," Jessie continued the story, "because that old groundhog that used to live in your garage decided to snack on it. So you went to the store to buy a new hose."

"And came back four hours later and found the stew was done. In fact, if you will remember, the stew was so done that you ended up throwing the pan away," Sally ended triumphantly.

"And you'd forgotten all about buying a new hose," Jessie added.

"Well, I got sidetracked," Sylvie mumbled, sounding more exasperated than embarrassed. "There was a new bookstore that had just opened up in the mall."

What would it be like to have friends like this? he wondered. Friends with whom one could be so carefree, could say anything without offense, could tease. Had he ever had such a friend? He didn't think so.

"The thing she cooks her rubber in," Jessie continued in that overly confidential tone, "is called a vulcanizer. Sylvie used to think it was from Mr. Spock's planet and could turn people into Vulcans. I think she got into making rubber stamps just so she could have one. It sort of looks like R2-D2 with a flat face. It weighs about a million tons. They had to use a crane to get it into her house. She'll never get it out."

"She even gave it a name," Sally added. "She calls it Leonard. As in the Vulcan, ha ha."

"Cut it out, you guys!" Sylvie pleaded. "The music is going to start."

He watched as—*wait a minute*. This was important, he realized. He was *watching*. This is how he lived much of his life, watching other people live theirs. He was not one to act, but one to react. The opening line from David Copperfield came into his mind; what was it? Something about whether or not he would be the hero of his own life, or if someone else would.

He had, long ago, without conscious thought, abdicated the role of hero in his own life. He sat stunned by this realization. How had this happened? And why? And what was even more important, would he be able to stage a coup and take the reins once more? For there was no way he would allow this to continue.

There was a slight tap on his shoulder.

"What's wrong? You look like you're in

shock," Sylvie whispered. "Is the music that bad?"

He turned his head to face her squarely. "No, it's fine," he lied. There was no way he could tell her that he had just come face to face with his own dragon.

Chapter Nine

So how, Ray asked himself the next morning, did one go about staging a coup in one's own life? How did one storm the castle of one's own life, as it were. How did one go about becoming St. George? He'd never seen, in the backs of comic books, any ads for a miracle cream or tonic that made one heroic. What was a hero anyway? Someone who helped little old ladies across the street? Someone who held doors open for women, as he'd always been taught to do? Today, many women didn't like to have doors held open for them.

He turned on the television while he sipped his morning coffee. It was a ritual, coffee with the news team. Maybe there was a burning building he could rescue someone from, a bomb he could defuse. No, until he got rid of these crutches he'd have to start small. Maybe he could find a kitten in a tree.

He glanced at the clock, and then reached for the phone. Time to call Harvey Schmedlapp and tell him what the doctor had said about his ankle.

After the requisite pleasantries with his supervisor, Ray got to the point. "The doc said I should stay off my ankle for a while."

"Let's see here, Ray. Let me look up your sick leave." Ray heard the unmistakable sound of a metal file drawer shoved shut. "Man, you don't get sick much, do you?" Harvey said. "Looks like you've never used any of your sick days. Tell you what. Why don't you take the week off? Call me again on Friday and we'll see how things are. And Ray, don't get hooked on those soaps, they can be dangerous."

So, Ray thought when he hung up. What would he do with himself for seven days? He would catalog his new stamps, and mail a birthday present to Helen, his foster mother. He would make his meat loaf today. Maybe go to the library and see if the new Michaelson book was in yet. Wash his car.

"Expect rain later this afternoon," announced the television weather forecaster, smiling in front of a weather chart and doing that vague directional pointing peculiar to weather forecasters. "We'll have a lovely morning, breezy and mild, but then shortly after lunchtime those clouds will roll right on in, bringing about half an inch of rain."

He wouldn't wash his car today.

But he should check his gutters to see if they needed to be cleaned out. That was the one drawback of the tall sycamore in the front yard. Its leaves were terrific gutter cloggers. He wondered if he could manage to climb a ladder. Sylvie probably needed to get back up on her ladder and clean out her gutters, too, he thought.

Now there was a heroic deed he could do. He could take his ladder over to her house and clean out her gutters. It was an ugly job, but a hero did what had to be done, regardless of how he felt about it. Regardless of his feelings about the person he helped. Even if the person he helped sent unwrapped cans of SPAM in the mail. And inflated beach balls, and plastic pumpkins at Halloween.

Yes, he told himself, it was perfectly legal. Yes, the post office would deliver those things. But it irritated him. Items in the mail should be properly packaged.

Even so, she did do all she could to help him. Even that vile witch's brew was supposed to be restorative. He shuddered at the thought. Yes, Sylvie was a generous friend—surely it was a matter of misunderstanding. Maybe she just didn't realize how irritating her little mail pranks were to all the good people of the U.S. Postal Service.

And putting his irritation aside, he knew how he truly felt about the possibility of seeing her again. He liked it.

Now don't get all heated up about her, he cautioned himself. *She's educated, comes from a family that's obviously wealthy and probably snobbish about it. If they think musicals are low-brow, what will they think of you with only a high school education? Not much, so you can forget any possibilities for anything there but friendship.*

Somehow it was not a comforting thought.

"Did you hear that, Jean-Luc?" Sylvie asked her dog as she scooped out his kibble. "Half an inch of rain this afternoon. This is not good. This means we can't open all the windows while we burn rubber. Yuck."

Jean-Luc, his gaze riveted on the bowl in her hand, ignored her.

"Jean-Luc, sit," she commanded. "Wait." She set the bowl of kibble in front of the dog and walked a couple of feet away, glancing over her shoulder to make sure Jean-Luc was still sitting politely in front of the bowl. He saw her peeking at him and wagged his tail hopefully.

"Yes, you are being a good boy," she told him, "a most excellent boy. But this is today. Last night you were a Big Bad Poodle and scared me to pieces. So Tanner says we have to back up to square one. This means you have to wait until I say you can eat."

Jean-Luc licked his lips at her.

She gave in. "Okay."

Jean-Luc whipped his head around and buried his muzzle in the bowl of kibble. Contented crunching ensued.

So there would be more rain today, Sylvie thought as she perched on a stool and sipped her cup of herbal tea. She shoved some counter clutter aside so she could set her cup down. For a moment she sat in thought, drumming her fingers on the counter. Then she glanced at the clock. It was almost 8:00. She had to shower and get dressed. Putz around until about 9:00 when she started her day. It took Leonard almost an hour to heat up. In that time she could start filling her mail orders for rubber stamps. Then, in between burning batches of rubber, she could get a start on typing the mailing labels. When Leonard was finished for the day, he could cool down and then she could take the filled orders to the post office.

Maybe the rain would hold off until then. Schlepping thirty-five boxes down to the post office in the pouring rain was not her idea of fun. *Think good thoughts to the rain spirits, Sylvie,* she thought while taking a last sip of tea.

She left her mug on the counter. There wasn't room for it in the sink, and wouldn't be until she put the dirty dishes in the dishwasher. And she had to put the clean dishes away first. Well, she'd get to it later. Right now it was time for a shower.

What would sound good this morning? Music to shower by. She felt too optimistic for Puccini, and Wagner was winter music. But Rodgers and Hammerstein would be perfect. Oh, June certainly *was* bursting out all over, she thought as she waltzed over to her CD player.

Damn! There was no way he would be able to climb a ladder and clean out gutters. He glared at his ladder, propped up against the roof of his apartment, as if it were at fault here. Indeed, it had been a struggle to maneuver his crutches and carry the ladder at the same time, but he'd done that. He'd set the ladder up, but couldn't manage to climb it. His ankle wouldn't work properly. He ground his teeth in frustration.

Maybe he could drive his ladder over to Sylvie's house and she could clean out her gutters. His ladder was longer, more fit for such a job, Now that would be truly heroic, he thought sarcastically. Howdy, ma'am, I brought you a ladder so you could do your own dirty work.

He tipped his head back to survey the sky. No rain clouds yet, but it was still morning.

"Hello," a worried voice called. "Can you help me?"

It was Sylvie, climbing out of her car. Jean-Luc tried to follow her. "No, Jean-Luc," she told him. "You have to guard the car."

He shook his head in amusement. That friendly poodle was not exactly a deterrent to crime.

"What do you need help with?"

"I don't know. It's never done this before. I've lived there for about five years and it's never done this. I tried to call Roger, he's Karen's brother you know, but he was out of town, so I drove by to see if Jessie had left for work yet because she always has tools for stuff, but she was already gone, and then I saw you standing here in your yard."

He felt out of breath just listening to her. And she was wringing her hands. He didn't know anyone actually did that, outside of novels. "Hold it," he told her firmly. "Stop right there. Start over. What is this thing that it—whatever it is—has never done?"

"It's smoking."

He gathered his patience in a neat little pile in front of him where he could see it. "What is smoking?" he asked, carefully and slowly.

"The outlet."

"What outlet?"

"The outlet where Leonard is plugged in," she said as she waved her hands around in what he could only assume was meant as some sort of explanation.

"Leonard is your machine?"

"My vulcanizer."

"The thing you use to burn your rubber?"

"Yes, only I don't really burn it, it just smells that way. And when I burn food it really doesn't—"

"Wait. Stop. Don't go off onto any side trails

now. The outlet you plug your vulcanizer into is smoking. When did it start smoking?"

"When I turned Leonard on." She sounded slightly impatient, as if it should have been obvious. Though with her—in his mind, anyway—nothing was obvious.

"How much smoke was there? Great puffs or little wisps."

"Little wisps." She waved her hands again, this time in imitation of the wisps.

"Then what did you do?"

"I turned Leonard off, and I sniffed around the outlet and it smelled hot. I tried to unscrew the plate thingy but I didn't have the right kind of screwdriver—I only had a Phillips and it needs the flat kind, I forget what they're called—so I shut off all the circuit breakers in my house. Then I tried to call Roger, but he—"

Ray held up his hand to stop her blathering. "You're *sure* you shut off *all* the breakers before you came over here?"

She nodded, even if it was a bit doubtfully. "I'm pretty sure I got them all. And I brought Jean-Luc. I didn't want to leave him in case my house caught fire. And I thought of loading up all my stamps but—"

"Stop," he told her again. He thought for a moment, quickly running through the tools he'd probably need to investigate. "Do you want me to take a look at it to see what I can do?"

"Oh, could you please?"

"Do you have a flashlight?"

She wrinkled her forehead. "I think so."

He congratulated himself on his great patience. "Do you know where it is?" He caught another thought. "Do the batteries work?"

A look of confusion came over her face. "I don't know. I assume they do."

He added a flashlight to his mental list of tools to take.

"It'll take a couple of minutes to get my things. Why don't you bring Jean-Luc inside so he doesn't worry. Don't lock your keys in your car again," he called after her as she took off for her car.

His answer was a flutter of her hand. "I won't. It's one of my dragons that I'm trying to conquer," she called over her shoulder.

Sylvie kept glancing at him out of the corner of her eye as she drove them in silence to her house. Ray had agreed to ride with her because his ankle made it difficult for him to drive his own car. He didn't seem to mind that Jean-Luc, from his seat in the back, was panting in his ear. He hadn't cringed when she scooped the mess of papers and things—mostly things—off of the passenger seat and plopped them in the back so that he could get in, fitting his crutches in as best he could. But, then they weren't at her house yet.

A feeling of dread seeped through her. The feeling she always got when someone new was going to come into her house. Martha Stewart she wasn't. Real women were supposed to be in control of their houses, not the other way around.

Stop it! she told herself firmly. *It is all right if he sees your messy house, after all, we are only going to be friends. It isn't as if you are trying to impress him or something. In fact, the sooner he sees your messy house the better it will be. Get things out in the open.* She was an uncontrollable slob. She admitted it freely and fully. There were just too many things to do to stop and clean her house. It would only get messy again, so why waste the time and energy in the first place? At least that was always her justification. But after seeing his white-glove-test clean apartment—well, when he saw her house he just might run screaming.

She didn't even own a white glove. She used to have one, a pair of them in fact. But when Jean-Luc was a puppy he chewed them up.

At least before she tried to turn on Leonard she'd finally gotten her clean laundry put away. And most of her dirty laundry was in the basket in her bedroom and he certainly wasn't going to go in there. She'd just have to make sure that door was closed.

Here they were, she thought as she pulled into her driveway. Disaster area, sweet disaster area. Maybe she should track down some hard hats.

* * *

Wordlessly Ray gazed around her living room. He had entered a new world jungle, a riot of color and texture. Books were shoved haphazardly on shelves along with magazines and what looked like little bits of pottery. The walls were covered with tapestries and rugs and plates and paintings. The hardwood floors were tossed with rag rugs. What furniture there was, and there wasn't much, was littered by more books and papers. Yet the whole room was alive. It was her, free and unrestrained. She obviously didn't feel the need to be in control of her surroundings, he thought, fighting the urge to close his eyes against the seething mess.

"So where's this smoking outlet?" He grinned as Jean-Luc, evidently much at home, nimbly stepped over a pile of books to leap up onto the back of the couch where he could see out the window. The window had strings of beads hanging in front of it, instead of a curtain.

"In the basement," she told him, leading him past the living room into a hallway and then the kitchen where he tried not to look too closely at the dishes piled in the sink. After all, he'd seen worse.

"Leonard is too heavy to be upstairs," she explained, "so he has to live in the basement."

"Leonard's Lair?" he suggested.

Her delighted laughter floated back to him as she opened a door and started down the steps. Jean-Luc came in a scramble to dash down behind her.

"I think this is where the flashlight comes in handy," he said as he flicked it on.

"Can I hold the flashlight and your tools while you get downstairs? I didn't think of your crutches. Can you even get down the steps?" She held out a hand expectantly.

He recognized the remorseful concern in her voice as he passed over the flashlight and small tool bag. "Of course I can get downstairs with crutches." *It just takes a little maneuvering,* he told himself grimly, determined to make it. At least he was able to put a little weight on his foot. *Remember,* he told himself, *this is heroic.*

"Hey, buddy, you get your nose out of the wood," Sylvie ordered. "Go lie down." Jean-Luc slunk over to what was evidently his place—a cushion under the stairs, heaped with dog toys.

Leonard's Lair was a different world, he saw in amazement. The basement was washed in a grayish gloom cast from the dim light that filtered through the big window wells. But here all was clean and orderly. Not a proverbial hair out of its proverbial place. A long worktable divided into several workstations, and with a jigsaw on one end hugged one wall. On the opposite side of the room was a series of wooden cubbyholes filled with small blocks of wood. Another wall was lined with pull-out bins, a picture on each one. The area under the stairs was devoted to shelves full of what looked like bottles of ink, and of glue, and a refrigerator and file cabinet standing side by side. A telephone with an answering machine sat primly next to a paper pad and pen.

"For telephone orders," she said, evidently realizing he was trying to read the printing on the pad. "My business, remember? People either send in orders, or call them in. Actually, I like to talk to people on the phone. I like to have the personal contact with them. I can learn a lot about what stampers think, and what new stamps they want to see. Sometimes I've made new designs because people have asked for them. My mermaids were like that."

"Mermaids?" he asked, hoping he didn't sound as dumb as he felt.

She darted over to the wall of cubbies and pulled out a small piece of something red. "This is a rubber die of a mermaid. See? The rubber it's in reverse." She reached for a small mirror and handed it to him. "Look at it in the mirror and you can sort of see what it'd look like if you stamped it."

Ray moved closer to the window, adjusted the angle of the mirror and rubber, and sure enough, he could see the reflection of a mermaid. The mermaid was doing . . . "What is she doing?" he finally asked.

"She's combing her hair. Mermaids have long lovely hair you know, so that means they have to comb it constantly or it would be a horribly tangled mess. She's the first mermaid I did. Her name is Lycene and she helped the Princess Delphine vanquish a great sea dragon. She was so popular that I did more mermaids, and even"—she reached into another cubby and brought out another rubber die—"a baby mermaid."

He looked at it closely, and sure as anything, there was a baby mermaid. Round and chubby, with one fist in its mouth, its other hand clutching something. "What is it holding?"

Sylvie drew him over to the cubby and pointed to the front of it. The cubby wall was in the gloom, away from the window. He held the flashlight to see. There, on a slip of paper attached to the wooden front was an image of the baby mermaid, fist still in its mouth. In its other hand was a teddy bear.

"Who is this princess?" he asked, still studying the baby mermaid. It could have been real, the expression on its face, it's hands, even the detail stitching on the teddy bear.

"My stamps all revolve around the adventures of Princess Delphine. She's over there in those bins, along with her faithful canine companion, Halcyon. Together they travel the world, helping those in need, fighting the dragons of those who can't fight them themselves. My dragons." She pointed out a row of bins for the dragon dies. There were dragons of various sizes and expressions, some were sly, some were nasty looking. Some were even somehow sleazy, as if they'd be at home in some B-movie.

He handed the mermaids and the mirror back to Sylvie and turned his attention to the row of Princess Delphines and caught his breath. He knew her. He had seen her. The Princess Delphine was Sylvie. The long, flowing, rippling hair, the slender legs, pixie face, even the arch of the eyebrow. This was the sylph he'd seen in his dreams. This was the girl he'd fallen in love with. There were images of her brandishing a flaming sword, resting peacefully with her dog at her side under a tree. In another she was standing straight, though her shoulders slightly lowered made her look as if she were tired, the kind of inner exhaustion. She was gazing off into the distance, and he knew that she didn't even see what her eyes were looking at. In yet another image, she was kneeling reverently in prayer. There was an image of her standing face front, her head tipped back in rapture, her arms stretched out wide as if embracing the world. Suddenly, he was seeing a side of Sylvie he'd never seen, he was seeing her as she saw herself, or maybe as she wished to be.

"Here is Jessie." Sylvie interrupted his thoughts. And he saw Jessie as an evil sorceress, and as an elf. And there was Sally as a princess, complete with a cat in her arms. He looked closely at the image of the vet, Melissa, as a wise woman. He could almost read the expression in her eyes. Karen as the peasant woman with a large furry dog beside her.

"And over here are the Angie flower children."

Flowers with the faces of children. And they

were all rubber stamps. There were probably close to three hundred cubbies lining the wall, each had a little piece of paper on the front. He could spend hours looking at them all. They were amazing. She was amazing.

"Anyway, this is my workshop," she said, as if it needed explaining.

Still astounded, stunned by the beautiful simplicity of the art before him, he nodded his approval. "I like it. It's nice." *What an understatement that is,* he chided himself. "But where's the patient?"

"He's over here." She tugged at his sleeve.

He turned around and came up close and personal with a flat-faced R2-D2. "Leonard, I presume?"

"Yup. Leonard, this is Ray Novino. He's going to fix you. Ray, this is Leonard. Isn't he beautiful?"

"I bet all the little girl vulcanizers think so."

She moved past him, some flowery fragrance wisping after her.

"This is the outlet."

He leaned his crutches against the wall and hunkered down so he could get a good look. It was a grounded outlet. Probably had to be in order to support a machine as powerful as Leonard. Sylvie set his bag of tools down next to him, and he pulled out a flathead screwdriver. He quickly unscrewed the outlet plate, pocketing the screws so they wouldn't get lost.

He carefully lowered the plate and aimed the

flashlight inside. He did not like what he saw.

"Lady," he said carefully, as he didn't want to scare her. "This must have been your lucky day."

"Why lucky? Do you know what's wrong? Can I fix it? I have to get Leonard going today. I have rubber to burn."

"Yes, I know what's wrong. And yes, it can probably be easily fixed. But you're lucky because you still have a house. It looks like this outlet was a whisper away from catching fire."

Chapter Ten

Now, standing in front of the myriad of objects that crammed the shelves of Hartley Hardware, Sylvie thought there was a solidity to all of it. Boxes and bricks, and metal things designed to hit and pound and cut. Maybe that was why it was called hardware. Whoever had designed this hardware store had made no attempt to be aesthetic about it. And there was the smell. Eau de Hardware. How different it was from a fabric store, where everything was soft and sensual, flowing, and full of color. Sylvie shook her head in resignation. They were looking for screws. Ray had said it was always good to have extras, just in case. "Okay," she said to Ray who was intently searching the little numbers in front of the little boxes on the shelves, "I give up. How do you know which one is which?" In spite of the long string of numbers on each box—and long strings of numbers made her eyes cross—they all looked alike.

Ray didn't look up from his search. "They're all different. Screws are not interchangeable. If we don't get the exact kind of screw we need, it won't work." He pulled out one box, peered in it, then slid it back in place. "Too long." He went back to his search.

"What are you looking for again?" she asked.

"The right kind of screw," he said patiently again without looking up.

She fisted her hands into her pockets and stepped closer to the shelves to study the little pictures on the ends of the boxes. She never knew there were *kinds* of screws. Of course, she'd never really thought about it. She knew they came in different sizes, different lengths, but wasn't a screw is a screw is a screw? Evidently not. At least, Ray didn't think so.

Okay, she saw it now. They *were* different. This one was flat, and that one was rounded. And they were different shapes. This one was hexagonal. Some had crosses on the tops, for Phillips head screwdrivers, some were for a common blade. And that one was—"Why are those blue? And why are those black?"

"They're for use with different materials. Those blue ones are for masonry. Those particular black ones are hardened steel."

"Are all black ones hardened steel?"

"Not necessarily."

"Where did you learn about electric stuff?" she asked. She didn't think she could ask him where he learned about screws—hardened steel ones at that—and keep a straight face.

There was an instant tightening of his shoulders, and a stillness. It was as if he'd become a statue, not breathing, all systems stop. Apparently this was not a casual question. She decided to wait it out, to see what he would do with it and at last he gave her an answer.

"My foster father was an electrician. I worked for him all through high school," he said shortly.

Foster father? A gazillion questions thrust up to the front of her mind, competing fiercely for her attention. What happened to his parents? Why did he have a foster father? And for how long?

But from the way Ray held his back to her and the way his knuckles paled on the handles of his crutches she could tell he didn't want to tell her any more about it. To ask him even one of her questions would be prying. Well, if they were going to be friends, she'd have to trust that he'd tell her someday. *You'll just have to be patient,* she told herself primly.

You're lousy at patient, she reminded herself sourly.

"Now, this is the one we need." Ray slid out a box and began counting out screws. "We'll get half a dozen of them, just to be safe." He shoved the screw box back on the shelf and led the way down the long aisle of hardware-store stuff. "The outlet plates are over here. If you want new ones—and I recommend you get new ones, they're inexpensive and will look better—you'll need to decide which ones you like. They're all different, too."

He made an abrupt turn and made his way down the aisle, leaving her there, in the middle of millions of screws and nails and bolts and nuts and whatever else inhabited the dark shelves of hardware stores. He needed some time, she realized. It must have been difficult for him to tell her he had a foster father. *Of course,* she told herself, *he could have just said he'd worked for an electrician while he was in high school, so he evidently wanted you to know that he had a foster family. Which means he wants you to know something—just not too much.*

"It might take me a while to look at the outlet plates. Is there something else that we need that you can get in the meantime?" she asked, swinging the red plastic basket as she headed after him.

"We also need the outlets themselves, and things to ground the outlet in your bedroom. I'll get those things while you're here."

"Good, then I'll meet you in ten or fifteen minutes in the front of the store." *That should be enough time for him to gain his composure,* she thought.

He glanced back at her, tossing her a brief and strained smile. "Okay."

So these were new outlet plates. As if they could possibly be of the least importance to her after he'd dropped that bombshell. She stared at the unoffending bits of plastic as her thoughts whirled and danced and surged.

Ray was a definite gentleman. When he showed her how the old outlet wires had almost caught fire, all the sawdust that had filtered behind the loose plates, he'd insisted on personally checking every single outlet and switch in her house. They all needed to have dust cleaned out and several of them needed to be replaced due to worn wiring, yet he had taken it all in stride as if it were no big problem. In her bedroom, where he had patently ignored her baskets of dirty laundry—at least it was in baskets—he told her the waterbed heater needed to have a grounded outlet. He even offered to ground it for her. Then he moved on to the kitchen, again not saying a word about the dirty dishes in the sink, or the spot of dried sugar and lemon juice that she'd hurriedly scrubbed at as he was looking the other way. He'd waited patiently as she'd shoved aside boxes of papers and junk, the flotsam and jetsam of her life, so he could get to the outlets in her computer room. Yes, Ray was a gentleman. He'd seen the worst of her house and he was still talking to her.

She picked up a plain white outlet plate and

turned it over and over in her hand, examining it from all angles. Then she looked back up at the display. Hanging on the next rack were light switch plates. She pulled one of them down as well. This one was ceramic rather than plastic. It had a plain flat white surface. Some of the others had ivy leaves on them, some had generic looking flowers. They certainly weren't very imaginative. Suddenly, her stamper's mind took over. Could she stamp on these? She'd have to use permanent ink so it wouldn't smear. She could send them in the mail! She could use that stamp of the plug, and maybe some of her sparks stamps. What a hoot! Then slap address labels on them, and some postage, and off they'd go to all parts of the country! Let's see. She needed one for Mad About Rubber, one for Princess Neutress, Sister Mary Rubber, and Rubber Dub Dub, Plum Crazy. She mentally ticked off the names of her stamp characters, pulling down a plastic plate for each one. Then she grabbed a couple of extras just for good measure. They would make great birthday presents.

"For someone whose house just almost burned down you sure look happy," he told her as she waltzed up to him fifteen minutes later. "That shopping basket is almost full." He set the new outlets in her basket and glanced at the things she'd put in. She had what looked like more than a dozen each of new outlet plates and switch plates. "Did you decide to replace all your light switches, too?" he asked, taking the basket from her.

"Are you being sarcastic?"

"No," he teased. "It's a perfectly good way to keep me busy all day."

Once again he was charmed by her laughter. And the light in her eyes, all crinkled up at the edges. In fact, suddenly he was charmed by all of her. Maybe she really was a sprite after all. Or at least some kind of magical being.

"May I help whoever is next?" called a clerk in a bored voice.

"I'm next," Sylvie answered, taking the basket back from him. He caught her saucy grin as she did a tiny dance step over to the counter to unload her basket. "Hello," she sang to the clerk. "Isn't it a lovely day?"

Ray ignored the clerk's gloomy reply about rain. He was too busy studying the pert figure before him. The wild red hair that reminded him of clouds on a breezy day was casually tied back in a loose ponytail. She wore a bright pink T-shirt, and blue jeans on those model long legs, and sneakers that—he stopped at her shoes. There were little fairies and dragons all over her shoes. He knew she'd done it. No one in their right mind would make shoes like that. No one would buy them.

A brief memory flitted past his mind. Once when he was in second grade he'd drawn something or other on his arm using one of those fine-tipped felt pens. "Why do you draw all over everything, Ray?" his mother asked plaintively as she scrubbed his arm until it was red. Then she'd hugged him and given him a new pad of drawing paper. "Draw on this, not on your arm, you silly goose," she'd told him, and kissed the top of his head.

When had he stopped drawing? And what would it be like to live with someone who insisted on putting fairies and dragons all over everything? It was amazing that there was a flat surface anywhere in her house that wasn't— The switch plates. He could see it now. Fairies and dragons on all the new switch plates.

Clouds were beginning to congregate over Hartley as Sylvie pulled into her driveway. "Rain is coming soon," she commented. It was more to make conversation than to impart information. She just liked to talk to people. She liked people.

Ray made a noncommittal sound of agreement.

"Soon it's gonna rain," she half sang half hummed the tune from *The Fantasticks*. "I'm not taking any chances with you right now," she told Jean-Luc as she snapped on his leash before she let him out of the car. "You might just get it into your curly head to run away, and right now I have more important things to do than to chase you down again."

Jean-Luc gave her a long-suffering look, as if being on a leash was totally below him, but it was also beneath him to protest.

"Let me take those." Ray reached around her to take the shopping bag before she could get them.

When had a man ever treated her as if she were someone to be cared for? She couldn't remember it ever happening. It made her feel special. "They say that chivalry is dead," she told him with a smile as she latched the gate behind them.

"Not dead. Just in a coma," he answered.

On the porch, she pulled out her keys and unlocked the front door. Suddenly there was a loud crack of thunder. Jean-Luc dashed past them into the house and hit the end of his leash. "Whoops!" Sylvie told him. She unsnapped his leash. "There you go." And he was gone.

"I'm glad we got home before the rain started," she told Ray. "That dog is terrified of thunder. Distant thunder is no problem, but he turns into a quivering mass of poodle when the thunder gets close. And he absolutely hates to go outside in the rain. He's a total wuss about it."

"Where is he?" asked Ray glancing around.

"He's probably in the bathroom hiding behind the toilet. For some reason he thinks that's a safe spot. I'll go get him." Sure enough, Jean-Luc was cowering in the bathroom. Sylvie took hold of his collar and hauled him out. "C'mon, you big lug. You have to go potty before the rain starts." She practically dragged him to the front door. As this was a common occurrence during thunderstorms, she was used to it. "Hey, silly, don't try to climb up Ray. He's not a tree. Yes, you're the best poodle in the world. Now go outside and go potty before there's more thunder and it rains." She shoved him out the door. "Get off the porch and hurry. Then you can come back in." She turned to take the bag from Ray. "He doesn't mind the rain itself, but he's terrified of the noise, and he hates stepping in puddles."

"I thought you told me poodles were swimmers."

"Oh, he loves to swim. But he doesn't like to get his feet wet. Go figure. Except for those two wussy idiosyncrasies he's quite a perfect dog. And also except for the fact that he doesn't come when he's called."

From outside on the porch, Jean-Luc yipped to be let back in. Sylvie opened the door. Jean-Luc threw himself upon Ray with frantic glee.

"I hear you're a fluff ball," Ray said to Jean-Luc as he petted him affectionately.

"Poodles aren't fluff balls at all," she told him. "Most people think they're airheads because they usually look so prissy and frilly and silly. Especially when their owners put them in bows and paint their toenails and all of that. Actually they're exceptionally intelligent. They're just judged by their looks all the time, which actually says more about the people who are doing the judging than the dogs. What? Why are you looking at me like that?" He'd trained his gaze on her, those eyes that were a luminescent version of Marvey color #33, clear and full of depth.

"Because you were talking about you, not your dog."

"When? Just now? I was telling you that Jean-Luc and his poodle brethren are very intelligent," she said curtly.

"Yes, but you were also talking about yourself."

She could only stare at him.

"Yoo-hoo!" Sally's voice came floating across the front yard. "Hello there," she called.

Sylvie's gaze was still locked with Ray's. "We're in here, Sally," she called back to her friend.

"That's good," Sally said as she opened the screen door and let it bang behind her. "Because I didn't want to eat all of this by myself. Hi, Ray, I hope you like chocolate. No, Jean-Luc, sweetie, this is people food. Not that *that* has ever stopped you."

Finally Sylvie was free of that blue gaze, breathless but free. "Hi, Sally, whatcha got?" she asked, with a quick glance out the door to make sure Sally had fastened the front gate. She had. Sally knew Jean-Luc.

"I don't smell burning rubber. Hey, do I have the wrong day? Is it Tuesday already? I get confused during summer vacation."

"I'm replacing some of Sylvie's outlets before she turns on her—Leonard," Ray explained.

"Evidently, my house almost burned down," Sylvie added cheerfully.

"Not cool," Sally said. "That would've been a big-time distress. Good thing Ray came to your rescue. Especially since I need to borrow some of your stamps today. Anyway, it sounds like too much hard work to do before lunch. It *is* lunchtime you know."

Sylvie glanced at her watch. "It's only eleven forty-five," she pointed out.

"That's lunchtime. And if you're lucky you get a whole half hour without playground duty. Of course with the rain coming we might have to stay indoors." Then her expression lost its usual teasing look. "Did your house really almost burn down?"

Sylvie nodded. "The outlet was smoking."

"But did it inhale?" Sally quipped. "Looks like your dragons and your house have joined forces." Then her face grew serious. "Sorry, I just couldn't help myself. Why was it smoking?"

"The wiring is old," Ray told her. "And the outlet was full of dust. It's a fairly simple matter to clean out the dust and replace the outlet. Rewiring the whole house would be more complicated."

"Enough of this talk," Sylvie ordered. "My house is going to be fine. As soon as Ray can change some outlets. So, no more talk about burning houses. Too depressing."

"Let's talk about lunch, then." Sally beamed at them and held out two bulging plastic bags.

"What did you do?" Sylvie asked.

"Ray, I hope you like chicken salad because I stopped at Lola's and bought a bunch of it. And I got some of her croissants, and she'd just baked some chocolate revival cookies so I also brought half a dozen of them. Sylvie, you're drooling." Sally leaned toward Ray and whispered conspiratorially, "She loves those things. They're so good they practically make your eyes cross. She'll do almost anything for one of Lola's chocolate revivals."

"Like Jean-Luc and frozen vegetables?" Ray asked, equally conspiratorially. "Will she sit, and shake hands?"

Sylvie burst out laughing. "Okay, guys, let's not pick on Sylvie this morning."

"We're not picking on you," Ray protested.

"You're teasing me."

"Yes," he agreed. "But that's not picking on you. That's teasing you."

"I suppose you think you have the right to tease me just because you're replacing my outlets."

"That's right."

She felt her insides go all mushy at his grin.

"So, Sally," Ray said, directing his grin at her friend. "Did you bring these particular chocolate revivals today as a bribe?"

"Yup," Sally said smugly. "I figured since I needed to use some of her rubber I'd bring her lunch as a bribe. I know the way to the kitchen, so give me about ten minutes and it'll be ready."

Ray held up the bag of outlets. "Care to help me? We can probably do the first one in ten minutes."

When he looked at her like that she'd follow him anywhere, she thought. She felt a slow blush creep up her neck and face. *Stop it!* she told herself firmly. *Forget this attraction bit, you're only going to be friends.* "Sure, what do I do?"

It was oddly relaxing, even comforting, Ray thought, to do this kind of work again. He liked working with his hands, liked fixing things. It gave him a sense of accomplishment, a sense of completion. He also liked Sylvie near him, handing him tools, holding the flashlight steady. Liked the way her arm accidentally brushed his from time to time. He shifted his position slightly so those accidents occurred with greater frequency.

"So that's all there is to it?" she asked, surprise filling her eyes. "You just use that thingy to strip the sheath off the wire—"

"That thingy is called a stripper," he corrected patiently. "The wire covering is called the insulation."

"I like sheath better," She said." "Okay. The stripper and the sheath. Sounds like a box-office hit. Oh no, that would be The Stripper and The Sheik." She grinned in obvious delight. "Anyway, you strip the wire, and when it's naked you put it in this little hole. And it makes electricity. That's it?"

Had she deliberately softened her voice, made it sound sultry? He hoped she didn't know what that kind of voice did to him. If she continued, it could be embarrassing. He swallowed. "Do you want it to be more complicated than that?" he asked, catching her gaze and squelching down impertinent images of making electricity with her. *Watch out,* he cautioned himself. *Talk about making electricity, buddy, and you're playing with serious fire here. Her house might really burn down.*

She still held his gaze in the glow of the flashlight. Her eyes were twinkling, and he could see into her very soul. He knew she could see into his as well, could see his desire, his longing. He was suspended, out of time, as a captive in the hands of an enchantress. He eased toward her, just a whisper closer, their gazes still holding. Would she lean toward him? After a fraction of a second, yes. Holding her gaze—was he the enchanter now?—he imagined what her lips would taste like, feel like. He imagined their softness as he moved another whisper closer. Then another. Still drowning in her gaze.

"Let's do it, you guys!" Sally called from the top of the stairs. "It's time for lunch. Can we turn the electricity on now? It's getting dark outside. Regular gray cloud convention out there."

He jerked away from Sylvie as if he'd just woken from a dream. Feeling himself turn red, he quickly turned his attention to screwing on the outlet cover. "Electricity to the kitchen coming right up," he called. "As soon as we turn the breaker on. And you—" He glanced over at Sylvie—at least he meant it to be a glance. But the glance turned into an actual look, and once again he was overwhelmed by the attraction he felt for her. She was so interested in everything—asking him question after question about how to do the repairs, how he knew which wire went where, why they were different colors. He could almost see the workings of her mind in the expressions that crossed her face. Was that regret he saw? Regret because he'd almost kissed her? Or was it regret because they were interrupted? He could watch her face forever. But forever would have to wait. "We can turn on the breaker to your workshop now and then you can turn on your vulcanizer."

Delight bursting forth in her eyes banished all traces of regret. "It's so good of you to help me," she said, somewhat breathlessly. "To spend your morning—when you should be resting your ankle—coming to my aid. How can I thank you? Name your reward."

When she looked at him like that, her eyes alight in the glow of the flashlight, he knew what he wanted as his reward. *Hands off,* he cautioned himself. *She's out of your league.*

Chapter Eleven

"Sally, look what you've done," Sylvie exclaimed. "This is wonderful."

"Aw, shucks, ma'am, t'weren't nuthin," Sally said in a faux cowboy twang.

But it was. Sally had cleared the kitchen table and had even ferreted out a tablecloth.

"The plates don't match," Sally told Ray. "Sylvie says that way everyone can pick out which one they like the best."

"Makes sense to me," Ray answered.

Sylvie wondered what was going on in his head, though. She remembered taking a peek inside his cupboard when she first went over to his house and made him tea. Was it only two days ago? He'd had what looked like a complete set of some of that unbreakable china. Everything matched at Ray's house.

"Chicken salad and croissants from Lola's," Sally went on. "Ray, you sit here by the window, and Sylvie you're here. Fruit salad from Abernathy's, iced tea à la Sylvie. Jean-Luc, get your nose away from the table. And I refilled the ice cube trays because Jean-Luc insisted on his fair share."

"For someone who doesn't like dogs, you sure spoil this one."

"I never said I don't like dogs," Sally replied pertly. "They have a right to exist. They're just not cats." She didn't even try to hide the tidbit she slipped to Jean-Luc.

"Have you ever had a dog?" Ray asked, an eyebrow raised.

"Never a one," was the cheerful answer. "Don't want one, neither. How could I let a dog stand where a cat once stood before?"

"That's beggar and king, you silly. Let a beggar stand where a king once stood before. Or something like that," Sylvie corrected. "If you're going to butcher poetry please get it right. I like the stuff."

"Isn't that a contradiction?" Ray asked, his eyes twinkling. "Butchering correctly?"

"Depends on whether or not you're a cow, I suppose," Sally answered, passing a platter of Lola's chicken salad. "Have you ever had this, Ray? It's truly scrumptious."

A short streak of lightning shot across the sky

outside. "One-one thousand," Sylvie counted. "Two one-thousand, three one-thousand, four one-thousand." There was a grumble of thunder. "There goes Jean-Luc, streaking off for the safety of the bathroom."

"Lucky again," Ray told Sylvie. "We got that first outlet done before the thunderstorm arrived. It's not a good idea to be working on electrical outlets when there's lightning around. There's only a slim possibility that you'd be hurt, but it's not worth the chance."

"I really appreciate this, you know," Sally said after lunch as she followed Sylvie upstairs to the Rubber Room. Ray remained downstairs, hard at work.

"Yeah, you've appreciated it every summer since I've known you," Sylvie teased.

"The kids appreciate it, too. They love getting a letter from their kindergarten teacher. Putting different stamps on each letter makes them even more special."

"So what do you need? A kitten for Caitlin, they're over there with the domesticated animal stamps. Also a dog for Angie. And over with the body parts, I even have a leg-in-a-cast stamp for Joshua Martini. And yes, I have purple ink, pens, pencils, watercolors." Joshua Martini's purple cast had been the talk of the kindergarten the previous winter.

Sylvie switched on the light and waved Sally into her Rubber Room. "It's all yours. Just clean the stamps when you're finished, and put them back where they belong or you're dog food."

"I always put them away," Sally pretended to huff. "I'm a good putter-awayer. I teach kids to put things away. What's this?" She dropped her stack of letters on the worktable and turned over a piece of paper on Sylvie's drawing board. It was the image of Ray as the sleeping prince. Sylvie had turned it facedown earlier that morning when she brought Ray upstairs to check the outlets.

Sylvie grabbed for it. "It's just something I've been working on."

Sally raised it out of Sylvie's reach. "Let Auntie Sally take a look at this. Hmm. Methinks I see someone I know here." She squinted dramatically at the page. "I spy with my little eye a prince that looks like your mailman." She raised her eyebrows at Sylvie. "What is the meaning of this?"

Sylvie squirmed under her friend's scrutiny. "No meaning at all."

"That's guano. And I'm a teacher, I work with school administrators. I know first-class guano when I hear it. You're smitten, aren't you?"

Sylvie felt herself turn the color of a fire engine. "No," she protested. "I'm not. I just thought he would be interesting to do."

"And it just happens to be a prince?"

"So, I needed a prince." She tried a careless shrug. She didn't think Sally was fooled.

"Yes, I know you do."

"Not for *me,* for Delphine. She needed a prince. Someone to be a human companion—not that she needed him around to rescue her or anything like that. Halcyon is a faithful companion, but she needed someone like her. Someone she could talk to."

"But you see, my friend, the lovely Princess Delphine is your alter ego."

"You've obviously been talking to Karen," Sylvie grumbled.

"But of course. And just wait until she sees this drawing! She'll really go to town! There is a certain air of sensuality to this prince. He's almost sexy, but not quite, as if you've not made up your mind. Or maybe as if you don't want to admit that you have. You really like him, don't you?" Without waiting for an answer Sally continued. "I'm glad. And I heartily approve. So does Jessie, by the way. And also Karen, and M'liss."

"I don't need your approval," Sylvie muttered. "I'm a big girl."

"Of course you are." Sally grinned at her. "But except for Florian, we're the closest thing to family that you have around this part of the world. You could always take Ray to Florian for approval, but he'd just tease you to death and embarrass you."

"I suppose the phone lines in Hartley were buzzing last night while you all dissected my friendship with Ray."

"Yup," Sally said, her expression catlike

smug. "We all think you should go for it."

"I'm glad I have your stamp of approval," Sylvie said glumly. "But speaking of good housekeeping, I don't. He does. Y'all haven't seen his house. I could never be happy living that neatly."

"You just say that to relieve your cognitive dissonance."

"You're beginning to sound like Karen again."

"Speaking of Karen, and your slovenly ways, why don't you hire her daughter to come clean your house once a week? It'd give you a sparklingly spotless house, and it would give Katie an outlet for her fastidious nature. You know she's horribly frustrated by their house, all the Newfoundland hair they sweep up every day. Not to mention all the dog nose muck on the windows. Karen says Katie always mutters darkly about Sisyphus when she cleans the house. C'mon, Sylvie," she coaxed, "do it. Do it for Katie if not for yourself. She's the daughter of one of your best friends, and she needs something to do that will keep her out of Karen's hair this summer. It'd be good for both of you."

Sylvie gazed out the window at the clouds. They weren't as heavy as they'd been earlier. She could see hints of blue sky behind them. "It looks like the thunderstorm might be over soon," she commented. "Jean-Luc will be able to rejoin the universe."

"Quit changing the subject."

"Quit being so bossy."

"I have every right to be bossy. I'm your friend and I love you."

"I'll think about it."

"Good. Think about it all you want, then call Katie and ask her to come over once a week and clean your house for you. Maybe even twice a week. Everyone will be happy."

Sylvie plucked the drawing of the sleeping prince out of Sally's hands and put it back on her drawing table. "I'll think about it," she promised.

"And I'll clean the stamps and put them away when I'm finished."

This was, Sylvie thought, a good time to make her escape. "Leonard should be all warmed up now and ready to go. I'm going to go burn some rubber. I'll be in the basement with the Beatles on, so yell loudly if you need me."

"Sylvie," Sally's voice called her back. She turned to see her friend, earnestly watching her. "You can't run away from your feelings. It doesn't work. People try it and they get all messed up inside."

Suddenly Sylvie found her feet to be very interesting. "I'm not running away."

"You sure could have fooled me. Big dragon here. It's name is Hiding From Life 'Cause Life Sometimes Hurts. This is one you gotta vanquish."

"Are you sure you don't need my help?" she asked Ray before she descended into the depths of her basement.

"Yes, I'm sure," Ray told her. "Jean-Luc will keep me company, won't you, boy?"

Jean-Luc, having just been coaxed out from behind the toilet, but looking ready to bolt at a moment's notice, eyed them nervously and licked his nose.

"I take that as a yes," Ray interpreted with a chuckle.

"Well, okay, if you're sure," she said doubtfully.

"I'm sure. Replacing outlets and switches is not rocket science. I'm also sure you have your rubber to burn." But most of all, it would be best if she weren't near him while he worked. As much as he liked it, being close to her made him feel things he wasn't sure he wanted to feel. He was here to do her a favor, to help her. To do a heroic deed. Nothing more. He wasn't here to be a prince to her princess. Even though that was an enticing thought, great fantasy fodder.

"Then I'll be in the basement if you need me. I hope you like the Beatles."

"I like the Beatles fine," he said, following her to the stairs. "And I have to come down to the basement anyway to turn off the breakers to this part of the house."

She spun around to face him, an unconvincing scowl on her upturned face. "No."

"No?"

"That's right. Not with that ankle. I can turn off breakers for you. Just yell down which ones you want turned off." She thrust her chin out at him.

Determined thing, she was. He grinned at her, knowing if he fought this skirmish he'd only end up letting her win.

"Then please turn off the breakers to the dining room, the kitchen, and your bedroom. C'mon, Jean-Luc, let's get this show on the road."

The poodle tucked his tail between his legs and followed him. Guys, even if one of them was a wuss, needed to stick together.

"Breakers are off," Sylvie's voice floated upstairs a few seconds later followed by the opening chords of *Sgt. Pepper's*.

"Thanks," he called back. Whistling the tune—he hadn't heard this in years—he consulted the piece of paper they'd scribbled on earlier that morning. Let's see. The outlet under the window in the dining room needed to be changed. Well, she called it a dining room, but the table couldn't possibly have seen a meal in eons. It was buried entirely under piles of papers, books, magazines, pieces of cloth, all the flotsam and jetsam of someone who had never learned to put things away. Although maybe they belonged on the table. Maybe they'd grown there. Now that was a scary thought.

He propped his crutches up against the wall and hunkered down in front of the outlet. Jean-Luc crouched down as close to Ray as possible and stuck his nose in the way.

"You're a good helper, Jean-Luc, but you need to move your nose so I can see what I'm doing."

Jean-Luc snorted.

"Well then, move over here." He patted the floor invitingly. Jean-Luc did not move. Ray tried to pry the dog away from his leg. Just then there was another lightning flash. Ray counted to eight thousand before he heard the rumble.

Jean-Luc licked his lips, but he didn't run.

"Good boy," Ray praised the dog. "You didn't run away. But you have to move. Well, I guess that will have to do. Time to learn how to change outlets. Are you watching? Test on Friday. Okay, first you unscrew this plate, like this here."

The outlet was quickly changed. But before he went on to the next one—in the kitchen, by the telephone—he took a look out the window. The clouds had broken up but rain was still sheeting off the eaves. Gutters. They were still clogged and right now he couldn't do a darn thing about it. He shook his head in annoyance. This ankle was truly a bother. Well, her gutters would have to wait until he was divorced from these blasted crutches. Unless—

"Say, Jean-Luc. Sylvie said you loved to climb ladders. I bet I could teach you to clean out gutters, do you think so?"

Jean-Luc licked his lips.

As Ray worked his way through her house, Jean-Luc stuck to him like glue. "She should've named you Elmer," he told the poodle. Ray wondered about the difference in the three levels of her house. Each was completely different, according to what Sylvie did in it. The basement, Leonard's Lair, where she made her stamps and filled orders, was neat and tidy, everything in its place. The upstairs, the large open space she called her rubber room, was likewise kept neat and unchaotic. This was where, she'd explained to him, she did her artwork, created the designs that she turned into rubber, and where she made cards to send to people. The main floor, however, was a disaster. It was as if she spent her working hours, her creative hours, in neatness. But in between, in the living part of her house, she couldn't be bothered.

Once again he regarded the room—color everywhere, splashes of it, waves of it. Varied in tone and hue. Her house, at least this floor, was like a modern painting, the color random and frenetic.

"Here's something," he murmured to Jean-Luc. He picked up the small silver frame to study the photograph in it. It was a family with a man, woman, three children and a dog, all in a manicured yard with a large mansion in the background. It was her family, he knew. He peered more closely. The girl—Sylvie, he'd know her anywhere—looked about ten, and had a great grin on her face as if utterly delighted by life. He'd seen that grin before. When she'd taken her first bite of chocolate cookie at lunch. Rapturous. As if she'd been given the world. He looked at the faces of her family. They, on the other hand, all shared expressions of distant calm, as if they'd never known gut-wrenching hurt, as if they'd never seen ugliness. He studied what he could see of the house. Big, expensive.

So this was Sylvie's family.

He was right. He didn't belong here. He, who had no parents, no sisters or brothers, who'd grown up in a working-class foster family, who was still working class and proud of it. It was probably a good thing Sally had interrupted them before lunch, or he would have kissed her. Somehow, knowing the interruption was a good thing did not cheer him up.

A wet nose thrust itself into his hand. "Well, Jean-Luc, we see the tracks. And I am definitely from the other side."

Jean-Luc wagged his tail, more in response to being spoken to, he hoped, than in agreement with what had been said.

She came from the house on the hill, so to speak, and she even had a poodle, for Pete's sake. No mutt for her. Still, he liked Jean-Luc. "You're a good guy, even for a wuss. You know that?" he said to the dog, scrubbing the curly head with his knuckles.

Yes, he felt sure, Jean-Luc knew that.

He paused by the door of her bedroom. He felt funny about going in, but the outlet where she plugged in the waterbed heater had to be grounded—it was a safety issue. She'd given him the go-ahead to her house, so he wasn't trespassing. There was really no need for him to feel strange. After all, he'd spent several summers going through people's houses doing electrical work. *Ah, but that was different,* he pointed out to himself. *Those people were complete strangers. Those people hadn't haunted your dreams. Those people weren't like magical creatures who would change your life. Those people weren't Sylvie.*

Jean-Luc, however, had no such apprehensions. He shoved the door open with his nose, trotted in, leapt gracefully into the center of the waterbed, nosed around in all the pillows and covers—flowered sheets and comforter of course, as he could have predicted. Ray didn't want to look too closely at the bedding, in case he might find fairies in between the flowers—then plopped down. A waterbed. The epitome of luxurious bliss.

"I know what you mean," Ray muttered to him. But he had to stop thinking about Sylvie as someone he wanted to explore, someone he wanted to touch, to kiss, to hold, to treasure. *Quit staring at her bed,* he scolded himself. So he looked at her wall. Instead of wallpaper, the wall was one huge seething mass of stamped art. It was literally covered by small scenes, dotted with stars, drifts of flowers, fairies flitting, gargoyles crouching, trees lifting their limbs to whatever was above. It was a fantastic example of graffiti raised to the level of art—and it *was* art. This woman had an amazing talent.

Ray shrugged and turned back to the task of grounding the outlet. As he unscrewed the plate a delicate scent teased his senses. He lifted his head and closed his eyes in concentration. Yes, it was still there, that elusive scent he'd first noticed, that scent that somehow reminded him of his mother. He closed his eyes for a moment, drinking in that scent, and memories of his mother. "You're a wonderful person, Ray," she used to say to him. "Don't ever forget that." Had he forgotten?

Suddenly, there was a new smell, acrid and indescribable. It smelled slightly like burning tires, but there was even more of a bite to it. He wrinkled his nose and shuddered. This must be the notorious smell of rubber cooking. It was not pleasant.

Several minutes later, the outlet grounded, Ray glanced out of the bedroom window. The rain had slowed to a mere sprinkle, dripping off the eaves. Didn't she care that clogged gutters were damaging to a house?

Movement in the street caught his eye. It was Tony, the substitute carrier, doing Ray's route. Ray watched him unlatch the gate, come up the walk, reach into his bag, pull out a sheaf of mail, and then struggle slightly to pull out something else. Something odd. It looked like—it couldn't be. It was.

Suddenly, all of Ray's burgeoning tender feelings for Sylvie were squashed flat, replaced by a familiar feeling of exasperation. He had forgotten the SPAM. He'd forgotten that she wasn't Sylvie the Sylph, she was that notorious thorn in his side, The Crazy Lady. He had forgotten the countless times he'd wanted to strangle this lady and all her wacky friends. Mailbags were meant for mail, not cans of SPAM, and not for the other objects that they sent each other.

There was the sound of Sylvie's mail being shoved in the box, followed by a slight thump on the front porch as the substitute mail carrier delivered the bicycle tire.

A bicycle tire.

Chapter Twelve

"So tell me what happened," Karen said. "So far all you've done on this walk is sigh and look piteous. And let me tell you, since you're obviously not in a frame of mind to appreciate it, that tonight is a lovely evening."

Sylvie smiled at her friend. It was a wan smile, though, for she really didn't feel much like smiling.

"That's a start," Karen encouraged. "Keep it up and the next thing you know we'll have an actual laugh. Brian, leave it." The Newfoundland dropped the piece of paper he'd nosed from under a drift of dried leaves. "Good boy." Brian swished his tail.

Jean-Luc, unleashed because they were safe in Karen's fenced-in acres, pranced brightly along next to Sylvie, head up, eyes darting in all directions. He wanted some excitement.

"Look at these two dogs," Sylvie said, trying to be conversational. "They are completely different. Jean-Luc is pure white, curly hair, fine boned. Brian Boru is pure black, long full flat coat, heavy boned. Jean-Luc prances, Brian plods. Yet they're still best buddies."

"Brian doesn't plod," Karen corrected. "He moves in a stately manner. He's powerful and steady and reliable. Jean-Luc is flighty and tends to be hyperactive." As if to prove her point, Jean-Luc danced up on his hind legs, batting at the Newfoundland. Brian simply ignored him and let out a great gusty grunt. "Jean-Luc is swift and fleet and probably has a higher metabolism. They both are exactly what they were bred to be. So what is your point?"

Sylvie shrugged, not meeting her friend's gaze. "I'm just saying that it's nice that they can be so different and still be friends."

"No you're not. You're using them to represent two other people. I'd guess you're really talking about you and Ray. However, it's usually easier to talk about your own life if you use proxies, representations, symbols. That's one reason we sometimes use dolls and toys when we work with children."

"That's why it's a pain in the neck to have a best friend who's a psychologist," Sylvie groused. "You can't make a simple little comment without her trying to read all sorts of things into it."

Karen let out a peal of laughter. "I only read things if they're there."

Sylvie stubbed a sneakered toe into a clump of dirt. "Well, maybe it is there," she admitted.

"Maybe," Karen agreed.

They walked a few more yards in companionable silence. It was one of the good things about Karen, Sylvie thought. She didn't feel the need to fill up all the silences with idle chatter. You could be quiet with Karen, could go on a walk and never say a word. Of course, Sylvie usually had something to say. She liked to talk. She'd talk anytime to anyone about anything. Her mother used to say that Sylvie had learned to talk when she was nine months old, and Florian would add that she'd never shut up since.

"Okay, I'll tell you," she said at last.

"Okay. Tell me."

"I don't know what happened." *That's not precisely true,* she told herself. *What happened is that Ray didn't kiss you.*

"What do you mean you don't know what happened?"

Sylvie shook her head miserably. "I don't know what happened. One minute everything was fine and so I went downstairs to burn my rubber and I turned off the breakers so Ray could do the electrical work. Then about an hour later I brought some boxes upstairs to put them in my car to take them to the post office."

"So?"

"Everything was different. Sally came downstairs because she was finished using my stamps, and I think she knew something wasn't right because she left pretty quickly. She didn't even stay to finish the last chocolate revival cookie."

"Yes, I can see how that's serious."

"Don't tease."

"I'm not teasing. Sally leaving without the last chocolate revival *is* serious."

Jean-Luc danced back to Sylvie for a pat. She looked down at him forlornly. "You still love me, even if no one else does, don't you, Jean-Luc?" Karen snorted derisively. Jean-Luc wiggled away from Sylvie and struck his Dignified Dog Looking Down Upon the Masses pose.

"So tell me about Ray when you came upstairs. What was he doing?"

Sylvie closed her eyes for a moment, so she could describe it better. "It was as if he'd closed the curtains to his soul," she said at last. "He was polite, said all the right things, did all the right things, but there was a distance in him, as if he were holding me at arm's length. No, even farther than that. As if I were a stranger to him, or someone he was acquainted with casually." She frowned in remembrance.

"Then what happened?"

"He'd finished doing the outlets, so I offered to drive him home on my way to the post office. He accepted, and so I went downstairs to turn off Leonard—I wasn't finished, but it was obvious that Ray didn't want to be in my house any longer. I loaded up all my orders, drove Ray home, went to the post office, returned home, turned Leonard back on, finished burning my rubber, fed Jean-Luc his supper, then I called you."

"Did you ask him about this change in his behavior?"

Sylvie felt her eyes grow big as she turned to look at her friend. "I couldn't do that."

"Why not?"

"Because . . . because . . . well, I just couldn't, that's why."

Karen smiled tolerantly. "Because it would have embarrassed you to ask?" she suggested. "Or because it might have embarrassed him to be asked? Or because you really didn't want to know? Or because by asking such a thing you might be making yourself vulnerable? Or because he might not tell you the truth?"

Sylvie thought for a moment, then nodded. "Yes."

"Which one?"

"All of them."

Karen chuckled. "You're saying you'd rather worry about all the possibilities of what might be wrong than deal with the truth?"

Sylvie let out a sigh of exasperation. "Why are you always so reasonable?"

"I'm not always reasonable, and you know it. In fact, when it comes to my own life I can hide from the truth and reality with the best of them."

"Yeah," Sylvie muttered, "that's when we all have to get together and whup you up the side of the head."

"That's right," was the cheerful reply. "That's what friends are for."

"Okay, friend, then tell me what I should do. Should I go over to his house tomorrow and demand to know why he was treating me as if I had something contagious? Or do I pretend nothing has changed? Or do I just shrug my shoulders and say it's been fun and *adios*?"

"What do you want to do?"

Sylvie growled at her. "I don't know what I want to do. That's why I'm asking you. You're my friend. You're supposed to tell me."

Karen shook her head. "Nope. I'll help you figure out what you want to do, but I won't tell you what that is."

Sylvie threw up her hands. "So help me figure it out. Before I go crazy."

Jean-Luc pranced over to her, followed by Brian in his lackadaisical stroll.

"Yes, you guys, I'm frustrated."

The dogs comforted her in their individual doggy ways. Jean-Luc stood on his hind feet to show her how cute he was, Brian leaned his bulky self against her, thwapping his tail against her legs. "You're such great guy dogs," she told them, reaching down to catch them both in hugs.

"They should be. They're both named after great guy heroes."

That reminded Sylvie of something. "Sally said Princess Delphine is my alter ego and because I think she needs a human companion it means that I want a human companion for myself. What do you think?"

Karen chucked. "I'd be more interested in knowing what you think."

"You're the psych. You're supposed to know these things. What good is all that knowledge if you don't share it?"

"All that knowledge tells me that what truly matters most in your life is what *you* think, and that what you think should not be colored by what *I* think."

"So forget your paper training. Be rebellious. Pretend I'm someone else and we're gossiping. Please?"

"I think there may be some truth in what Sally said."

They had come to the flat grassy back part of Karen's property. Karen pulled two tennis balls from her pockets. She handed one to Sylvie. "You throw for Jean-Luc that way," she said, pointing. "I'll throw for Brian this way."

Sylvie nodded in complete understanding. It didn't work to throw the balls in the same direction. Jean-Luc was just too speedy for Brian's loping gait. This way the game was kept fair.

Sylvie and Karen settled on the grass, back to

back, and on the count of three, they each threw a tennis ball. The dogs took off.

"So you think I'm subconsciously telling myself it's time for me to find my prince?"

"Maybe."

"Am I right?"

"Sylvie," her friend groaned. "I can't tell you that. I don't know. But I sometimes think you're trying to hide from life, shut yourself up in a make-believe world, where everyone lives happily ever after. That is not life. Life is not perfect. It's full of pain, and disappointment, even heartache. It's messy and tangled and sometimes ugly. But it's the living, the struggling, the times that we stumble and fall and get back up again. It's our battle scars that make us beautiful. And interesting. And compassionate. Trust me, you really wouldn't want a Stepford life."

"I know that."

"Yes, I know you do. And I also know that you've heard Tanner's lecture on Everything You Ever Wanted to Know About Pack Behavior But Were Afraid To Ask, because you've taken his beginning obedience classes. But, Sylvie, pack behavior doesn't just apply to dogs. Remember that people live in packs also. I think you might be trying to tell yourself it's time to create a human pack."

Sylvie threw the ball again, this time farther. Jean-Luc bounded after it with absolute glee. "You and Melissa and Tanner are just doggier than I am. I don't necessarily relate everything to dogs."

Karen hooted. "No. You relate every thing to dragons. At least dogs are real."

"Dragons are real. They're just metaphorical." With a sad smile that signaled she no longer wanted to discuss the situation, Sylvie turned. "Speaking of dragons, I could almost feel the ground shake as Brian brought his ball back just now."

"That's my great guy dog," Karen said with affection in her voice.

Ray stared unseeing out into the gathering gloom. Gloom certainly fit his mood, he told himself. Really, though, there was no reason for it. Why should he be gloomy? He turned and gazed around his apartment. Everything was clean, neat. Spartan. The way he liked it.

Is this really the way you like it? a sly voice whispered in his mind. The image of Sylvie's sly dragon stamp insinuated itself into his mind. It was mocking him, taunting him.

He tried to slam the door on the whispering voice but it had already done its damage. *Was* this the way he liked his life? Organized, predictable, controlled? Suddenly he realized that the only color in his living room came from the spines of the lined-up books on the shelves, and from the CDs, in order on their rack. Everything else in the room was either black or brown or gray. The couch was brown and gray. Even the painting on the wall lacked bright color—it was a Wyeth print. He'd always found it soothing.

You've always found it safe, came that whispering voice.

Safe from what? he wondered.

Safe from life, was the answer. He imagined the dragon chuckling slyly.

But he wasn't afraid of life. He didn't run from responsibilities. He had a job, paid taxes. His bills were always paid on time. He'd never bounced a check.

That's not living, that's existing.

Well shouldn't existence count for something?

Not at the expense of life. Heroes are not content to merely breathe. Heroes live. Heroes have families, and dogs and cats.

I did a heroic deed today, he protested. *I helped Sylvie.*

Men who want to be heroes and the women who drive them crazy, the voice taunted.

Go away! he commanded the voice.

If this were a movie, he thought, he'd now hear the cackle of evil laughter and see the burst of smoke as the dragon disappeared. He snorted at himself in disgust. He'd just wasted a couple of hours staring outside at the sky. Really, he had to stop this self-evaluation. He had things to do. He had to make dinner.

He turned his back deliberately on the living room, strode into the kitchen, and opened the refrigerator. By now it was too late to make meat loaf—that would have to wait until tomorrow. For tonight he'd have to settle for the leftover macaroni and cheese in the freezer.

But when he set his single place at the table he gazed for a moment at his plate. It was plain white, unadorned. Sylvie's plates were gold rimmed, and flowered, looked like they were all flea-market alumni. Sylvie's table had flowers in vases on it, unmatched napkin rings with cloth napkins. Certainly she could afford matching things, she just preferred things that were . . . unique.

Dammit! He had to stop comparing his apartment to her house. They were too different. She was from the house on the hill, remember? He was from the wrong side of the tracks. Her family was cultured, wealthy. He never knew who his father was, and when his mother died he'd been placed with a foster family. She'd gone to college, to graduate school, for Pete's sake. He had gone to work right out of high school.

"You're a wonderful person, Ray," his mother's voice came back to him. *"And I love you more than anything in the whole world. Don't ever forget that."*

Wonderful he may be, but he was still out of Sylvie's league. Besides, she drove him crazy. Her drawings were lovely, but this hobby of hers was a menace to the post office. It showed a diseased mind—an indescribable frivolity. What with all the outrageous things she and her friends sent each other in the mail. A bicycle tire, for Pete's sake! He just had to remember that and everything would be fine.

That's right. It was the taunting voice again. *Forget about truly living. Be content to continue to merely exist. Content to merely use up space and oxygen. You're good at it. Nothing will change. Your life will be safe. And you'll always be as lonely as you are now.*

Chapter Thirteen

Sylvie spent the rest of the week making stamps, filling orders, readying her new catalog supplement, chatting via E-mail with stampers from all over the country, chatting with them on the phone when they called in orders, and working on stamped cards to send out to her mail buddies. She made preliminary preparations for her booth at the rubber stamp convention that was coming up next month. Anything and everything she could think of to keep busy.

She received a pair of child's safety scissors from Princess Neutress, a straw hat from Sister Mary Rubber—the postage had come loose from the straw and copious amounts of tape had been used to refasten it—a bag of Oreos from Mad About Rubber, the *nom d'stamp* of

Melissa's cousin, Madeleine. Most of the Oreos had been crushed, but the bag was still intact.

"No, I'm not thinking of Ray," she told Jean-Luc firmly on Friday afternoon. "I'm not thinking of him at all."

Jean-Luc pawed the ground in front of him and looked haughtily down his aristocratic nose at her.

"I am, too, telling you the truth. You don't believe me? Would I lie to my great guy dog?"

Jean-Luc made a show of looking the other way.

"Watch it, buddy, or I'll clip your coat in a checkerboard."

Jean-Luc did not appear impressed.

"Besides, it doesn't matter if I'm thinking of him or not. He obviously doesn't want to see me, or he'd call. And I don't want to throw myself at him, I've already done that. Besides, it's undignified."

Jean-Luc ignored her, preferring to study the wall rather than look at her.

"Actually, it's just fine if he doesn't want anything to do with me," she told him as she checked her stamp bins. "Mermaids, both the big one and the baby one," she muttered as she made a note on her clipboard. "Getting low. Because, my dear dog, I don't have romantic relationships. And if Ray and I just stay friends that's terrific. And friends don't have to live in each other's pockets, now do they? Dragon eggs." She made another note. "Friends don't have to see each other every day. After all, sometimes I don't see Jessie for a week. So I'll just assume Ray and I are friends." She reached the end of the row of bins. She had five images to turn into stamps next week. Mermaids, dragon eggs, the lady-in-waiting, and one of the flower children she'd modeled on Melissa's stepdaughter, Angie. She'd make two dozen of each of them. Maybe a dozen of the archer as well, just for good measure. The archer was one of her longtime best-sellers. Her archer stamps were all over the world.

"Finished, Jean-Luc. Let's go upstairs."

At the top of the stairs she flipped the light switch. She did like her new switch plates. She especially liked the ones she'd stamped with blue ink.

Still, there was a heaviness to her step as, followed by her faithful canine companion, she put Puccini on the CD player and trudged up to her Rubber Room. There, on the worktable was a row of switch plates, all stamped. Each had an address label stuck on it. All they needed was postage and they'd be on their way to the far reaches of the country.

"Maybe I ought to send one of these to Ray. What do you think, buddy? Do you think he'd like a switch plate? Let's see. I could put some crutches on it. Or maybe a row of gargoyles." Gargoyles always seemed so sad. Maybe it was because people thought they were ugly. She thought they were beautiful. "Yeah. I like that idea. I don't have any stamps that will fit, but I can draw them on with a permanent pen."

Jean-Luc stood up on his hind legs and stuck his cold wet nose in her cheek. "Thanks, pal," she told him, putting her arm around his sturdy body and hugging him. "I needed that."

Jean-Luc gave her cheek another swipe. Then he trotted over to his cushion where he made the requisite number of circles, then plopped down in a sprawl, his chin on his front paws. But every time Sylvie glanced his way, she found his gaze pinned on her face.

She was almost finished with Ray's switch plate, and *La Boheme* was near the end of Act IV, when the doorbell rang.

Jean-Luc was up in a heartbeat, leaping down the stairs in a barking frenzy. Sylvie grabbed his collar and held him back while she opened the door.

"Hi, Jess."

"So why have you been hiding out all week?" her friend demanded.

"Is that your idea of a friendly greeting? Jean-Luc, knock it off."

Jean-Luc ignored her and continued being obnoxious. Jessie ignored her, too. "You've been avoiding us," she said bluntly.

"No I haven't. Jean-Luc, settle down."

Jean-Luc, tired of being ignored by Jessie, barked plaintively.

"Shut up, will you!" Sylvie told her dog in exasperation.

"Hello, Jean-Luc, you great big sweetie," Jessie said, finally nose-to-nosing with the wiggling dog. "Your mom has too been avoiding us, hasn't she? We all think so. So we've decided." She turned away from the dog to grin up at Sylvie. "We're all meeting in fifteen minutes at Lola's for dinner. Go put your shoes on." Then her grin turned to a scowl. "And wash your hands. They're green."

"Well, I was working with permanent ink," Sylvie explained. "It won't all wash off."

"Green?"

"Trees and dragons tend to be green. Except the ones that are gold and red. Dragons that is, not trees. But then, trees can be gold and red in the fall."

Jessie sighed. "You're changing the subject. You're trying to distract me." She wagged her finger in front of Sylvie's nose. "But it won't work. Your best buddy, Jessie, is too smart for that old trick. Go wash your hands and get your shoes on."

"Really, Jessie, I don't feel like going out. I was going to watch a video and go to bed."

"You can watch a video after we eat dinner. Get your shoes on." Jessie, followed by the adoring Jean-Luc, trotted down the hallway to stick her head in the kitchen. "Gee, Katie sure does a good job, doesn't she? We ought to find a way to clone her. Much more practical than sheep."

"I'm going to watch *Braveheart*," Sylvie called

after her. "And it's a long movie. I don't want to be up all night."

"So watch half of it tonight and the other half tomorrow. You don't want to watch Mel Gibson die right before you go to bed anyway. Much easier to take in the morning." Jessie cocked her head and listened hard for a few seconds. Then she turned to glare at Sylvie. "I hear Puccini," she accused in an overly dramatic tone. "Okay, that does it." Her voice was back to brisk and normal. "We're getting your shoes on right now. Jean-Luc, you big sweetie pie, you're on your own tonight. I'm kidnapping your mom. We'll take real good care of her and bring her back after dinner, so don't worry." She headed into Sylvie's room.

"You really are the most insufferable bully in the world, you know that?" Sylvie called after her friend.

"Yeah. That's why I was appointed the kidnapper. Do you want to wear socks? Do you have any clean ones? Oh, here they are. Gee, Katie even put away your clean laundry. I ought to hire her to come over and clean my apartment." She reappeared in the doorway with a pair of socks in one hand, and Sylvie's shoes in the other.

"I don't suppose you'll take no for an answer?"

"Put it this way. Lola baked her special chocolate brownies today." Jessie thrust the socks at her. "Take these. Sally called and got some reserved for us. She said if you don't come she'll have to eat her brownie and yours also and then it'll be all your fault when she gains more weight. Hurry up, now. Get your socks on."

Sylvie sighed and reached for the socks. "Okay. But I really can't stay out late."

"Fine. We'll bring you home before you turn into a pumpkin."

They were waiting for her at Lola's. Her best friends. Sally, Melissa, Karen. They had a table outside on the wooden deck, under the trees, overlooking the river. On the other shore was a small park that was currently host to a kid's soccer game. Parental cheers and the accompanying shouts of encouragement periodically erupted from the crowd and floated across to the diners. A Friday night in Hartley.

"She was listening to Mimi die," Jessie announced without preamble as they reached the table.

"That always means trouble," Melissa said, a twinkle in her eye.

Sylvie rolled her eyes. "It does not," she protested, settling her purse strap over the back of her chair.

"Yes it does," Sally pointed out reasonably. "And we already ordered iced tea for you. You listen to Mimi die when you're feeling morose."

"Can't I even listen to opera without everyone turning it into a major issue?"

"Sure." Jessie nodded, scooting her chair

loudly on the wooden deck. "You can listen to *The Magic Flute* anytime you want and we won't say a thing. Even *Carmen*, and that stuff by Wagner that only you actually like. But when you put on Puccini it means you need cheering up."

"And we're here at Lola's to see that you get it," Karen added.

"One for all, and all for one. Complete with Lola's chocolate brownies," Sally put in.

"Say, Sylvie." Jessie grabbed one of Sylvie's hands, held it up high and studied it thoughtfully, turning it side to side. "Didn't you wear green hands to Melissa's wedding?"

"You know she did," Sally nudged Jessie's elbow. "Give Sylvie her hand back and get your elbows off the table. Roger took that picture of the group of us with Sylvie giving you green devil's horns. Remember?"

Melissa chuckled. "Angie was thrilled that a grown-up person had ink on her hands. For weeks after, she tried to use Sylvie's green hands as an excuse not to wash her own. Every time she played with that stamp set you gave her, she'd make a lovely mess."

"Shh!" Sally hissed in a stage whisper. "Don't let Sylvie hear you say the words 'play' and 'rubber stamps' in the same sentence. She thinks stamps are serious stuff."

"Oh come now," Jessie said loftily. "Sylvie loves to play with her rubbers. She does it all the time." She exploded into a fit of giggles.

Sylvie looked around the table at her friends. They were all so very dear to her. What would she do without them. "Thanks," she started to say, then had to clear the sudden clog in her throat. "I appreciate it." The waitress arrived with their drinks, and Sylvie was able to busy herself unwrapping a straw.

"Say, M'liss," said Jessie after a beat, as if she hadn't heard Sylvie's words, but Sylvie knew they all had. "I talked to Madeleine the other day. And yes, Karen, the dogs are fine. She got suckered into adopting a kitten that she says is truly ugly."

"Hey," Sally exclaimed. "You're talking of a cat here, not a dog. Kittens are, by definition, beautiful."

"This one isn't." Jessie chuckled. "At least not according to Karen. But this tiny kitten, as yet unnamed, is not the least bit intimidated by two monstrous, hulking Newfoundlands drooling all over it."

"My Newfoundlands do not hulk," Karen pointed out in a faux huff. "And they are not monstrous. They are *exactly* the size they're supposed to be."

"That's *exactly* my point," Jessie answered. "The last time you saw them was when they were itty-bitty babies and you sent them out to Madeleine. Although even speaking of Newfoundland puppies as itty-bitty simply boggles the brain. That was then, this is now. Now they're big mamas. One hundred something pounds is huge any way you slice it."

Melissa, with a tolerant smile, leaned forward, arms crossed on the table. "I talked to Madeleine, too. She said this kitten has decided that Belle, the bigger dog, you know, is her mother. Speaking of kittens, Mrs. Shoemaker brought her new kitten in today. She's darling."

"What did she name her?" Sally wanted to know.

"Cinnamon."

"Life without cats would be like cooking without spice," Sally began.

"Life without *dogs* would be like Cheerios without milk," Jessie added.

"Life without dogs *and* cats," Melissa said with a quelling look at Sally and Jess, "would be like a movie without popcorn."

Karen was next. "Life without dogs would be like strawberry shortcake without the strawberries."

She had the best friends in the world, Sylvie thought as they all looked expectantly at her to continue their game. "Life without dogs would be like rubber without ink," she said. "And," she added, trying to keep her voice steady, "it would be almost as awful as life without you. Thank you, my very dear friends." For they were dear, as dear to her as anything. She took a long sip of raspberry iced tea, her favorite.

"See, Syl," Jessie said cheerfully. "Mel will just have to die later. I told you we'd be better company than *Braveheart*."

Sally gasped loudly. "Jessica Virginia Albright, that's sacrilegious!"

But it was Karen who intervened. "No, Sally, it's very religious," she said gently. "Friendships are sacred."

"Are you sure you'll be ready to go back to work on Monday?" Jessie asked him.

"Yes, I'm sure." It was Saturday morning and Jessie had accosted him as he was opening the garage door. Saturday was grocery shopping day. "Look, Ma, no crutches," he quipped, taking another careful step.

"But can you walk your whole route?"

"No. There'll still be a sub, but we never run out of things to do." He grinned at her. "Are you trying to keep me an invalid?"

He enjoyed her blush. It wasn't often he got the chance to make his friend turn red.

"No, it's just that . . . well, I guess I don't want you to overdo it, that's all. Maybe you should stay home another few days. I can even call Sylvie if you don't know her phone number, and I'm sure she would be happy to bring you some more of her herbal tea."

He shuddered.

Jessie chuckled. "Yeah, I know. It's lethal. But Sylvie has this obsessive need to take care of people who are hurt. Karen says it's probably related to her mother dying. Except Karen hasn't ever had to drink Sylvie's herbal tea. Somehow she's always managed to escape. I know!" She stopped suddenly and snapped her fingers. "I'll ask Karen how she does it, and then you can stay home and when Sylvie brings over her tea, you'll know how to get out of drinking it."

He crossed his arms and leaned against the front of his car, gazing at her speculatively. "Your concern is overwhelming," he said dryly. She was up to something. Her face was a dead giveaway. He wished he knew what it was.

"Oh, stop teasing me," she said, an unconvincing pout flashing across her face.

"That's what friends are for. Isn't that what you used to tell me?"

"Yeah, I guess so." She shrugged. "Well, have fun at the grocery store. Don't buy any junk food."

"You know I never buy junk food."

"But who knows? Some day you might just give into temptation. And the world as we know it will undoubtedly end."

He chuckled. "Never fear," he told her. "I'm not the junk food type."

"Maybe you should be."

"Why?"

She practically bristled with excitement. "You're always so unruffled, so perfect. Maybe you ought to live dangerously, even if it's only once in your life. Maybe you should be completely rash and do something totally out of character. Like, maybe you should buy a bag of circus peanuts and eat the whole thing at one sitting."

He shook his head in disbelief. "That sounds almost as bad as Sylvie's tea."

"That's what Sylvie used to do in college during exams."

"What? Eat a whole bag of circus peanuts?" He shuddered again at the thought.

"Yeah. Madeleine—they shared a house in grad school you know—always says it was the most disgusting thing in the world. But then what could you expect of someone who sat through classes drawing dragons in the margins of her books? She also draws princesses. And princes. You ought to see them. Of course, Madeleine always draws anatomically correct body parts. She's a medical illustrator, you know. Once she sent Sylvie a birthday card of an anatomically correct dragon. It was a scream." She beamed up at him guilelessly. If he didn't know her any better he'd think she was just making idle conversation. What was she up to?

"How can something that doesn't exist be anatomically correct?" he had to ask.

Jessie shrugged. "Dunno. But don't tell Sylvie that dragons don't exist. You know how you don't want to tell little kids that Santa isn't real because it'd wreck their realities and warp their lives? Sylvie's sort of like that."

"You're a nut," he told her without rancor.

"But I'm a nice nut," came the chipper reply.

Now her wacky friend, on the other hand, was an outrageous nut.

You're wrong, buddy, he corrected himself. *Sylvie may be outrageous, but she's also . . .*

No. He deliberately shut the voice off. He didn't want to know what Sylvie was. It was safer that way.

"You think I need more danger in my life? Is that it? Are you sure eating a whole bag of circus peanuts is dangerous enough? You don't want me to take up skydiving? Or lion taming? Or bungee jumping?"

She tapped her foot on the driveway. "Stop it. You're making fun of me."

"Yes, I am."

"And you admit it," she exclaimed in mock amazement.

"So why don't you go ahead and confess what you're up to."

"I'm not up to anything," she answered quickly. Too quickly, he thought.

"Then why are you blushing?"

She groaned in mock despair. "I always blush. You know that. I have overactive capillaries or something."

"So what are you up to?"

"Nothing."

"Methinks thou dost protest too much."

"I am not. I can't protest if there's nothing to protest about. Besides, isn't that a double negative? I mean . . ." She stopped and scowled at him. "You're getting me all confused. Whenever people quote the Bible at me I get all confused."

He chuckled. "That's Shakespeare, and you know it. But I didn't mean to confuse you. I only wanted to know what you're up to. Why you have this sudden interest in making my life more dangerous."

"Oh, I dunno." She stubbed her toe into the grass, then shot him a perky grin. "I just thought some excitement might be fun. You might enjoy it. But I guess I'll let you figure that out for yourself. You're bright, you shouldn't have a problem."

But something she'd said had caught his attention. "Say, Jess. What happened when Sylvie's mother died?"

"Well, I don't know all of it. Sylvie never *ever* talks about it. And if you know anything at all about Sylvie, you know that she'll talk to anyone about anything, at anytime, and forever. But she never talks about her mother's death. All I know is that her mother was in the hospital. Sylvie used to go visit her every day. They all did, Sylvie's dad and her brothers, I mean. But the day she died, Sylvie didn't go. She stayed home painting. I think she was painting a picture to take to her the next day. Something like that. Anyway, she wasn't there when her mom died, and I think she feels guilty about it. But that's really all I know. And the only reason I know that much is because I bullied it out of Florian."

For a flash of a moment he felt as if he'd been

slugged in the stomach. Memories of his own mother's death flooded over him, threatening to drown him if he wasn't careful.

"Whoops!" Jessie exclaimed. "Look at the time. I better be going. I have to get to work."

"Do you want a ride? I'm going past the clinic."

"No, thanks. I'm biking. I need to work off the brownie I had last night. We all went out for dinner."

"You and Sylvie?" He couldn't resist an excuse to say her name again.

"Yeah. And the others. You know, Melissa and Karen and Sally."

"Oh, yes. You're all friends."

"We're more than just friends. We were Siamese quintuplets in a former life. Bye." She abruptly turned and trotted off. Then she turned around and jogged backward. "And remember, sprains take a long time to heal. If you need to stay home another week, I'm sure the post office people wouldn't mind." Once again she whirled around, and then was around the corner.

For several minutes after Jessie left, Ray stood in thought, leaning against the side of his car. Death was such an emotionally intense topic, he didn't let it into the forefront of his mind very often. Not at all, in fact. But now, after Jessie had cracked it open, those thoughts began to swarm free. Well, he thought, he didn't have time for them right now. They'd just have to get shoved back where they belonged. Out of sight. Out of mind. Out, out damned thought.

Speaking of back where they belonged, he should return his library books. Whistling, he headed back into his house to gather them up. As he was unlocking his door, his phone rang.

"Hello, Ray." It was Helen, sounding homey and cheerful as she always did, as she always was. Helen was round and warm. "I wanted to thank you for the lovely birthday present. It was so nice of you to remember, but then, you always were a thoughtful person. How is your ankle, dear?"

"Getting better. I've graduated from my crutches and I'm going back to work on Monday."

"Are you sure you're ready to go back? With all the walking that you do?"

Ray grinned to himself. Who would've thought his foster mother and Jessie would have so much in common. Though he doubted Helen had anything up her sleeve. Helen was as straight an arrow as ever there was. "I'll still have a sub for my route, but there are plenty of chores I can do that don't require walking around town. Besides, I've had some time off, now I'm ready to get back to work."

"Well, if you're sure," she said, but her voice sounded doubtful. "Ray, in your note, you didn't tell me how you sprained it."

"I fell on my route. Now don't worry, it's nothing serious."

"Not serious? You're a mailman, Ray, your ankles are very important to you."

He chuckled. "Helen, I'm fine. The woman who lives in the house where I fell called Harvey for me. Then she made me sit on her porch with a bag of frozen vegetables wrapped around my ankle until Harvey arrived." Knowing the way Helen's mind worked, he tried to sound as if Sylvie was a little old lady. He wasn't sure he succeeded.

"Frozen vegetables? That's very resourceful. It probably helped with the swelling."

"It did, but I'm fine now, graduated from crutches and I'm on my way to hobble to the grocery store."

"Well, all right," she said doubtfully. "But remember, you have always been a poor patient. You always wanted to get out of bed much before you were well."

"Now, don't worry. I'm fine." Then he took a deep breath. "Helen," he said, "Helen, I've never said this before, and this is long overdue. I want to thank you and Phil for taking care of me for so many years. I know I probably wasn't the easiest foster kid in the world to raise. I mean, I was angry a lot."

"Oh, honey," she cried in a voice that sounded suddenly thick. And after a short pause she continued. "Oh my dear, you were hurt. Your mother had just died. Of course you were angry."

"But I know I wasn't always polite, or pleasant. So, thank you for all your patience."

"Ray, dear, Phil and I understood that you didn't mean it. We didn't take it personally. Besides, there were also times when you were a delight. And you still are. Like the way you always remember to send perfect birthday presents." There was another short pause. "Why have you all of a sudden, now, decided to tell us thank you? What's *really* been happening in your life since we saw you last?"

Trust Helen to be perceptive. "I met someone," he said at last, knowing that she wasn't being nosy, but that she was genuinely concerned.

"Tell me."

"It may take a while. This is long distance, you know."

"Oh fiddle pish. You're part of our family. Now tell me."

So he told her. All of it. Including Jessie's recommendations that he have a bit more excitement in his life.

"Do *you* think you need more excitement?" she asked.

"I don't *want* excitement," he said emphatically. "I don't like excitement. I like things to be calm and reasonable."

She sighed. "Ray, dear, you know I love you. But you were always nervous about unexpected things. You never liked surprises. You always wanted to know what was going to happen. You've always needed to plan for things, which was a great help when we were going on vacations. I've never told you this, but Phil and I talked to the social worker about it once. He said it was probably because you wanted some control over your life. But you know, Ray, the few times you told me things about your mother, you told me how sometimes she'd do things on the spur of the moment. That sounds pretty spontaneous."

"Yeah," he muttered.

"Ray, listen to me. If you think this woman is wonderful, she probably is. You have good sense about people. But you'll never know how wonderful she is until you get to know her better. And remember, it's our eccentricities that make us interesting."

"I guess you're right."

"Of course, I'm right." He could almost hear her smile. "And I love you. Now. My advice is to spend some time with her. If you end up thinking she is the right woman for you, then bring her back here for a visit and we'll give her a good third degree ourselves. Just to make sure."

"You've got a deal."

"Good. Now, I know you have errands to do, so I'll let you go. It was wonderful talking to you, Ray."

"I love you, Helen." He'd rarely said it, but over the years he'd realized it to be true.

"Phil and I love you, too, dear." And he knew they did.

* * *

The library was busy every day, but today seemed even busier than usual. When he saw a mother encouraging a pair of squirming toddlers, one in each hand, up the front steps he quickened his pace to hold the heavy door open for them. As she passed with her charges, the mother gave him a grateful smile. "Thanks," she said breathlessly.

"No problem."

As he followed them through the heavy doors into the library he was hit by a rush of cool air, heavy with the scent of books. And people. He slid his books into the return slot and dodged a young boy who was paying more attention to the book he was reading than where he was going. Reading and walking at the same time was a skill that needed lots of practice, he thought as he made his way to the reference desk.

"You giving away something for free?" he teased Liz, the librarian who had become an invaluable friend and advisor.

"The children's summer reading program is in full swing. You better watch your step. With all the babies in strollers and crawling around using bookshelves to try to stand, it can get hazardous." She shot him a quick grin, then checked her watch. "There's going to be a puppet show in about ten minutes, so it'll be less chaotic while the kids are in the meeting room. Then, when it's over we'll be a veritable zoo again. This is summer. We love it. So, what did you think of the Michaelson book?"

"I think she gets better with each book."

"I think so, too. Oh, that reminds me, I saw something the other day and thought you might be interested in it. It's Carl Sagan's last book. I know you've been reading philosophy recently, and Sagan was an astronomer, but he was also quite philosophical. Let's see." She shoved her glasses higher on the bridge of her nose and rapidly typed a title into the library's computer. "Here it is. It's in. Let me write the call number and then I'll find it for you." She scribbled a string of numbers and letters on one of those slips of paper that were always everywhere in the library.

"I don't want to take up your time, Liz. Besides, you know I can find my way around this place almost as well as you can. After all the hours I've spent in this library over the last couple of years."

"I know. But it's part of my job to put the book in your hand. So, if for any reason you can't find it, let me know, okay?" She handed the slip of paper to him along with her lovely smile.

"Thanks, Liz. I'll track it down. Also, is there a good general book on European medieval history? Nothing specific. Just whatever you happen to know is good."

"So you're going to read history now? From the space age to the distant past?" she teased. "Let's see. There's a book by Tuchman that's a classic. Let me see if it's in." She checked her computer again. "Yes, it is. I'll write down that number for you as well." As she handed the second slip of paper to him she said, with a twinkle in her eyes, "You know, Ray, by now you've probably read enough solid nonfiction to have the equivalent of two college degrees."

"And I owe it all to you, Liz, my favorite librarian who pushes books on me unmercifully," he teased.

"Occupational hazard, I guess," she answered cheerfully. "When we find a reader, pushing books is an automatic response, like Pavlov's dogs. I suppose I'll have to start keeping my eye out for good things on the Middle Ages for you."

"Thanks again, Liz. You're great."

"So are you," she said with a grin and a nod.

Typically for a Saturday morning, the parking lot of Abernathy's supermarket was also packed. He found a spot in his usual row, plucked a cart from the cluster that had gathered between the parked cars, and wheeled it into the store. He didn't need a list, he knew what he needed. The same things he bought every week. First stop was the produce aisle. One head of lettuce, carrots, onions. Fruit. Then on to the—

He stopped. Was Jessie right? Did he need some excitement in his life? Was he set in his ways? Was he staid and stolid? Rigid, inflexible? Was Helen right? Was it a need on his part for control over his life? He looked down at the cart of groceries. He'd been eating the same meals for years. Yes, they were easy to cook, provided leftovers for his lunch, and were based on sound nutritional principles—thank you, Helen. But they were predictable. Safe. Unexciting. And, now that he thought about it, boring. Was this what he wanted to be? No.

Suddenly, he wanted something different, something outrageous. He wheeled his cart around and headed down the long row of aisles, scanning the shelves until he found it.

A little while later he opened the door of the Hartley Veterinary Clinic.

Suzette, the receptionist, looked up from the other side of the counter, surprise splashing her face. "Hi, Ray, how's you ankle? You're dressed like a regular person today. What's up?"

"I have something for Jessie. Can I leave it with you?"

"Sure," came the chipper reply. "She and Dr. March are in with a client right now, but is it an emergency? Do you want me to get her?"

"No. I was just at the store and I picked up something for her. Tell her it's a thank-you present." The stiff plastic rustled as he handed her the bag.

"I'll be sure and tell—Oh. Circus peanuts!"

"Thanks, Suzette. She'll understand. I'll see you later."

He had one more stop. One more delivery to make. He threaded his way through Hartley, heading out toward the tree-lined street at the edge of town. Soon he was there.

He waved to little Joshua Martini, proudly riding his bike without training wheels. He passed the house where the elderly couple lived, then he came to the second-to-last house on the street. The one with the picket fence, and the lilac bush, and the gutters that he'd bet were still clogged. The house where she lived.

Her car wasn't in the driveway.

He unlatched the gate and limped up the walk to the porch. Only silence greeted him when he knocked. No Beatles music blaring, no Jean-Luc barking.

She wasn't home.

Disappointment sluiced through him.

He sank down on the porch swing for a moment to consider his options. It hadn't occurred to him that she wouldn't be home. This meant that he still had time to change his mind. He still had time to back out. He could leave right now, just drive away. No one would ever know. *And you can go back to your black-and-white life,* he said to himself. *You can go back to eating meat loaf every Sunday, and never again see nasturtiums in potato salad, or violets in lemonade. Freshly squeezed lemonade.*

On the other side of this door was a house teeming with living color. Vibrant, screaming, passionate color. *If you walk away now,* he told himself, *you'll spend the rest of your life wondering what if*. Heroes didn't wonder what if. They were too busy charging once more into the breach.

Ray, it's time you put a little color in your life.

But am I ready?

Maybe not. But, if people waited for things until they thought they were ready, no one would ever do anything new, anything unfamiliar. And besides, we're not exactly talking bungee jumping, here.

So he would leave the things he'd brought in her mailbox. Along with a note. He loped back to his car where he always kept a small tablet of paper and a pen in his glove compartment. What should he say? How should he word it? He thought for a moment, then wrote.

When he was finished, he rubber-banded the note around the small box and slipped his gifts inside of Sylvie's mailbox. Leaving them wasn't as personal as giving them to her face to face, but still, it would do. He only wished he'd be there to see the smile break over her face. He hoped she'd smile. Well, with any luck she'd call him.

Chapter Fourteen

"Where did this come from?" Sylvie asked Jean-Luc as she held up a bag of circus peanuts. Jean-Luc stood up on his hind legs to give the bag a better sniff. Then he dropped to all fours and nosed around the porch some more. Sylvie examined the bag. No address label, no postage, so it wasn't from one of her stamping buddies.

"Jean-Luc, get your head out of—Oh. There's something else." His tail quivering in excitement, Jean-Luc's nose followed Sylvie's hand as she reached into her mailbox and drew out a small box with a piece of lined paper rubber-banded around it. "It's a note. *Hello Sylvie,*" she read. *"There isn't a circus in town, so I would like to take you to the movies tonight instead. If you can go, please call me. I'll be home this afternoon.*

Ray. P.S. The candy is for you, the dog cookies are for Jean-Luc. Look Jean-Luc, it's those realio trulio dog crackers that are shaped like people."

Jean-Luc had already figured out that something good and tasty was in that little box.

"And he wants to take me to the movies," she whispered. "Tonight." She held her arms wide. "Tonight . . . tonight." She sang the tune from *West Side Story*.

Jean-Luc barked.

"Obviously no ear for Bernstein," she chided him. "With a one-track mind. Yes, you're incredibly cute," she added. "And you're brilliant and yes, that's a lovely dance, but you'll have to wait till we get inside and then I'll give you a cookie," she told him as she shifted the things to her left hand so she could rummage around in her purse for her keys. No keys. Where were they? She patted the pockets of her shorts. Still no keys.

Oh no! Not again.

Just to make sure, she perched on the porch swing and emptied the contents of her purse onto the cushion. Jean-Luc leaned against her knees and watched anxiously for anything that might prove to be edible. Wallet, wrinkled store receipts for the past decade at least, her address book, several pens, half-empty packages of gum, an ink pad, that moon stamp she'd been looking for, loose change, a dog comb, a paperback—always take a book with you in case there's a flood and you need something to read—but no keys.

Her shoulders sagged in defeat and she sighed heavily.

"Well, Jean-Luc, I guess the dragon is back."

She leaned against the swing and stared morosely out into her front yard. If she'd stayed home this morning and watched Mel Gibson die like she was supposed to, she'd have been here when Ray came by. And her keys would be where they belonged. In her purse. But no, she had to go take the last of her stamp orders to the post office. Once more she'd tried to be efficient and look where it got her. And while she was dropping off her orders, he was here dropping off circus peanuts for her.

Speaking of circus peanuts . . . She carefully eased open the bag and pulled out one of the orange candies. She hadn't had these for a long time. At least three weeks. She popped one into her mouth and sighed in utter bliss. Then, while reaching for another, her gaze stumbled on her car. Wait a minute.

"Eureka!" she crowed. She leapt up and bounded down the steps to her car. She'd forgotten to roll up the back window. It wasn't open all the way, just enough so Jean-Luc could stick his nose out and snuffle smells as she drove. It was also open enough so she could reach in and unlock the door. And there were her keys, not a care in the world, dangling innocently in the ignition.

"Take that, you dragon!" she cried triumphantly doing the Rocky dance, her arms upraised, one fist clutching the wayward keys.

Whirling around in her moment of triumph, she suddenly faced disaster.

"Jean-Luc Picard Taylor! You rat! Get your nose out of there this instant," she yelled at him as she charged up the porch steps to rescue her bag of candy.

"Don't you dare give me your innocent look," she scolded him. "I know you too well. And, you have orange sticky stuff on your chin."

"I didn't think you'd like science-fiction movies," she commented as they were standing in line for their tickets.

"What gave you that idea?" Once more he found himself fascinated by the expressions that flitted across her face, as if she invited the world to know what she was thinking, what she was feeling. As if she were hiding nothing.

"All those books by dead poets in your living room."

He let out a shout of laughter. "Do you think that dead poets and science fiction are mutually exclusive?"

She wrinkled her forehead. "No, of course not."

"Do you have something against dead poets?"

"Not at all," she answered airily. "In fact, some of my favorite poets are dead. It's just that they were in the past, and science fiction is looking into the future."

"Is that an odd combination?"

"Some people might think so."

"Some people have no imagination."

She looked at him, amazement in her face. "That's what I think."

"Now you, for instance. You have imagination. No one in their right mind could ever say you weren't overloaded with it."

"You're teasing me."

"Yup," he answered smugly. "Jessie told me you had double master's degrees in medieval history and in art. Then you name your dog after a starship captain. Now there's the past and the future for you."

She sighed in resignation. "Yes. Everyone in my family thinks I'm eccentric. Why didn't you name him Vincent? they asked me. Or Brueghel. Or Seurat—there's a good French name. That was from my brother Florian. I told him poodles were actually German. Then Gareth, my other brother, asked me why I named a poodle after a bald guy."

"What did you tell him?"

"I told him I didn't name him after a bald guy. I named him after a man who is courageous, intelligent, witty, with lots of élan. He said dogs don't have élan. I said they do, too. When I picked Jean-Luc up at the airport—I got him from a woman in Minnesota—he was eight weeks old. I'd never met him before. I didn't know if he'd be frightened, or nervous from the plane trip. But I opened the pet carrier and he stepped out, proud as anything, and surveyed the freight office. He didn't merely look around, he actually *surveyed* his surroundings. I was sitting on the floor, to be on his level, you know, and I told him hello, that I was his mom, and that we'd go home now. He looked up at me, and I swear he almost said 'Make it so.' So you see, if you at all watch *Star Trek*, you'll know that there was simply never any other name he could possibly have."

"I take it your brothers aren't into the voyages of the Starship Enterprise."

She gave a moue of disgust. "They both think," she said in imitation highbrow, "commercial television is so pedestrian. They support public television." She shrugged and dropped the highbrow. "I support PBS, too, but I also think that they're incredible snobs."

Here it was again, he thought. The tracks thing. There was simply no way around it. If he and Sylvie ever had anything other than friendship . . . She'd stand up for him, as she stood up for Jean-Luc, and that—the fact that she had to stand up for him at all—was intolerable. He had nothing to be ashamed of, nothing to apologize for. *Then why do you feel like you should be apologizing?* he asked himself.

Because she is so used to her house on the hill that I don't know if she can see the other side of the tracks. I don't know if she is even aware that it's there. Her upbringing, her education is something she takes for granted. It doesn't occur to her that someone else may not know who Brueghel was.

Suddenly he realized she wasn't saying anything. He glanced down to see her gray eyes focused intently on him.

"Yoo-hoo!" she said softly. "Anybody home?"

"I'm sorry," he said apologetically. "I was thinking."

She cocked her head to consider him. "Must have been deep thoughts. You were somewhere in a galaxy far far away." There was in her voice a tone that told him she'd be happy if he shared that distant dreamworld with her.

"The line is moving," he said to her in relief. He had no intention of letting her in on those thoughts, at least, not now. He motioned her ahead of him, but she continued to gaze at him for a moment. Then, as natural as spring, she reached out, slipped her hand into his, and together they followed the crowd into the theater.

What was it about Ray, she wondered, that one moment he could be actually flirting with her, and the next minute closing her out. He'd done it again, outside the theater, just before the line started to move. Then she'd taken his hand, and after all, sometimes people who were just friends held hands, and he was back again. Did he even know he was doing it? Maybe not.

Karen said people did all sorts of things they weren't aware of on a conscious level. Maybe she should pretend it didn't happen. Maybe she should ask him about it. On second thought, no. She didn't have near enough chutzpah. Still, she wanted to say something to him. Wanted to talk to him. She didn't feel uncomfortable sharing silence with him, she just wanted to share her thoughts.

Then the theater lights began their slow dimming.

"Don't you love the moment in a theater when the lights go down?" she whispered. "Right before the movie starts there's a feeling of anticipation, of expectation. You're about to enter a new world. Like you're about to take the first step of a journey. Anything could happen."

For a long moment he didn't answer, just looked at her, gazed at her, stared at her, devoured her in the dimming theater lights. Devoured her with his bluest of blue eyes. Even though color was disappearing in the darkness she knew his eyes were the perfect color. And then the lights were completely gone, and the theater was filled with the glow from the film company logo on the screen. His gaze still held.

"I wonder where this journey will take us," he whispered at last.

The intensity in his voice sent a shiver shimmering through her. It was as if he'd missed her point about the movies and was talking about something else altogether. Something about her and him, the two of them together, like a quest. Only the quest was something personal. Something private. Something romantic.

She wrenched her gaze from his and fastened her eyes firmly on the screen. She folded her hands firmly in her lap. *Movie time, Sylvie,* she told herself. *Pay attention to the movie. Don't think about personal considerations with Ray. You seem to be forgetting your number-one rule. You don't have romantic relationships, you have friendships, remember?*

Friendships were safe. Romantic feelings and mushy stuff, those things were not safe at all.

Chapter Fifteen

"I know it's late, but I want to show you something," he said as he turned his car into a long driveway lined with tall trees.

"Is it bigger than a bread box?" she teased. On the ride back from the theater, they'd had a spirited discussion about science-fiction movies in general, and the one they'd just seen in particular. They'd talked about books they'd read—he read Michaelson, too. Sylvie was still feeling playful. "Is it animal, mineral, or vegetable? Shall I close my eyes and hold out my hands?"

"It's larger than a bread box, it's all three of them, and it doesn't matter if you close your eyes or not, because it's dark back here."

She remembered the earlier look in his eyes and a delicious shiver shot its tendrils through her. She shook it off. After all, she wasn't in high school anymore. She was a sensible adult. And they were just friends, she reminded herself. They were buddies. Their relationship was completely platonic. And she was ready to buy a bridge.

"Where are you taking me?" she asked. She was curious, and totally unafraid. At least, she wasn't afraid of being alone with him. After all, since they were only friends there was no problem in being alone with him at night, in the dark.

But what if they weren't just buddies? What about those feelings of destiny she'd felt the day she first met him? she asked herself. What if they were going to be more than buddies? What if her life *was* going to change?

Well, relax, Sylvie, it isn't likely, given the fact that you're a slob and he's a neatness addict. Even his car seats are clean enough to eat off of. So there is absolutely no chance of that romantic thing happening, which is very good because as soon as it happens, things change. You know that. You stop being friends and start being lovers and when the relationship ends you've lost your best friend. Remember this. It's important. No matter what the books say.

Yet that very danger, that very definite possibility of change, was tempting her, seducing her. Like a siren from Homer's Odyssey, she thought. Or like a sprite in the forest sent to steal a human down to the fairy realms to be held captive for all eternity by the king of the fairies.

Suddenly she realized he'd said something.

"What did you say? I'm sorry, I was gathering wool," she apologized.

"You ask me a question and then don't listen to the answer," he teased. "Now that's nerve."

"I agree. It was nervy of me, wasn't it?" She grinned into the dark night passing by the open window of his car. "It's a habit of mine, I do confess, kind sir."

"Kind sir?"

She could almost hear him raise his eyebrows. But before she could formulate a response, he pulled into a large paved space and turned off the engine.

"We walk from here," he said, switching off the headlights.

"Walk where? Is it far? What about your ankle? Are you sure it isn't hurting too much?

"Calm down," he said, chuckling. "You're acting like Jean-Luc. My ankle is fine."

"But where are we going?" she insisted.

"You'll just have to wait until we get there."

"You sure sound cheerful about keeping me in suspense," she pointed out.

He came around the car and opened her door. "You've never been here?"

"Nope. Well, actually, I'm not sure. I have no idea where we are." She looked around, but all she could see were trees and more trees. She looked up to see a myriad of stars, pinpricks of light in the darkness.

"This is the back of Kedrick Park. You'll know where we are in a few minutes. Down this path."

He led her toward a spot darker than the surrounding forest. "Path?"

"It's here, don't worry."

Like a human following a sprite, she found herself compelled to go where he led and found, just as he'd promised, that there really was a path. Then, after only a minute or two, he stopped suddenly, and she almost crashed into him.

"I'm sorry, I should have warned you. Now, I want you to close your eyes, and take my hand. I won't let you run into anything."

She took the hand he held out, took a breath, closed her eyes, and, fighting the urge to reach out into the nothingness with her other hand, took several tenuous steps in the direction he guided her. They stopped. She felt his hands on her shoulders as he positioned her, pointing her.

"Open your eyes."

She did.

"Oh," she gasped. "It's beautiful!" And it was.

In front of them was a small grassy area leading down to a lake, glassy and still. But in the distance, on the opposite shore, were the lights of Hartley.

"Why, we're on the other side of the lake," she said in surprise. "There's the band shell. And over there," she pointed, getting her bearings, "is that new development." She glanced quickly at him, standing quietly beside her, watching her. Just as quickly, she glanced away. "And if you look closely at the water you can make out the reflection of the stars. If Jessie were here, she'd point out different constellations, and name the stars," she said, gazing upward. "But I've always been content to merely look." She glanced at him again. He was still watching her—though watch was a passive word, and the expression in his eyes was certainly not passive. Their gazes caught and held, and she wanted to do more than merely look at him. Look was another passive word. What she wanted to do, to him, with him, for him, was very active.

Sylvie was suddenly aware of her pounding heart, of the tingling of her senses. She knew his heart was pounding, took it for granted that his senses were tingling, too. She could see it in his eyes. Those eyes in a face that was coming closer. And closer.

He was going to kiss her!

Hey, wait a minute! She yelled at herself. *Danger, Will Robinson! If he kisses you, you'll kiss him back, and then you'll never be just friends again. And you'll run the risk of losing him. Are you sure you're ready for that?*

She jerked back, took a shaky step toward the water, and fixed her gaze firmly on the reflections of the lights of Hartley. She cleared her throat and tried to speak normally. "How did you find this place?"

For a few beats he was silent, but she kept her gaze glued to the water.

"I used to deliver mail to that new development." He sounded distant again. This time she knew that she was the cause of it. "One day I wondered what was on this side of the lake, so I explored. This is what I found."

What could she say to him that would tell him she still wanted to be friends? "This would be a wonderful place to bring Jean-Luc to swim."

"That's what I thought," Ray agreed, still sounding distant.

She'd hurt him. "Tomorrow is Sunday. If you don't have any plans, why don't we bring a picnic and Jean-Luc?"

Jean-Luc knew they were going somewhere special, Ray realized, watching the poodle trying to stick his nose out the window. Sylvie had said not everyone appreciated the finer points of having a wet dog in their car. She'd shoved some papers and things into the trunk, brushed off the passenger side front seat, and declared her car fit for human passage.

Now, Jean-Luc whimpered and yipped noisily at some sort of big dog walking politely at the side of an elderly gentleman. The big dog pointedly ignored the poodle.

"Knock it off, Jean-Luc," Sylvie scolded him. "You can hurl threats and insults from inside the car, but you can't stick your whole head out the window, it isn't safe. Only your nose. You should know that by now."

"This is an adventure for you, isn't it, buddy?" Ray told him.

Jean-Luc gave him a quick lick, then went back to intently staring out the window, his whole body alert.

"Why don't you have a dog?" Sylvie asked him, glancing over from the road. "You obviously like them. You're the kind of person who should have one. Or two."

"Not everyone who likes dogs has one. Look at Jessie. It's a huge commitment, and I haven't had time. What with work and all." Ray winced as Sylvie shifted too soon. The engine lugged for a moment before she shifted back down again. He should offer to look at her engine, earlier he'd noticed that the idle sounded too fast. And he'd bet any amount that she hadn't changed the air filter for a while. If she ever had.

"And when Jessie gets her puppy, she'll move into the apartment above Melissa's vet clinic. If you ask Jessie when she's going to get her puppy, she'll become perfectly obnoxious about how people should only have a breed with the correct temperament for them. Then she'll tell you all about *her* search for her perfect breed, and then she'll tell you she's on a waiting list for an Irish Wolfhound puppy."

"Waiting list?"

"A woman out in Wyoming breeds them. Jessie wants one of her puppies. Evidently so do a lot of other people, so the woman's got a waiting list. But what about you? Wouldn't you like to have a dog to welcome you home every day?"

"Someday I'll have one." *And a house, and a wife, and children,* he added to himself. *Maybe children who love to draw all over everything.*

"But why not now?" she persisted.

"Get into the turning lane up here," he cautioned her. "The road isn't well marked, and it's easy to miss it." When she'd made the turn, he relaxed for a moment to consider her question. "It just hasn't been the right time for me to get a dog."

From her noncommittal sound, he wasn't sure whether she believed him or not. Jean-Luc gave up on his window and scrambled over the back of the front seats.

"What are you doing, boy?" he asked.

"Jean-Luc, get in the back," she told him at the same time.

Jean-Luc ignored them both. The dog appropriated Ray's lap and stuck his nose against the cool air vent, inhaling nosily.

"Jean-Luc, you big curly doofus, get in the back where you belong."

Jean-Luc flicked a glance at her and then returned his attention to the air vent.

"That does it," Sylvie said with a sigh. She braked the car and came to a stop on the shoulder.

"What's wrong?" Ray asked.

"Jean-Luc, this is your boss speaking. I won't let you ignore me," she added firmly, and before Ray knew it, she'd taken hold of her dog around the middle and hefted him into the backseat.

"That is your place," she told him firmly. "Don't you forget it. Don't even pretend to forget it, because I won't believe you."

Ray tried to hide his grin.

"What's so funny?" she demanded.

Evidently his grin was not hidden well enough.

"You look so fierce," he chuckled.

"I am fierce," she said and scowled at her dog again. Jean-Luc merely looked the other way, obviously avoiding the stern look in Sylvie's eyes. "This guy has decided he doesn't have to pay attention to me and he's wrong."

"What'd you expect? You named him after someone who had a habit of following orders selectively," he pointed out. "And creatively."

"Starship captains and dogs are two different things," she retorted. "When starship captains disobey they're merely stripped of their rank. When dogs disobey they have to go to dog school. Jean-Luc is starting remedial dog school Wednesday night."

Ray gave up all pretense of hiding his amusement. "Remedial dog school?" he asked through his laughter.

"For recalcitrant dogs," Sylvie explained as she turned the key in the ignition. "Do you know Tanner Dodge? He's a friend of Melissa and

Karen's. He's a terrific dog trainer and teaches classes. Jean-Luc and I went through his basic classes, but after this guy here took off at the park last weekend, I talked to Tanner and asked if we could take the class over again."

"I take it he agreed."

"Tanner's as much of a dogaholic as Karen is. He's sort of devoted his life to helping people learn how to communicate with their dogs better. I think it's an ingrained behavior kind of thing with him."

"Sounds like a good thing."

"He says—is this where we turn?—that the challenge is—he sees things as challenges not problems—Jean-Luc is so smart that he gets bored easily and dog school gives him something to think about. And Tanner says I've probably been losing ground in the boss department. Anyway, I have to learn to think more quickly than he does so I can stay ahead of him."

Ray raised his eyebrows. It seemed to him that Sylvie thought rather quickly.

"Tanner is going to start teaching agility classes, you know, where dogs go through obstacle courses and stuff. Jean-Luc'll love it, you know how he adores ladders. Or course, ladders aren't part of agility courses, but there's an A-frame that's sort of similar. Here we are," she called out as the car rolled to a stop and she set the parking brake. "Okay, buddy, let's get your leash on so you don't get into trouble."

While Sylvie got all the dog paraphernalia out

of the backseat, Ray unlocked the trunk and pulled out the deli bags. He'd offered to bring lunch if she brought a blanket to sit on. He didn't want to have to smile his way through baby goosh again. Or nasturtium petals. Or something even worse. Besides, Helen always said to feed people before you had a serious talk with them. It put them at ease. In the years since he'd been on his own, he'd often found Helen's advice to be sound. Right now, he wanted to spend a wonderful afternoon with Sylvie. He wanted to put her at ease, and then find a way to convince her that he was . . . *what? Good enough for her even without an education? Don't put yourself down, buddy. Don't sell yourself short.*

I'm not.

You are, too.

Am not.

Are, too.

He simply refused to squabble with himself. He slammed the trunk instead.

Sylvie was holding onto Jean-Luc's leash with one hand, an overflowing tote bag in the other.

"Do you think you might have left the kitchen sink at home by mistake?" he asked, nodding at the bulging bag.

"Don't be silly," she replied with a perky grin. "We don't need the sink when there's plenty of water in the lake."

He liked her grin. It made him feel good. It

made him feel very good. He liked feeling very good.

"I'm stuffed," she announced inelegantly two hours later. She stretched out on the blanket, fingers interlocked behind her head, and closed her eyes. What a pleasant afternoon this was, she thought. Jean-Luc was worn out from swimming, his sodden curls making a damp spot on the blanket next to her. Ray was . . . Where was Ray? She opened one eye to take a quick peek. There he was, on the other side of the blanket, plain blue shirt bright against a backdrop of forest, propped up on an elbow, a bottle of soda in his hand. His clothes, at least the clothes she'd seen, were all monochromatic. Maybe he was uncomfortable around bright kaleidoscopic splashes of color.

A slight movement caught her eye. "Jean-Luc, keep your beautiful nose away from the leftover food," she cautioned him.

Jean-Luc immediately left off his sniffing and pretended to be the epitome of accused innocence. Sylvie was not fooled. She stared at him fiercely until he lowered his eyes and looked away. With a great sigh, he put his head back down on the blanket. She glanced over at Ray.

He was watching her. He seemed to be pondering something deep and meaningful. Well, she had something deep and meaningful of her own to ask him. She'd waited till they were finished eating, and now it was time. Except she wasn't sure how to bring it up. The indirect method would probably be best, she thought. Start from the outside, and work herself around to where she wanted the conversation to be.

"Why don't you ever talk about yourself?" she asked.

Suddenly he was still. He hadn't been moving before, but this was not merely the absence of movement. This was the kind of stillness that comes when someone stops breathing, or when the earth stops its rotation. Or when someone is asked something they're not expecting, something they might not want to answer and so, just for a second, they're not sure what to say.

Any motion now—even the twitch of a toe—and the spell will be broken, she cautioned herself. *You'll break into his stillness and he might never give you the answer he'd have given you if you hadn't broken it.* Then she grimaced to herself. *That's sure convoluted, Sylvie. It might not even be true.*

But it sounded good. So she prepared to wait until he was ready to answer.

Chapter Sixteen

"I talk about myself." His voice broke the silence, but his whole body remained still.

"Actually you don't," she corrected him gently. "You joke, and tease, and you listen when I talk, but you very rarely say anything about *you*. I mean, I know the kinds of books you like to read, the music you listen to, the movies you watch. But they're all external things. You never say anything about what you think deep inside, or about your dreams, or about what you want to be doing in fifty years."

She thought he was on the way to becoming a statue. Maybe she'd gone too far. Maybe it was too nosy of her to bring this up. No maybe about it, it *was* too nosy of her. Maybe she should switch gears and talk about the weather and forget what she'd just said. She obviously hadn't thought it through completely. *So what else is new?* She asked herself. *One of her first dragons was named Sylvie Leaps Before She Thinks.* It was a dragon she'd never been able to slay.

"What do you want to know?"

"Everything," she exclaimed, leaping at the opportunity. What she wanted to know most of all was why he had a foster father. What happened to his parents? But she couldn't ask that outright, it would be rude. She had to work her way around to it. "Have you ever seen *The King and I?* You know the song, 'Getting To Know You'?" She sang the first couple of lines. "Like that. I want to know all about you. What you named your teddy bear when you were little. I want to know what your favorite book was, and how many times you saw *Star Wars*, and how old you were when you had your first crush on a girl, and why you only read poetry by dead poets—not that I have something against dead poets or anything, I read their stuff, too—and if you collected baseball cards when you were little, and what's the first thing you ever wanted to be when you grew up, and . . . What's wrong? Why are you looking at me like that?"

"Like what?"

"Like you're trying not to laugh at me."

"I'm not laughing at you." But he had relaxed.

"Good. Because I absolutely hate being laughed at." She looked away from him, feeling suddenly shy. She watched an ant, struggling under a bread crumb load, make its erratic way across a paper plate. Ants had such determination! She wondered if they ever got too tired and just gave up. "My brothers used to laugh at me just because they knew I hated it. It made me so mad that I'd start to cry. And then they'd really laugh at me and I'd get even more mad." There. She'd admitted it. The most humiliating trait about herself that she could think of and she admitted it to him. Then, before he could say anything, she rushed on. "So what did you name your first teddy bear?"

"Charles E. Bear. He was dark brown with golden glass eyes. And before you ask, I don't know how old I was when I got him. I think he was original equipment. My favorite book was *The Book of Three*. I probably saw *Star Wars* thirteen times, but *Return of the Jedi* was my favorite. My first crush"—he shot her a grin, brilliant and slightly wicked—"was on Katherine McGill who sat in front of me in second grade. She always wore dresses. I collected stamps not baseball cards. And when I was four I wanted to be a paleontologist. What else? Oh, yes. Dead poets again. What is it about dead poets that fascinates you? I assume you're referring to the books in my living room. I usually read books by authors who are alive. Those books are . . ." He stopped, took a deep breath, and slowly let it out. "Those books," he continued, "belonged to my mother. And I always wanted a sister, or a brother. But I didn't have either until my mother died and I went to live with my foster family."

Whoa, Sylvie! Time to tread carefully now, instead of tromping in as you usually do, wearing steel-toed combat boots. Tact was not her strongest point. "How old were you when she died?"

"Twelve."

Though it was said simply, she knew there was nothing simple about it. Losing a mother at any age was beyond devastating, and lasted forever. Of all the people in the world, she knew this. So she would wait, silently, until he continued to tell her, or not. But it would be his choice.

Ray shifted slightly on the blanket, readjusting. *Was he also shifting his mind?* Sylvie wondered. *Was he also trying to become more comfortable with her? With sharing history*. She waited through his silence again, her fingers gently combing through the curls on Jean-Luc's head.

"I never knew my father." Ray spoke in an even tone, as if he were distancing himself from the meaning of the words he was giving her. As if he were talking about someone else, a stranger with whom he had no emotional connection. "He left my mother before I was born. There was just the two of us, no relatives that I know of. When she died I was sent to live with a foster family. Helen and Phil, and their two kids, Sam and Kathy. They were about my age. I lived with them until I graduated from high school."

He stopped again, and Sylvie watched him reach out to pull up a blade of grass and absently twine it around his fingers. She doubted he was even aware of what he was doing. It was probably a way of getting rid of nervous energy.

"Was that around here?" she asked, trying to match his even tone so she wouldn't interrupt his thoughts. She realized she was tapping her toe to some tune or other in her head, her own method of dealing with nervous energy. She made a conscious effort to hold her foot still so she wouldn't distract him.

"In New Jersey. I moved here shortly after high school to work for the post office."

"Why the post office?"

He shrugged. "Why not?" he said sharply. He dropped the blade of grass and raised the soda bottle to his lips. After a long swallow he lowered it. "I'm sorry," he said apologetically. "That sounded rude. I got a job with the post office because it seemed the logical thing to do."

What was logical about working for the post office? Then she realized. "Because you collected stamps?"

He nodded. "Sort of. But, it's more than that." Suddenly there was more expression in his voice. In one fluid motion he was suddenly sitting cross-legged on the blanket, his eyes alive and alight. "I always wanted to travel to the places my stamps came from. I could never afford to travel, but I thought that working for the post office would somehow give me a way to participate in the world. If I couldn't go there myself, at least I could carry the mail that went there."

He suddenly looked young and vulnerable. But rather than making him appear weak, it made him even more appealing. Sylvie found herself wanting to reach out to him, to touch him, to make a connection, to offer to take him anywhere in the world he wanted to go. But to do so would interrupt the spell. This was a dream of his, and he was sharing it with her! "Dreams are important," she agreed. "If we didn't have them we'd die. As a species, I mean. I really believe that. You know the line in *South Pacific* where Bloody Mary sings the song 'Happy Talk'? 'You got to have a dream. If you don't have a dream, how are you going to have a dream come true?' "

He was silent for a moment, staring out across the lake, but Sylvie knew he wasn't aware of the water, it was just something to focus his eyes on. He was somewhere in his mind.

"I never went to college." The even tone was back, and there was a slight stiffening to his shoulders.

She frowned, puzzled over the change in him, and in the subject. Unless—"Did you want to go?"

"I couldn't. My grades weren't good enough for a scholarship, and I didn't have any money."

"That's not what I asked," she pointed out gently, carefully. "I asked if you wanted to."

"There was never any point in thinking about it because it was never going to be an option for me."

Sylvie kept her gaze trained on him while she pondered this. For her, going to college had been a given. There was never any question about it, it was expected. The only point of discussion was where. Evidently this was, for him, one of those dreams that had died before it was even started.

"Would that bother you?" he asked, his voice slightly strained.

"Would what bother me?" she asked.

"Going out with someone less educated than you are."

She barely managed to catch herself before she laughed at the sheer absurdity of it. It might be a ridiculous notion to her, but evidently it was important to him. *Think tact, Sylvie, forget your normal bulldozer personality made in America by John Deere.* She thought for a moment, then answered him. "A college degree does not necessarily make one more educated," she answered quietly. "It only proves that you've studied enough to pass some tests. There are many different kinds of education, and just as many ways of acquiring them. College is only one way. It may not even be the best."

He was silent. Considering.

"And education and intelligence are not necessarily the same thing," she added. "Sometimes I think they're probably not even related. I know lots of people with college degrees who have the intelligence of a brick. College usually teaches you to answer questions. It does not necessarily teach you to think."

She waited.

Finally he nodded, and a slight smile came out to play on his face. "I think it's time to wake up Jean-Luc and incite another game of ball."

Jean-Luc, hearing the magic word, sprang up onto his toes, all senses alert, anticipation in every curl on his body.

"He wasn't really asleep, you know," Sylvie said, reaching out to hug her dog. "He was just playing possum." Jean-Luc, his mind obviously on a game of ball, shrugged her off.

Sylvie sat on the picnic blanket, her knees drawn up under her chin. Her eyes followed Ray as he threw the ball for Jean-Luc. She wondered if the death of his mother had anything to do with the white glove thing, or if he was just one of those people who were obsessive about picking up after themselves. It really wasn't quite human. Maybe Karen would have some wisdom on the matter.

What would it be like, she wondered, to lose everything at the age of twelve? She wasn't much older when her mother died, but she had her father and her brothers, aunts, uncles, cousins, grandparents—the whole family tree.

Ray had practically lost his own life when his mother died. Yes, he was still breathing, but dying was only one way of losing your existence. If she hadn't had her family she didn't know how she'd have survived. Ray hadn't had a family. Yet not only had he survived, he'd grown up to be a most rare kind of man. *Ray Novino,* she said to herself, *you're truly a nice guy.* His mother must have been a terrific lady to raise him up to be so sweet. Nice in the best sense of the word. The woman he ended up with would be lucky. Very lucky indeed. Then, in a heartbeat, Sylvie realized that she wanted to be that woman. Maybe if she could learn to be a better housekeeper . . .

Jean-Luc caught the ball on the fly—good boy—then dashed back to drop it at Ray's feet. By the time Ray had raised his arm to throw it again, Jean-Luc was already on an outrun.

"Why are you sitting around like that?" he called to her, a big grin of delight on his face. "Come join us."

She scrambled to her feet just in time to catch the ball he threw. It was covered with doggy slobber and bits of grass and dirt. Oh well. Jean-Luc didn't seem to mind. She drew back her arm and let it fly.

The ride back to Sylvie's house was silent. *She isn't chattering as she usually does*, he thought.

He wondered if something was bothering her. He thought it was. Would it be intrusive of him to ask? He thought it would.

Jean-Luc, however, plastered his nose to the window and stared out, as if for dear life.

Finally, she pulled into her driveway. She took her keys out of the ignition and raised her hips up to slip them in her pocket. Then she turned and smiled at him. "There. I know where my keys are."

"Do you always have this problem with your keys?"

"Yes, I do," she admitted with a sigh. "I have locked my keys in my car more times than I can count. It's totally humiliating. It's a big mother dragon that's been impossible for me to slay."

"Why don't you get one of those magnetic key boxes that stick onto the underside of your car?"

"I keep meaning to, but I always seem to forget when I'm at the store. Maybe I should write it down on a grocery list. Then I might remember. But I usually make lists and then forget to take them to the store, or something." Her voice seemed to run out of steam. Then she brightened. "Well, that's the way it is." She smiled at him. "Let's get this car unpacked. Jean-Luc, where's your leash?"

Carrying an armload of picnic gear, he followed her up the steps of the porch. At the door, key in the lock, she stopped. When she tilted her head up to him, he could see the distress in her eyes.

"You asked me if I minded going out with someone who didn't have the same pieces of paper that I have."

He nodded, wondering where this was going.

"I don't mind that at all, but do you mind going out with someone who's a total slob?" she asked in a rush. Then before he could answer, she added, "I mean, I always try to organize things, to keep things picked up. But it all seems to get away from me. If this were a sporting event it would be House 325, Sylvie zip. It's my biggest dragon, and one of my oldest, keeping a clean house. I know your apartment could pass for a *House Beautiful* ad, and I also know that mine couldn't. Maybe if I bulldozed it down first, or if I had a month's notice and an army of maids." She sounded glum.

"No."

"No what?"

"No it doesn't bother me if you're—" he paused, trying to be diplomatic—"not the most dedicated housekeeper in the world. But it obviously bothers you."

She stubbed her toe into the doorjamb. "Yeah, it does."

"Why?"

"Women are supposed to be in control of their houses," she said in a low voice, "not the other way around."

He couldn't help laughing. He really couldn't. "Who said that?"

"Everyone. The magazines, the advertising people. I've read billions and billions of books on how to organize your closets, and your time, and your life, that kind of thing. But it never works for me. I always start out with the best intentions, and then, before I know it, wham! My house has won again and I don't even know how it happened. It's as if Superwoman is thumbing her nose at me and blowing raspberries."

"You mean you're not Superwoman?" he said, trying to cheer her up. "And here, all this time, I thought you were."

Jean-Luc leaning against his leg, panting, nudged his hand, encouraging a pat or two.

"Superwoman doesn't continually lock her keys in the car," Sylvie said miserably. "Superwoman always manages to get the dinner dishes washed before next week, and never lets the dirty laundry breed like rabbits."

There had to be something he could say to cheer her up, Ray thought. Then he knew what it was. "Superwoman is boring."

When her eyes immediately brightened he knew he'd been right. "You really think so?" she asked hopefully.

"Absolutely. Besides, if you really wanted a sparkling clean house, you could hire a maid."

"Actually, I did. I had Katie, Karen's daughter, come over. It took a couple of days, but she whipped my house into livable shape and had it cowering in the corner."

"So why does it bother you?"

"Because I can't do it myself. Sure, it's clean right now, but give me a week and it'll be back to normal chaos. Karen's brother, Roger, says it's called entropy. Some law of physics that I don't understand."

Chaos. No, he didn't like chaos. But there were always solutions. "Then have her come back next week. And the next, and the next. *Ad infinitum*." It seemed an obvious solution to him.

"That's what Karen said."

"Karen is smart."

She nodded, but didn't say anything.

"This doesn't solve the issue?" he asked.

She shook her head.

"You think you should be able to do it yourself?"

She nodded. "It's a girl thing," she explained.

"Must be," he agreed. "Then again, maybe it's a talent. Like playing an instrument, or drawing castles and fairies. Some people have it, some don't."

"Maybe." She sounded as if there were a possibility there. Then she turned the key and opened the door. Jean-Luc barged in and headed toward the back of the house. They followed the dog, the screen door banging behind them.

Yes, it was cleaned up, he thought as he surreptitiously looked around. He could actually see the floor in the living room.

From the direction of the kitchen there came a tinny rattle, and a sharp bark.

"Okay, buddy, I'm coming," Sylvie called to him.

There was another tinny rattle. Jean-Luc's answer.

"His water bowl must be empty," she explained. "Just bring all that stuff into the kitchen," she said, moving down the hall.

Ray followed more slowly, peeking into the dining room on his way. The table was cleared off, and a vase of flowers sat in the middle of it. Even from here, he could see a reflection in the shine of the wood. On the other side of the hall he glanced in her computer room. It was no longer a fortress of randomly piled papers and boxes. Katie had indeed worked wonders. It didn't look like the same house. Oh, the color was still here, the life, the vibrancy, but now it was a controlled riot, not a house running amok.

"Where did you go?" she called.

"Right here," he answered, giving the room one last look. He had to turn slightly sideways to maneuver through the kitchen doorway with the picnic gear still in his arms.

"Where do you want these things?"

"On the table is fine," she said from the sink where she was filling Jean-Luc's water bowl. "Here you go, buddy." She set the bowl down on a towel on the floor and Jean-Luc immediately stuck his head in and lapped noisily.

Ray set the things down, noting that there was actually a place to set them down, and looked around approvingly. It was a nice kitchen. In fact, it was a nice house. He liked this house. It had tremendous potential. She really should keep it clean. Then, on the spotlessly clean counter, his gaze hit a disembodied hand.

Chapter Seventeen

The hand was made of rubber. He took the three steps over to the counter and picked it up. On the palm, in black ink, was the address. To someone called Mad About Rubber.

"This hand is on its way to Colorado," he said, struggling to keep his voice calm.

"That's right," she answered cheerily, opening the refrigerator door to put away the leftovers. "We're doing a body thing right now. We're each sending out body parts. That one's for Madeleine. You know, Melissa's cousin. The body part thing was her idea. She's a medical illustrator. She's a rubber stamper, too. Her *nom d'stamp* is Mad About Rubber. We all have rubber names."

Suddenly his exasperation erupted. "Why do you do this?"

"Do what?"

"Send objects like this in the mail?"

"Because it's fun." She was still busy in the refrigerator, moving things aside to make room for the pitcher of lemonade.

"Fun for whom?"

She shrugged and closed the refrigerator. "It won't fit." She held up the pitcher. "We'll just have to drink the rest of it." She opened a cupboard and took out two glasses. Like most of the dishes in her house, they didn't match.

"Fun for whom?" he repeated.

"For the person who sends it, and for the person who gets it. Wouldn't it brighten your day if you found something unexpected in your mailbox? Something like, oh, maybe a coconut, or a squirt gun, instead of plain old boring white envelopes."

"No it wouldn't."

For just a second, she paused in the act of pouring lemonade, as if she'd just remembered to count to ten. "Plain white envelopes are so boring," she said without looking his way. She finished pouring and thrust a glass at him.

"I like plain white envelopes," he told her. "I'm a mailman. The address is easy to read on a plain white boring envelope. You don't have to search for it. It makes the mail move more smoothly and arrive at its destination more quickly."

"But something unexpected, something silly, exotic, something out of the ordinary." She waved her glass in the air, sloshing lemonade. Her glass was too full. She took a quick sip before she continued. "I'd think that would break up some of the monotony of the mail. Now, tell me," she said, pointing her glass at him. "When something unusual comes into your post office; what does everyone do?"

"Sometimes they make a joke about it." She still didn't understand, he realized.

"Well then, it's done some good!" Her feet were planted firmly on the blue linoleum, her glass-filled hand held toward him, the other was fisted on her hip. Her chin was out. It was a challenge plain and simple. She was a spitfire, a fighting tiger. Jean-Luc, evidently sensing a coming altercation, slunk out of the kitchen. "If it makes people laugh," she insisted, "if it raises their spirits, then it's a good thing."

But it wasn't a good thing, Ray thought. *It wasn't in accordance with the spirit of the rules, even if it kept to the letter.* He liked things neat and tidy. He didn't like chaos. Chaos was unpredictable, it was out of control. It was having your mother die when you were a child and then being yanked out of everything you'd ever known and thrown into a new life and left to fend for yourself. He didn't like chaos. He had to make her understand.

"The post office in Hartley delivers three million pieces of mail every year. Imagine what my job would be like if everyone did this."

"Most people don't have the imagination," she snapped, fire in her eyes.

"Most people have more sense," he shot back. Then he saw the look on her face and knew he'd gone too far. He carefully set his still full glass of lemonade on the counter next to the hand. "Good-bye, Sylvie. Thank you for the pleasant afternoon." The words came out sounding stiff and formal. He didn't care. And if he did care, he'd certainly keep it to himself.

Her mouth opened, as if she wanted to say something, but nothing came out. There was nothing to say, anyway. Filled with a sense of having lost something special, Ray left her, standing there, unmoving. Not even the look of desolation in her eyes could make him stay.

He closed her front door quietly as he left, careful not to let the screen door bang.

"C'mon, Jean-Luc, I'm going to put on my pajamas and then we're going to watch *Braveheart*," Sylvie gritted out. Followed by her faithful canine companion, Sylvie stomped down the hallway to her bedroom. The nerve of that wretched man! She jerked open her drawer and yanked out her nightshirt. Just when she realized that she liked him, that she was actually thinking of maybe going ahead and trying to have a romantic relationship with him, he practically told her she didn't have any sense! "That's what he thinks!" she said to her dog as, changed into her comfort clothes, she stomped back to the living room. She was full of sense.

"I have lots of sense," she grumbled to Jean-Luc as she shoved the videocassette in the player. "Maybe I'll make the Princess Delphine discover that the prince she'd saved is really an emissary of the Wicked Wizard. He's really a lizard, or a rat, or a skunk, under a glamour to make him *look* gorgeous," she muttered. "But the princess discovers his true nature before it's too late. That's because she's brilliant and he's a skunk."

While the previews played she stomped into the kitchen to rummage around in the cupboard for the bag of circus peanuts. Jean-Luc came to sit at her feet, looking up hopefully. "I'll give you one, too, don't worry," she told him. Then she saw the box of people crackers for dogs. She'd show Mr. Male Man Ray Novino!

She ripped open the little cheerfully colored box and pawed through the contents looking for . . . There! She found one. Then another. And another. With a humph she shoved the mutilated box in the back of the cupboard and slammed the door.

"Here, Jean-Luc," she announced haughtily. "Here's a cookie in the shape of a mailman. Bite his head off."

"Morning there, Ray," Harvey called to him across the busy mailroom. "How's that ankle doing?"

The mailroom was doing the early-morning hum, Ray thought as he made his way down the box-strewn aisle to the supervisor's desk. Other letter carriers called out friendly greetings to him. Then he was at Harvey's desk.

"Doc recommended not to walk my route until next week. I decided to come in anyway. There's always plenty to do around here."

"Didn't want to take off another week? You sure have enough sick leave, man."

No, this was where he belonged. The mailroom with all the comings and goings of mail was what he knew best. He was comfortable here. But he didn't want to admit that to Harvey. So he merely shook his head. "Nah," he said. "I feel fine."

The supervisor whistled. "I wish I could feel fine and still get to take sick leave." It was a standing joke at the post office.

"You just don't want to miss all the soap operas," Ray pointed out. More of the joke. "You ought to get a VCR and record them."

Sometime later, while Ray was casing mail, putting each piece into it's slot in the order in which it was to be delivered, he heard furtive whispering. It was fairly close to him. Then a quiet chuckle.

"Hey, Ray," someone called out to him. "Be glad you're not walking your route today."

"Why?" he asked, not looking up from the mail. He liked to get a rhythm going, liked to see how quickly and efficiently he could case his route. Of course, he wasn't casing his own route right now, that would be done by the substitute carrier. This case was for one of the rural routes whose carrier was on vacation. That carrier had taped photos of his children on the metal sides, and some of the house numbers were peeling off the slots. The case for Ray's route, on the other hand, was not cluttered with personal memorabilia, and he kept all the numbers neatly affixed on the metal slots.

"Lookit this." Tony, the substitute carrier, came around the corner of the metal case. "It's going to that lady on your route."

Ray lifted his gaze from his handful of mail to take a quick glance.

The 'It' was a red plush stuffed heart. The address was embroidered on a piece of white cloth sewed onto the heart. It was too big to fit into the mailbag along with the legitimate mail.

"I mailed my heart . . . from San Francisco," one of the older carriers sang out lustily. He received a round of loud guffaws and a smattering of applause from the others.

"C'mon, Ray," Tony said. "Aren't you glad you're not carrying this today?"

"Sure, Tony," he answered shortly, turning back to his task. "Why should I get all the fun? I like to spread it around. Let you carry the strange stuff for a change."

"Yo, Tony," called one of the other old-timers. "You can use it for a pillow when you take your nap. Maybe you'll dream of the girl you're going to marry."

More loud guffaws and a wolf whistle.

Ray ignored them. Then he thought of something. "Tony," he called after the substitute carrier.

"Yeah?"

"When you deliver mail to that house, remember to put the lock back on the gate. She has a dog who knows how to open gates."

"Sure thing, Ray," Tony answered.

Ray hoped he would remember. Tony was apt to be casual about things.

Turning back to the mail he was sorting, he started up his rhythm once more. Pick up a piece of mail, read the address, slip it into the correct slot. Pick up the next piece of mail, read the address, slip it into the correct slot.

"Hey, Novino," someone called out from the aisle of cases across from him. "What's the strangest thing you ever delivered to her?" Everyone knew who the 'her' was. Sylvie's strange mail was a constant source of good-natured amusement among the mail carriers.

"I bet it was that cast-iron skillet," someone offered.

"Nah, it was the toilet plunger," another carrier suggested.

"Yeah," someone else agreed. "That was a good one."

"Okay now, here's the really big question.

What is the most memorable thing she ever sent?"

Shouted out in near unison came the answer, "The squirt guns!"

Yes, he remembered that, Ray thought. About a year ago Sylvie had mailed a dozen squirt guns in the shape of dragons. All had addresses written on them somewhere in permanent pen. All had the correct postage. At least, he thought now, she hadn't filled them with water. He bet she'd thought about it.

"Ray, my man, why aren't you saying anything?"

"He disapproves," someone called out in explanation.

Evidently his opinions were well known, Ray thought. "Mail should be properly packaged," he told them. They were mail carriers. They knew this.

"As long as it has the correct postage who cares what we deliver? I don't."

"As long as it's not illegal," came another voice.

"Or flammable, or whatever. Hey, the strange stuff breaks up the day. Makes it interesting," said still another.

Martin, the first buddy Ray had made at the post office, wandered over from the next case, still holding a handful of uncased mail. "Don't be so rigid," he said quietly. His voice was full of good humor, but Ray felt there was a hint of caution there as well. "Loosen up," Martin added. "Life's too short to worry about strange stuff in the mail. If you want to worry, worry about the big stuff, like falling satellites, or the sun going nova, or the coming ice age."

"Yeah, Martin," Ray said. "Thanks for the advice."

"Anytime, pal. That's what I'm here for."

From over in the corner there came a burst of loud laughter followed by some hoots and catcalls.

"Ray Novino. Ray Novino. This is your letter carrier calling." It was Schumann, who delivered mail to where Ray lived. "Look at this, everyone. Someone sent our very own Ray Novino some strange stuff in the mail." Schumann was doing his Steve Martin imitation. "Wild and crazy strange stuff."

"Go see what it is, man," Martin urged.

"Make sure we all see it," Tony added. "Inquiring minds want to know."

Ray quickly finished casing the mail he had in his hand. Then, not wanting to appear overly concerned, he strolled over to the corner of the room where the cheers were coming from. He came to a stop in front of Schumann.

"What is it?" he asked, as if he really didn't care one way or another. He didn't think he fooled anyone; they had all known one another too long.

"Who do you know in Minnesota?" Schumann asked, holding something behind his back. "Postmark says Anoka, Minnesota."

He frowned. "Anoka, Minnesota? I don't know anyone from there."

"Well, someone sure knows you," Schumann said with a wide grin as he held out a large wooden spoon, elaborately painted with roses, and bluebirds, and lacy hearts.

Still frowning in confusion, Ray took the wooden spoon. Sure enough, it had his name and address on it. He turned it over and over. There was no return address, but the postmark stamped across the postage was Anoka, Minnesota.

He looked up from the spoon to the grinning faces around him. "I have no idea who sent this," he told them.

"Sure thing, Ray."

"Hey, I believe you," said someone else, then turned away, a grin on his face.

Ray hefted it thoughtfully as he walked back down the aisle, showing it to the other carriers.

"I have no idea who sent this," he insisted, feeling totally bewildered. "No idea at all."

"You have a secret admirer," Martin said, the grin evident in his voice.

That was Monday. On Tuesday someone sent Sylvie a heart-shaped cake pan. Someone from Cicero, New York, sent Ray a big white plastic mixing bowl. To make matters worse, it had fire-engine red hearts painted on it. On Wednesday Ray received a box of cake mix. Sylvie received a place mat, painted with hearts and flowers. There was an address label on the place mat. It had a stamped image of two women, one asking the other, "Do you still have the hots for the mailman?" Of course, Schumann took great delight in reading these words with just the right enthusiasm. This was, Ray thought, enough to transform the normally reasonable letter carriers into a troop of testosterone-ridden teenagers. The group in the mailroom began to eagerly await each new day's arrivals. Bets were taken on what the next item would be. By far, the most popular suggestion was lingerie.

Each morning, Tony reported delivering the previous day's object. He said he never saw Sylvie, so he couldn't share with them what her reaction was. But he said he heard some fancy opera music coming from her house. He couldn't help hearing it, he said. It was turned up so loud he could hear it clear down the street.

She didn't want to deal with anything anymore, she thought as she closed her eyes. She was stretched out on her porch swing, one foot on the porch, rocking. Back and forth, back and forth. Without conscious reasoning, bits of lullabies began to form in the back of her mind. As she rocked, they grew louder and louder, joined their bits together and turned into a regular song. The one her mother used to sing. Sylvie's Comfort Song, Mom called it. Whenever she was home from school sick, or when she was cranky and tired, Mom used to draw her over to the rocking chair, up on her lap. They'd rock and rock, and Mom would sing Sylvie's Comfort Song. Whatever the matter was, Sylvie would feel better. There was magic in that song.

For the past ten long years, she'd had to sing Sylvie's Comfort Song to herself. It still worked, but the magic was dimming. Maybe by the time she had her own daughter or son to sing to the magic would be all gone. Or maybe the magic that came with a new baby would renew the magic in the song. If she ever had a baby.

Oh, Mom, Sylvie silently called. *If you're up there, playing a harp, would you please go find Ray's mom, she's up there somewhere, and tell her to shake some sense into her son*?

Jean-Luc barked. She ignored him. She rocked. He barked again. She ignored him again. She rocked again. Wretched beast, he'd give up eventually, she told herself with a long sigh as he continued barking. She stayed still, and this time he went away. Sylvie was left to rock alone, singing quietly to herself.

What kind of a woman was Ray's mom? she wondered. And Helen, his foster mother, what kind of a woman was she? Were the two mothers anything alike? They must have both been terrific women to raise such a sweet son—even if he was bullheaded. Even if he thought she didn't have any sense.

Plop! Something landed on the pillow next to her head.

She opened an eye. She saw a tennis ball, very close. Evidently the wretched beast wanted to play ball. She set her foot to stop the swing. "You really need to play b-a-l-l now do you?"

Jean-Luc bounced up and down.

"You sure about this? You don't want to go think it over a little more?"

Jean-Luc raised to his hind feet and did a perfect pirouette. A very masculine pirouette, though, she told herself.

"Okay. You win."

She pulled herself into a sit, heaved herself off the porch swing and together she and her dog traipsed around the house to the backyard. Not as much room as Karen's, but enough. She threw the ball. Someday she'd get all the brush hacked down and grass planted. Jean-Luc brought the ball back again, and once more she obediently threw it. She'd like to have more of her land fenced in. More space for Jean-Luc. She threw it again, and again, until Jean-Luc started slowing down, panting. It was time to quit. "That's enough, buddy," she called to her dog. The beast was insatiable. He didn't know when to stop. He'd keep going until he dropped. She could retrieve him to death. Death by retrieving.

How did Ray's mom die? What would he have been like as a young boy? What would it have been like to meet a foster mother for the first time? What would it have been like for Helen? Slowly she got to her feet, pondering questions that had no answers. She called her dog, and, worn out at last, he came to her immediately. Good boy. Together they wandered back inside where Jean-Luc stuck his nose into his water bowl. When he was finished, Sylvie said to him, "Let's go up to the rubber room. I need to draw, and you can sleep off your b-a-l-l fix upstairs and keep me company. Okay?"

Jean-Luc gave her a few good-natured wags and followed her, slowly, panting. His dark eyes were full of satisfaction. He was happy.

Upstairs, Jean-Luc settled on his cushion, his teddy bear under his chin. Sylvie sat down at her drawing board, paper in place, pens close at hand. She stared at the white paper, thinking, pondering, focusing on Ray and Helen. She allowed herself to remember the overwhelming pain of the loss of her own mother. After a few minutes, she picked up her pen and began to draw.

By Thursday morning, on the drive to work, Ray actually found himself feeling curious about what strange new package would arrive today. He squashed his curiosity. Might be nothing at all. Maybe the person who was behind this was getting tired of it. If he just ignored all of it, it would eventually stop, he told himself. Best thing was to pretend nothing odd was going on. Nothing at all.

Flashing yellow lights suddenly appeared in front of him. Ray stopped his car at a detour. Road closed up ahead, said the sign, construction must be going on. This wasn't too unusual. People around here joked that the state flower was the orange construction barrel. He must have missed the detour sign. He turned his car around to backtrack to the alternate route. He'd be late for work.

Sylvie never had that problem, he found himself thinking. She worked from her home.

What does Sylvie think of all these items coming in the mail? he wondered. Of course, she didn't know about the things he'd gotten. She only knew about what was sent to her. She was probably enjoying it. She undoubtedly thought it was hilarious.

Bright images of Sylvie's smiling eyes flashed across his consciousness. Over and over and over again in his mind he heard the rippling sound of her laughter.

So you had an argument, he chided himself. *Is this the end of the world? It takes two people to argue, so get off your high horse, as Helen used to say, and go apologize.*

Maybe he should. Maybe the argument was an orange barrel in their friendship, a detour. Maybe he should go over to her house this evening. But how could he apologize for feeling the way he felt? he asked himself as he pulled into the post office parking lot.

Not for how you feel, you idiot, came his conscience. *For the way you said it. She's a bright lady. Certainly there's a way to make her understand. You've always believed in solutions to things. Well, look for the solution.*

As he pushed open the doors that morning, he glanced at the big wall clock. Five minutes late. He'd have to allow for the detour tomorrow.

"He's here!" came the excited cry. "Ray's here!"

"Wait'll you see what you two got today!"

Chapter Eighteen

"Yes, ma'am," the flunky said in a couldn't-care-less voice. "I know you ordered the O-rings on Monday, but as we should have told you then, we had them on back order. They arrived yesterday and we sent them overnight to you. You should get them today."

"That's why I'm calling," Sylvie tried to remain calm as she talked to the flunky on the phone. She could see him in her imagination chewing bubble gum and blowing bubbles as he talked to customers. Probably leaning back in his chair, feet on his desk. He was the epitome of poor customer service. But she needed the O-rings. She needed them now. "I want to know if you have any idea what time today they will arrive. I need them for my vulcanizer so I can get my orders out. I'm already almost a whole week behind schedule just waiting for these O-rings."

"I'm sorry, ma'am," he said without a smidge of sincerity in his voice. "We just send 'em out, we don't drive the trucks." Sylvie could almost hear him say, 'next,' in his tone of voice.

"Can you find a tracer number for me?"

"Yeah. I guess. Hold on."

"Thank you for your trouble," Sylvie told him, holding her sarcasm firmly reined back. She wondered if this guy was trying to get fired.

Finally she got the tracer number and called the shipping company. All she found out was that the package would be delivered sometime that day. She hung up the phone and bent down to hug Jean-Luc. "Well, buddy," she told him mournfully, "we're going to be even further behind. And we still have that stamp convention to get ready for."

Jean-Luc leaned into her sympathetically, then he bounced out of her arms, turned around, and made a play-bow, inviting her to play.

"I can't, buddy. I have to get the rest of these orders ready to go out today and hope that the rush on mermaids is over. But we'll go visit Melissa tonight after supper. You can play with Hugo and Lady. I promise."

Jean-Luc looked supremely unimpressed with such promises. He sneezed at her.

Sylvie shoved herself up from her desk chair

and wandered back into the kitchen to start a pot of iced tea.

She filled a big old pickle jar with water, floated four teabags in it, and set it out on her back porch in the sun. She trailed into the living room to peer out the beaded curtain. No delivery truck in sight. Yes, it would be an incredible coincidence if the delivery truck pulled in right after she'd called the company, but stranger things had happened. "But I guess strange things won't be happening today, buddy."

Jean-Luc stood up on his hind legs next to her to stare out the window.

"Speaking of strange things," she told him, "we need to think of something great to send back to the group."

Jean-Luc licked at her cheek and went back to staring out the window.

"Evidently, we decided to send each other stuff with a heart theme and I forgot." She shrugged. "Let's see. What heart things can we send back? Heart-shaped sunglasses have already been done. And Jell-O molds. I know." She snapped her fingers. "That store in town that sells yuppie toys. They have those little anatomically correct hearts that you squeeze when you want to get rid of tension and stress. Then they return to their original shape and you squeeze them again. That would work."

She reached out to tousle Jean-Luc's topknot. "I knew you'd come up with something. You're such a great guy dog." Her fingers found the beginnings of a small mat. "Uh-oh, we have trouble right here in River City, bud," she told him, pulling the mat apart with her fingers. "Your hair is too long. Pretty soon people will start thinking you're a rock star, or an old hippie. Time for a shave and a haircut."

Squeezie hearts. She could think of a heart she'd like to squeeze. A heart that belonged to a certain male man she knew. Remember what happened, she reminded herself. Just as she was beginning to think that there might possibly be the remotest hint of a chance of something maybe starting to develop between the two of them, it blew up right in her face. Oh well. It would have blown up sooner or later. You win one or two and you lose most. One has to be philosophical about it and keep on going. At least, that's what she told herself.

"You would probably love another people cookie, wouldn't you?" she asked her dog. Yes, he most certainly would.

She found the box and tossed him a police officer. "Sorry there aren't any more mailmen. You ate them all up already."

Jean-Luc was not particular. He would crunch up a police officer just as happily as he would a mailman.

As Sylvie leaned against the counter and tossed the confectionary police officers one at a time to her dog, her gaze fell once more to the heart-shaped cake pan from Plum Crazy. She set down the box of dog cookies and picked up the cake pan. It wouldn't have gone through the automatic sorters at the post office. The postage would have had to have been canceled by hand.

What would happen if everyone in the world started sending cake pans to each other? she thought. *Cake pans, or plastic baseball bats, or baby dolls. What if even half of the people in the world, only once a year, sent something creative? That would be about half a gazillion strange things that all had to be dealt with by hand.* Yes, it would take longer. Yes, it would be a serious problem. Ray was right.

A little niggle of unease wormed through her. She didn't like it.

Wait a minute! Maybe Ray was right that it would gum up the whole works, but *she* was right that such a situation would never happen because it would never occur to most people to send something fun, something outrageous, in the mail. There. Now she felt better. *But wait a minute,* her conscience reined her in. *You and your buddies don't send things once a year, you guys try to outdo one another with your creativity.* Well—she didn't want to think about it right now. She had other things to do.

"Time for a shower, Jean-Luc." She led the way to the hall closet for a fresh towel while she hummed a tune from *South Pacific*. Yes, she was going to wash that man right out of her hair. Then she was going to fill the orders that had arrived yesterday. Then give Jean-Luc a haircut. And whenever the wretched O-rings arrived she had lots of rubber to burn. After supper, on the way over to Melissa's she'd stop at the yuppie toy store and buy a dozen squeezie hearts to mail to her stamp buddies. She'd buy an extra one for her to keep and squeeze the dickens out of. Yes, it would be a good day. No doubt about it.

If only she would stop thinking about Ray.

"Can't possible be real silver," one of the carriers argued, jerking his thumb at the object he'd just handed to Ray. "My wife inherited some little silver bowls and stuff, and they're worth a mint. No one would be dumb enough to send a real silver candlestick unwrapped like this, in the mail."

Yes, they would, Ray said to himself. He knew someone who he was sure would do just that. He turned the candlestick over and over in his hands. It was lovely. Complete with roses and hearts—why was he not surprised? Sylvie's address, along with the postage, was on the bottom of the base.

"Maybe it's silver-coated aluminum," suggested one of the rural carriers.

"Weighs too much," Ray said, shaking his head. "Well, Tony, it looks like you get a heavy bag today." He handed the candlestick to the substitute carrier.

"Wonder what *you* got today," Tony said, taking the candlestick. "Hey you guys," he called out to the room in general. "Has anyone seen

Schumann? I wonder what the phantom folks sent Ray today. Anyone know?"

"It's over here," Schumann called back.

His voice sounded somewhat ominous, Ray thought. Or maybe he was trying not to laugh.

"Is it lingerie?" called one of the younger carriers. "Something from Victoria's Secret? Or Frederick's of Hollywood?"

"Wouldn't Ray look cute in some of their slinky underwear?" chuckled another. There was a series of loud catcalls and *woo woos*.

"Cut it out, you guys," Ray said tolerantly. "Enough is enough. So Schumann, what is it?"

"You gotta see this," Schumann said, coming down the mail-crowded aisle. "This is really amazing. I wouldn't've taken this at the counter, wherever it was dropped off. I really wouldn't. Lucky it didn't get broken. This is just amazing."

It was an old vinyl record, an old LP. Without its cardboard sleeve, unwrapped. Just the record. Ray reached for it, wondering. He looked over the record, looking for a postmark. He found it on the record label. "Hawaii," he muttered. "Someone sent an unwrapped vinyl record all the way from Hawaii. And it didn't break."

"Hey, what is it? Old Rolling Stones? It might be worth something."

Ray held the record up so he could see the label more clearly. "No, it's—" he began. Then he stopped. No way could he read this out loud.

He cleared his throat. "It's just some old tunes." He hoped they wouldn't demand he be more specific. He should have known better.

"What kinda tunes?" came a plaintive cry. "C'mon, Ray, we wanna know."

"You guys act like you're all still twelve," he muttered, feeling his face turn hot.

Schumann, a broad grin on his face, a twinkle in his eye, said, "Do you want to tell them, or should I?"

Wordlessly, Ray shook his head. "No way, man," he muttered. Wooden spoons were one thing, this was something else. Something way else. Knowing the reaction he was going to get when the title of the album was announced, he took a few deep breaths to steady himself.

"Listen up, men," Schumann ordered, standing on a stool and tipping his head back slightly so his voice would carry better over the rows of metal casing units. Evidently, Ray thought with a slight shudder, Schumann didn't want anyone to miss this.

"As we all know, today the delightful Miss Taylor received a silver candlestick. Today our good buddy Ray Novino was sent an old vinyl LP. You all remember them? Now it appears that Ray here, our very own buddy Ray, is a wee bit embarrassed by this record. He feels too shy to tell you what it is. So I will. It's called"—Schumann put his hand to his heart, hamming it up to the max—" '*The World's All-Time*

Greatest Romantic Hits; Songs to Share With the One You Love.' "

A roar of cheers and wolf whistles filled the room.

"Way to go, Ray!"

How was he ever going to live this down? As he made his way down the aisle with the mail he had to case, the other carriers kept the enthusiasm up, reaching out to clap him on the shoulder. The guys would be talking about this one for years to come. Finally he reached the case where he'd be working this morning. With the metal sorting slots on three sides, there was at least some sense of privacy.

Martin stuck his head around the case Ray was working in. "It's all in good fun," he said quietly. "They're just teasing you about it."

Ray whipped his head around. "I know it is, Martin," he answered seriously, "I know there's nothing malicious in it. It's just embarrassing. I'm not used to being the center of something like this."

"Do you know who's behind it? Who's sending these things?"

Ray shook his head. "I have no idea. It has to be one of Sylvie's . . . Miss Taylor's friends, though. They do this kind of thing all the time."

Martin nodded, "I've noticed," he said dryly. He turned his gaze to the address on the top letter in the pile in his hand. "Still, it makes work move more quickly when we have something to laugh and joke about. It changes the atmosphere in this place. Makes it more cheerful or something."

Ray frowned in thought. "Sylvie said almost the same thing."

Then he became aware of Martin's scrutiny. "So you really do know this Miss Taylor, ah, personally?"

Ray shrugged. "I sprained my ankle at her house, when I was delivering mail." That was a slight understatement, he knew.

"When did she say that about the weird mail?" his friend asked.

"I asked her what she thought would happen if everyone in the country sent these kinds of things in the mail."

"Most people don't have the imagination," Martin answered with a slight chuckle. "Lucky for us."

Ray looked up at him in surprise. "She said exactly the same thing. That most people don't have the imagination."

"Bright woman. And imaginative, too."

Ray nodded. "She has more creativity than anyone I've ever met. She's an artist. Most of her artwork is of fantasy worlds. It's pretty good." And as he said it, he realized it was true. Her art was pretty good. In fact, it was more than pretty good. It was excellent. He didn't have a formal background in art, but he knew Sylvie's creations were good. They had that spark of life in them.

"This is more than casual? This friendship you have?"

Ray felt himself redden again. But before he could say anything else, Martin's face broke into a broad, slightly wicked, grin. "Ray, I like you. You're a good guy. But sometimes you're just too straitlaced. Take some advice from your buddy Martin here. If you like some lady who's really creative, and full of imagination, then don't be such a stick-in-the-mud all the time. You'll get further in life, and you'll have more fun. Okay?"

Stick-in-the-mud, Martin said. Was he really a stick-in-the-mud? It was worth thinking about. "Thanks," he muttered.

"Anytime, buddy," Martin said, slapping Ray on the arm. "Anytime."

You'll have more fun, Martin had said. Sylvie knew how to have fun, he thought, his mother had known how to have fun. But did he? Helen had once commented that he was too serious too often.

"Are you gonna just stand there all day? Or are you gonna case mail?" Martin's voice jerked him back from his thoughts.

"What?" he asked.

"I said," Martin repeated patiently, a broad grin on his broad face, "you've been standing there holding that handful of mail for the last five minutes. Must be having good thoughts, eh?" He punched Ray lightly on the arm. "Good luck, buddy. Don't do anything I wouldn't do."

"Thanks," Ray said.

"Hey, are you all right, man?"

"I'm fine. Just a little tired, that's all."

"Well, take it easy. And remember, don't be a stick-in-the-mud."

Trouble was, he thought that afternoon pulling out of the parking lot, he didn't know how to *not* be a stick-in-the-mud. But, whatever he was, he decided, the first thing was to go over to Sylvie's house and make that apology. Maybe he'd stop at Abernathy's and buy her a bag of circus peanuts. He'd also stop at his house to pick up his ladder. The weather forecasters had predicted early evening rain. He would clean out her gutters for her, actions speaking apologies louder than words ever did. Then, he had another idea. So he'd also have to make a quick stop at the hardware store.

An hour later, circus peanuts on the seat beside him, along with a little brown paper bag from the hardware store, and his ladder tied onto the roof of his car, he drove down her tree-lined street. He waved to young Joshua Martini who was riding his bike on the sidewalk. "Hi Joshua, see you next week," he called out the window.

"Hi, Ray," the little boy called, a huge grin on his freckled face. "I'll have some new jokes for you."

"See ya later, alligator!" Ray called back.

"In a while, crocodile!" Joshua yelled jubilantly. He waved his whole arm so enthusiastically that he lost his balance for a moment and the bike swerved crazily. Ray braked slightly and glanced in the mirror to make sure the boy regained control of his bike again.

He'd have to call Liz at the library and ask her to look up some new knock-knock jokes. Of course, Joshua would probably know them already. That kid had a repertoire of more knock-knock jokes than Ray even knew existed. Maybe Liz could find him some other joke books. Maybe he should introduce Joshua to chicken jokes. Or pig jokes.

Then he was at Sylvie's house. He pulled into the driveway and turned off the engine. He was lifting the ladder off the roof when her front door slammed open and she burst out, tearing across the yard to the gate. There was panic in her face.

"Oh, Ray, I'm so glad you came," she gasped. "Jean-Luc is gone!"

Chapter Nineteen

"Gone? What do you mean?" Ray set the ladder against the side of her house before he opened the gate to her yard.

"He's gone," she repeated wildly. He could see tear tracks on her cheeks. She was shivering slightly. He took her by the shoulders to make her hold still.

"Calm down," he said in a deliberately quiet tone. "Start from the beginning and tell me what happened."

She gulped a few times, and reached up to smear new tears across her cheeks.

"I needed some O-rings for my vulcanizer," she began in a shaky voice. "I usually keep some on hand, because there's one on the jack that has to be replaced every once in a while. And it needed to be replaced on Monday because the hydraulic fluid ran all over the place when I was—anyway, I looked in the place where I always keep the spare O-rings. Only they weren't there. I think Jean-Luc ate them. He loves to chew up rubber anything—which is why I have to be careful of him in my rubber room—and he's done it before. Chewed up my O-rings, I mean. So I had to order a new supply of them."

"So you ordered new O-rings. What happened to Jean-Luc?" He'd bet that Sylvie saw a connection here, but he sure didn't.

"They were overnighted. They got here this afternoon." She balled her fist and smacked it into her other hand. "And I was so stupidly impatient to replace the worn-out one and get my rubber burning that I didn't make sure the gate was latched properly when the delivery guy left. I'm so stupid," she wailed miserably. "I should've known he'd get out! I should've checked the gate!"

"Don't cry," he told her, knowing it was a useless thing to say, but saying it anyway. "What time did the delivery guy leave?"

She sniffed loudly. "About three-thirty."

He glanced at his watch. It was now five o'clock. "When did you discover Jean-Luc was gone?"

"Just now. A couple of minutes ago. I came upstairs to make a phone call and I couldn't find him. I thought he was taking a nap or something. Or maybe he had gotten into something he shouldn't be getting into. Only I couldn't find him inside, so I looked outside and saw the gate open. Wretched dragons!" she added in a mutter.

"Does he have his collar and tags on?"

"Of course he had his collar on." She sounded insulted. Well, he thought, that was an improvement. "He *always* has his collar on. And he's tattooed *and* microchipped. And yes, the numbers are registered. Melissa stood over me while I did it just to make sure I didn't forget."

He held up his hands in surrender. "Just making sure. Do his tags have your phone number on them? So if anyone finds him they can call?"

She nodded.

"I take it he's done this before?"

She nodded. "He used to be a career escape artist. Then I took him to dog school and put a new latch on the gate and that stopped him for a while. But he still checks the latch, just to make sure. It's this routine of his. At least he's never learned that he could probably jump over the fence it he tried."

"Is there a particular place he liked to go when he used to run away?" He wanted to make her think, not react. Thinking logically would help her find him, reacting to the situation would not. At least, that was his theory.

She wrinkled her forehead in thought. "Sometimes he'd go to Karen's, and sometimes he'd go into the fields in back of my house.

Sometimes he'd go down the street to visit people."

"Did you call Karen to see if he was there?"

"She isn't home yet."

"Then let's go see for ourselves. Is your answering machine on?"

When she nodded, he took her hand and led her to his car, opened the door on the passenger's side, and gently shoved her in.

Jean-Luc wasn't at Karen's house, but from the inside of the house, Ray heard the deep woofing and woo woo-ing of a number of Newfoundlands. A curtain twitched and a big Newfoundland looked out the window.

"It's just me, Brian," Sylvie called to the dog. "We're looking for Jean-Luc. Have you seen him?"

The big black dog let out a powerful woof.

"If you see him, send him home, will you?" Sylvie answered.

When they went around to the backyard, where the lawn ended and the grassy fields began, Sylvie climbed up on Karen's redwood picnic table to search the fields with her gaze. "Back there is Karen's pond, and where we play ball a lot. Jean-Luc loves Karen's house. But I don't see him."

Good, Ray thought. She'll feel better if she's doing something positive to find her dog.

"No." She sounded totally dispirited.

He held out his hand to help her climb down from the table.

"Do you have any idea when Karen will be home?"

"She's usually home by about six."

"Let's leave her a note, ask her to keep an eye open for him, and we can drive up and down the streets looking. Unless you have another idea."

Sylvie didn't.

As they searched the small neighborhood, they stopped to talk to everyone they saw. No one had seen the white poodle, but all promised to call Sylvie if they did.

Finally, there was no more neighborhood to drive through.

"Sometimes he used to go into the fields in back of my house," Sylvie said, still staring out of the car window. "Will you come with me to look?"

"Of course," he told her as they pulled back into her driveway. "Why don't you get some long pants on, and some shoes and socks and we'll go find him."

She turned to face him, her large gray eyes brimming. "Thank you," she whispered tremulously, blinking back her tears.

Suddenly, he realized he wanted to make the sun shine for her. He wanted to give her the stars and the moon. But all he could do right now was help her find her lost dog. The sun and the moon and the stars would have to wait. "You're welcome," he said softly. "Go get changed," he added. "I'll wait here."

* * *

She tossed her shorts on the floor and jerked her jeans out of the drawer. Her sandals were kicked aside as she shoved her feet into socks and shoes. It had taken her less than three minutes. The light on the answering machine was a steady red. There were no calls. *Please,* she whispered to no one in particular as she grabbed Jean-Luc's leash off its hook and crammed it in her pocket. *Find Jean-Luc and call me.* The screen door smacked shut behind her as she leapt down the porch steps.

And there, she saw Ray, leaning against his car, waiting for her. Ray who had made her angry enough to spit, yet who had also spent a whole day fixing her outlets. Ray who had eaten *baba ganoush* without complaint, even though she could tell he didn't like it. Ray who had teased her, had laughed with her. And almost kissed her. He had come to her aid just when she needed him most. Maybe Delphine's prince wouldn't be an emissary from the Wicked Wizard after all. Maybe he would help the princess rescue her faithful companion, Halcyon, from the clutches of a dreaded and dastardly dragon. Then she saw the ladder. "Why is that here?"

"I brought it. It's supposed to rain this evening, so I thought I'd clean out your gutters for you."

She felt her eyes grow large. "My gutters?" she asked faintly. "That's very kind of you." No one had ever offered to clean out her gutters for her.

"And I have some things for you," he said.

"For me?" she asked. "What is it?"

He reached in the window of his car and drew out a plastic bag. Circus peanuts.

"I bought these on the way over here."

The tears that she'd thought were turned off came in a flood again. He was just so nice. He was the nicest man in the world. "I love these things," she said through a clogged throat.

"I know," he murmured. "And I have something else." He reached into his pants pocket and drew out something in his closed hand. "It's smaller than a bread box."

She held her hand out and he placed something in it. It was a small black metal box, with a magnet on the bottom. "It's a spare key magnetic holder thingy," she said in wonder.

"Yes, it is."

She looked up at him, expecting to see amusement in his eyes. But she saw something else. All the curtains on his soul were open, and she saw something warm and dark. She gave up the war with her tears, and immediately, his arms were around her, holding her close while she cried. A button on his shirt pressed into her cheek but she didn't care. She cried because he was going to clean out her gutters, and because he brought her circus peanuts for the simple reason that he knew she liked them. And because he bought her a spare key magnetic holder thingy. That was a stupid reason to cry, she told herself, but she cried anyway. She cried because she'd been so impatient to get her rubber burned that she hadn't thought to check the latch on the gate, so it was her fault that Jean-Luc had escaped. She cried because Ray's mother had died when he was twelve and he had lived with a foster family and had grown up to be the nicest man she'd ever known. She cried because when she was fifteen years old her mother had died before Sylvie could tell her how much she loved her. And because she still missed her mother like the dickens. She cried because it had been so very long since anyone had held her and it felt so good. She cried because the dragons in her life had been winning.

And Ray held her and let her cry.

He reached into his car to bring out tissues for her and let her cry until the tears had dried up, leaving sniffles and gulps in their place. She was left feeling drained, yet somehow more hopeful. After all, the dragons might be winning, but now, for this battle, Ray was with her.

She gave her nose one last inelegant blow. "Thanks," she told him, knowing that her eyes were bright red. "I needed that."

"Crying can be very cathartic," he agreed soberly.

Hand in hand, they made their way around her garage to the fields beyond. Determined, they shoved through the tangle of weeds, trompling down the tall grasses in their path. "Someday I'm going to get rid of all this bushy weedy stuff," she told him, trying to explain, "and plant a garden in this jungle."

"Two mighty explorers," Ray said with a grin as he flattened a young prickly bush with his foot. "Off to find a missing dog."

"We need Madeleine and her dogs," Sylvie added.

"More dogs?"

"Madeleine's dogs are bona fide search and rescue dogs," she explained. "They're Newfs. She got them from Karen when they were puppies. Then she trained them. They live in Colorado and track down people who are lost in the mountains."

"Sounds like a good thing for dogs to do. Watch those nails, they'll go right through your shoe." He pointed near her feet.

Sylvie stepped over the board. "Ugly things, rusty nails."

Ray stopped, stood gazing at the board for a moment. He picked it up, then turned it over so the rusty nails were pointing into the ground instead of in the air. He stepped on the board to drive the nails in the ground. "If I had a hammer," he said, "I'd pound them down flat. But right now, this is the best I can do."

They waded on through the fields, stopping now and again to call Jean-Luc. There was no answer.

"You need to teach your dog to come when he's called," Ray said emphatically.

"I know. I talked to Tanner about it. He says he'll show me a way I can do it so that Jean-Luc thinks it's a game."

"Good idea." Ray stood for a moment, surveying the field around him. "I'd say we're about halfway through, what do you think?"

"Those trees, over there." She pointed to the far end of the field. "That's where I've found him before. The wretched beast."

"What's on the other side of those trees?"

"Another field. Like this one. Then another row of trees, and another field. Et cetera, et cetera, et cetera."

He looked at her, confusion clearly written across the planes of his face.

"Yul Brenner in *The King and I,*" she explained, and they tromped on.

"Looks like I'll have to wait until after this rain to do your gutters," he said as the sky darkened and a light sprinkling of rain began.

"That's okay. They'll still be clogged tomorrow."

After a few more minutes, she stopped tromping and called for Jean-Luc again, listening intently for any answering woof. The only thing she heard was an ominous rumble of distant thunder.

"Oh no," she cried. "Not thunder. He's terrified of thunder. Jean-Luc! Where are you?"

"Jean-Luc, here, boy!" Ray hollered.

Then the rains came, pouring down. In seconds they were soaked as they continued to slog through the field.

Lightning and thunder came closer and closer in a game of atmospheric chase.

"Jean-Luc," Sylvie hollered again and again, rain streaming across her face like tears. Or maybe they were tears. Jean-Luc would be frantic in the thunderstorm. He might even be too terrified to answer her. "Jean-Luc!" She could just picture him, terrified, huddling under some bush or something, desperate to get away from the thunder. "Jean-Luc!" she tried to call, but her voice gave out.

Ray took over. "Jean-Luc!" His voice boomed over the pounding rain.

Then she heard it. A yip. Sylvie whipped her head around toward the line of trees.

"Jean-Luc!"

The yip sounded again.

"This way." Ray grabbed her hand and she stumbled after him through the brush and rain, heading for the trees.

"Jean-Luc!" she called hoarsely, "We're coming!"

"Jean-Luc," Ray shouted.

They were answered by another bark.

They burst out of the brush to come upon the row of trees.

"Where are you?" Sylvie called.

She heard a whimper.

"There!" Ray said, pointing.

And there she saw her dog. Huddled, trembling, under the overhanging arms of a huge and ancient berry bush.

She bent down.

"Hi, sweetie," she crooned, reaching for him. Thorns pulled at her arms, leaving long scratches, but she didn't care. She only wanted her dog.

Then the thorns were gone. She looked up. Ray stood next to her, holding back the thorny branches with his bare hands. Not even Mel Gibson had ever looked so glorious to her.

"Thanks," she whispered.

"You're welcome," he answered.

She turned her attention back to her dog. "Come here, you. Let's get you out of this bush." She was coaxing him out when another clap of thunder boomed. This one was overhead. Jean-Luc panicked, and dug his legs in, trying to scoot farther under the bush.

Sylvie threw herself down on her belly and reached for him. She got her hand around his collar and dragged him toward her. She threw her arms around her trembling dog, not caring that he was wet and muddy. She had him back again. He was safe.

"Jean-Luc, you creep. You ran away. You know better than that. No, don't try that innocent act with me, buster," she chided him, putting all her love for him in her voice. She hoisted him onto her hip, and with the other hand, pulled his leash from her pocket. Ray took it from her and snapped it firmly on Jean-

Luc's collar. "Thanks," she told him again.

"No problem."

"You're in the doghouse, buster," she told her shivering poodle. "And you get a bath and a haircut tonight. That's what you get for running away and scaring me half to death."

"He's really impressed, I can tell."

Sylvie squinted up at him, standing tall in spite of the drenching rain. "Are you teasing me?"

"Yes, I am." Then he added in a softer voice, "Do you mind?"

She was caught up in his gaze, as Jean-Luc was caught up in her arms. She knew Ray would not let her go, just like she would not let go of her dog. Did she mind? Did chickens have lips? Did rubber stamps grow on trees? "No," she whispered back.

He put his arm around her. "It's wet out here. Let's go home."

"So how do we give this guy a bath?" Ray hoped he didn't sound too breathless. Hauling around a mailbag all day was one thing. Carrying a standard poodle, a wet poodle no less, was altogether another. For one thing, poodles did not come with shoulder straps. For another, mailbags didn't flail and thrash about in panic when they heard thunder. He shifted Jean-Luc in his arms to get a better hold. He was glad he'd insisted on carrying the dog. There was no way they could have let him walk. Not in this thunderstorm. He'd have hit the end of the leash and kept going. Sylvie simply wasn't strong enough to carry him, not in his turbulent emotional state.

"Usually I comb him out thoroughly first. Poodles are easier to wash when they're free of mats and junk. But he's so filthy that I think I'll just toss him in the washing machine." She slanted him a grin.

He caught it and tossed it right back. "He's French. Isn't he dry clean only?"

"Poodles are German," Sylvie insisted. "Very washable."

"Don't they shrink in the dryer?"

"They're preshrunk."

Thunder blasted across the sky.

Terrified, Jean-Luc trying to take a dive out of Ray's arms.

"Cool it, dog," Ray muttered, struggling mightily to keep hold of him. "The thunder can't hurt you. It's the lightning that you have to worry about. Besides, we're almost home. See, there's your back door."

Jean-Luc trembled.

"I don't know how I can possibly thank you."

"All part of our friendly service, ma'am. You know. Snow and sleet and all that."

"I don't think there's anything about terrified poodles in the postal code, though."

"You just haven't read the whole thing." His arms and back ached with the unaccustomed strain.

"Have you?" she asked.

"No," he answered shortly. Jean-Luc started to struggle again. Ray tried to shift his grip. "But I'm sure there's something about poodles in there. I'll look in the index on Monday."

"Are you sure he's not too heavy? With your ankle and all?"

"My ankle is fine," he insisted. He hoped it was fine. Just a few more yards and he'd be able to put Jean-Luc down. He'd carried lots of strange things to Sylvie's door before, but never anything as awkward as fifty pounds of petrified poodle. Cans of SPAM were nothing compared to Jean-Luc.

"Let me get this for you." She rushed ahead of him to push the door open.

Finally. They were inside. The door was closed. He could put the dog down. He did. The furry beast made a mad, mud-splattering dash for the bathroom, and the safety of the spot behind the toilet.

Ray closed his eyes in relief and sagged against the closed door. "So where do we do the deed?"

"What deed?" she asked.

He loved watching her eyebrows when she was puzzled. Sometimes they arched, and sometimes they dove. Right now they dove together over the bridge of her nose. "Give him his bath," he answered.

He watched in satisfaction as her eyebrows

arched high and her eyes grew wide. "You don't have to help me give him his bath."

"I know. But I'm so wet I might as well. Besides, when I do get my own dog, I'll need to know how to bathe him. This will be good experience."

"Have you ever bathed a dog?"

"Only with a garden hose in the backyard."

"Well, are you sure?" she sounded doubtful.

"Of course I'm sure." He rolled up the sleeves of his already wet shirt. "Lady, bring on this dog and let us bathe him."

As soon as she hung up the phone after talking to Karen, Sylvie heard the water in the shower go off. She ducked quickly into the laundry room to turn on the washing machine. Ray would be out soon. He'd helped her comb the burrs and prickers out of Jean-Luc's curls, then bathe him. Since Jean-Luc was not particularly fond of baths, Ray had emerged from the experience even more wet and muddy than before. There was nothing she could do but offer him her shower, and offer to wash his clothes. She hadn't expected him to accept, but he had. But, he insisted, she was as wet and muddy as he was, and it was her house, and she was the lady, so she would take her shower first.

"Are you being a chauvinist?" she'd challenged.

"No. I'm being chivalrous." *What a great guy!*

There'd been a glimmer in his eyes when

she'd offered him her terrycloth bathrobe to wear after his shower, until his clothes were dry. It was ankle length on her, so it should fit him, and after all, it wasn't pink.

Her bathrobe was blue. Now, as he stood in the doorway to her kitchen, wearing nothing but her bathrobe—and she knew that was all he was wearing because she'd put his clothes, all of them, along with hers, in her washing machine—she almost dropped the eggs. He was beautiful. Even more beautiful than the prince. She would draw him standing like that, leaning against the doorjamb, his hands in the pockets. His damp towel-tousled hair curling, the bare hint of stubble on his cheek. But this was a drawing she would not turn into a stamp. Oh no, this one was for her alone. And there was no doubt that it would be sexy, sensual. And when he ultimately left her, she thought out of habit, she would have the drawing to remember him by.

What makes you think he will leave? she asked herself.

What makes you think he will stay? she countered.

The expression in his eyes.

She looked again into their deep blue depths, and she knew she was right. He would stay. And even if he didn't—but she knew he would—he was worth the risk. Her biggest, most feared dragon, the mother of all her dragons, sensing its imminent death, roared in furious protest.

But she stood firm against it. She raised her mighty sword and with all her strength, thrust it deeply into the dragon's heart.

"You're still holding those eggs," he said.

She looked down at her hands and noticed, with surprise, that he was right. She was still holding the carton of eggs. Eggs had babies in them. She'd just vanquished the mother dragon. Were there any eggs in the nest? And if there were, if the baby dragons hatched, could they be tamed and made friendly? If they didn't have a vicious mother dragon to teach them to be nasty? Could the Princes Delphine maybe, after defeating a dragon that had been the scourge of the countryside for many years, find that dragon's nest, discover dragon eggs, and hatch them? Maybe dragons went through an imprinting kind of thing. Like geese. They could imprint on the princess and Halcyon. Instantly, images for new stamps flocked and flurried around her mind.

"Sylvie? Are you okay?"

"Oh, yeah," she mumbled, blushing. "I was thinking." She set the eggs on the counter and turned back to the refrigerator. Not only that, but Delphine could find out that the prince she'd saved really wasn't an emissary for the Wicked Wizard, he was only pretending to be one. So Delphine could have her prince and her dragonlets, too. And Sylvie could have Ray. Ray who was the way life came from the sun to the earth. What could be better than this? The cold air felt good on her burning face. But she couldn't stay in the refrigerator forever. She had a man to feed.

"Not much to feed you for supper," she told him as she pulled out a pitcher of iced tea. He crossed the kitchen in one step and took it from her. She turned back to the refrigerator. Katie had cleaned it out and had thrown away everything unidentifiable, which was almost everything in it. "Tomato and cheese and ham omelets. Do you like omelets? Jean-Luc, get your nose out of here and go back and lie down on your towel. I love you, but you smell like wet dog and shampoo. And when you shake yourself you get drops of doggy-smelling water all over the kitchen."

Ray chuckled as Jean-Luc, with a very dejected look on his face, slunk back to his towel under the table.

"It's an act. Don't feel sorry for him," Sylvie cautioned Ray, handing him a glass of iced tea. Only instead of a glass, the iced tea was in a mason jar. "He'll go to great lengths to take advantage of you. So do you want an omelet?"

He didn't want food, Ray thought, he wanted her. Still, he was raised to be polite. "I like omelets," he told her.

"I make terrific omelets."

"I'm sure you do." He was. He refused to wonder if she put flowers in her omelets.

"Why don't you find something to put on the

CD player while I get this show on the road," she suggested. "Instead of standing there staring at me."

"I'm not staring."

"Yes, you are."

So he went to stare at her CD collection. Lots of things he didn't recognize. Lots of things he ignored. Then he found something that looked promising. He picked it up. *Songs of Seduction*. He had no idea what these songs were, but maybe he'd put it on later. And if they even half lived up to their title he'd be a happy man. Hold it, seduction was not a good thing to think about right after a shower, in her house, wearing nothing but her bathrobe—her bathrobe that carried her special scent—while she was in the kitchen still damp around the edges from her shower, wearing some sort of soft sweat clothes. He'd never seen sweat clothes that looked so soft and touchable. No, thinking about seduction was not a good thing at all. Well, it really *was* a good thing, but it would also be embarrassing as all get out. Right now he needed music for dinner. Something non-seductive, something safe. Ah, there was Bach. She liked Bach, he remembered. So did he.

He pressed the open button on the CD player. There was a disc in the frame. He picked it up and looked at it. Puccini. Ah, there was the case for it. He put the disc in the case. Now, to put it away. Did she keep her CDs in any order? None that he could tell. He sighed. How did she find what she was looking for? He set his chosen CD in the player, slid the drawer in, and pressed the play button. Her house was filled with Bach.

"Great choice, Novino," she called to him.

"Glad you approve," he called back. Yes, he thought, this was a start. But there was something else he had to do. He headed back to the kitchen. To Sylvie.

She stood in front of the stove, dropping bits of chopped tomato into a pan.

"Sylvie."

She looked up at him, the impish expression perfectly comfortable on her face. Then he glanced into the pan, at the omelet. She had dropped the bits of tomato onto the eggs in the shape of a heart. Think safe, he told himself quickly. Think Bach.

"Sylvie," he said again. His voice was hoarse, she thought. Maybe he was coming down with a cold. Not surprising after traipsing around in a field in a thunderstorm all afternoon.

"Yes, Ray."

He cleared his throat. "This past week, I've thought about our disagreement." The hesitation in his voice was obvious.

She slanted a glance at him, then went back to the omelet pan. "What about it?" She filled in the heart with bits of ham.

"I think a group of your friends are up to something."

"Why?"

"Every day this week, I've received an anonymous *thing* in the mail."

"Thing? What kind of thing?"

He cleared his throat again, and this time, when she took another peek at him, she could see a red blush creeping up his neck and face. He was blushing, she thought in amusement. He was actually blushing. Then her gaze fell to where the front of her bathrobe closed. His chest. It looked warm and—She took a deep breath and willed her heart to slow down.

"What kind of thing?" she asked again.

"Cake mix," he said, still not looking at her. "A wooden spoon."

"Someone is sending you cake mixes?" she asked incredulously.

"Not just a cake mix." He took a few deep breaths. "You see, the things they've been sending me have gone along with the things they've been sending you."

"How do you know what—oh." Realization struck her like a brick. "You work in the post office. Of course you'd know what people sent me."

"I'm not the only one who knows. Everyone in the post office. You see, when you put the things they sent to you with the things they sent to me, they—whoever they are—are trying to tell us something."

"I know who they are. It's no big secret." She slid a spatula under the edge of the omelet to check for doneness. Not quite.

"So who are they?"

"A group of my stamping friends. Every month we decide on a theme and send stuff to one another. This month we decided to send stuff with a heart theme. Only I guess I got mixed up about this one because I thought we were doing a body parts thing, and I had those hands just about ready to send out . . ." She let her voice trail off as she slowly put the pieces together. No. They wouldn't. They wouldn't dare. They couldn't. Could they? "What besides the spoon and cake mix did they send you?"

"A mixing bowl. And today I got two things, a record, old vinyl, and a candle. The candle, incidentally, fits perfectly in the candlestick they sent you. But it was the record that clinched it." He reached up to scratch the back of his neck.

"So tell me about this record," Sylvie said. "What is it? Where is it?" She kept one eye on his as she carefully flipped the omelet. She simply would not look lower than his face. At least, not until the omelet was finished.

"It's all in the backseat of my car. I'd go out and bring it all in to show you, but I don't think your neighbors should see me wearing your bathrobe."

"Yeah. That's a good point. But tell me, what is this record?"

"It's an old recording of some romantic songs. The guys at work are all taking bets about what will come next. They think you and I are being set up for a romantic evening."

"Why, those rats!" she exclaimed softly. "Where in the world did they get this idea?" The only people who knew about Ray were here in Hartley. Suddenly she knew. "Jessie!" she exclaimed.

"Jessie?"

"Jessie knows Madeleine. And Jessie has a warped sense of humor." She set the pan back on the stove with more of a bang than she'd intended. "Jessie said she'd talked to Madeleine, but I didn't think anything of it."

"I thought she was up to something," Ray said thoughtfully. "I saw her Saturday morning. She tried to encourage me to stay home another week. I thought she was up to something then."

How could one of her best friends do this to her? Sylvie thought in exasperation. And after that time with the guy with the Irish Wolfhounds Jessie promised she'd never interfere again.

"Anyway," Ray said, "this week, the guys at work have all had something to look forward to."

"What was that?" Sylvie asked, not really listening, not really caring. She was still thinking about Jessie and all sorts of medieval tortures.

"Wondering what's coming next. Hey, are you listening to me?"

She realized he was gazing into her eyes with incredible intensity. For a moment she couldn't breathe, couldn't do anything to escape his gaze.

"You're right," she said breathlessly, breaking away from his gaze and opening the cupboard. Taking them from inside, she held out two plates. "It *is* thoughtless of us. We've never really thought of what it would mean to your job. We only thought it would be fun to do. So we did it."

He took the plates from her and set them on the table. "What are you talking about?" he asked with a frown.

"Sending cool stuff in the mail." She opened the silverware drawer.

"It's okay. Don't stop."

Now it was her turn to frown. "Don't stop what?"

"Sending your things in the mail. It's what I was trying to tell you. The guys at the post office think it's funny. They get a big kick out of it." He took the silverware from her, too.

"But what about you?" No way could she imagine him being anything but annoyed.

He looked up from where he was setting the table and gave her a grin, somewhat shamefacedly. "I guess I started to get into the spirit of it all, too. I found myself looking forward to seeing what they'd think up next." He shrugged apologetically. "Someone at the post office told me I needed to loosen up. Said that our jobs were safe because, as you'd said, most people don't have the imagination to send 'cool stuff' in the mail. He told me that I was a stick-in-the-mud."

"Who told you that?" she asked incredulously. "You're not a stick-in-the-mud. In fact," she found herself bustling to his defense, ready to fight this infidel who obviously had no sense. "In fact, you're the nicest man I've ever known. And I—" She grabbed the words before they were out. Whew! She breathed in relief. She stopped herself before she told him she was in love with him. No, Sylvie, this would not be good. Not yet, anyway. "I think you're terrific," she amended. She dropped two slices of bread in the toaster and shoved the lever down.

"Thanks for that vote of confidence."

"You're welcome, but you still didn't tell me what you think."

"You were right that coming upon something unexpected, something silly, something absurd, it does make people smile. So go ahead."

"We really don't need your approval, you know," she told him smugly.

"I know. As long as the object has the correct postage, and isn't explosive or illegal."

She grinned at him. "Still, it's nice to know that you're not going to think I don't have any sense."

He stood very still. "Sylvie Taylor," he said in a soft voice that sent wiggles of shivers up her spine. His eyes were darkening. "I think you're wonderful."

So this was what it's like, Sylvie thought in absolute wonder, *when books say that time stood still.*

The dinger dinged. Time was again. And the omelet was done.

Jean-Luc, from his towel under the table, whined. It was a short, tiny whine. The kind that was meant to earn himself a cookie. Or an omelet. Or anything else, for that matter. He wasn't particular.

"You're hungry, are you, guy?" Ray asked, bending down so he could see under the table. Sylvie kept a surreptitious watch, in case his—her—bathrobe proved to be too short for such activity. It wasn't. Rats! See if she ever got another bathrobe from Victoria's Secret!

"Doesn't Sylvie have any ice cubes left?" he asked her dog. "Or something equally frozen? Vegetables, perhaps?" Jean-Luc wagged his tail encouragingly and licked his lips.

"You men always stick together?" Sylvie asked. She cut the omelet in half, and carefully slid it onto the plates. The toast popped up with a tinny sound of the toaster.

Ray's answer was a cheeky grin. "Absolutely," he added.

"Frozen peas in there." She reached for the toast and jerked her head in the direction of the freezer. "But only a couple of them. And make him shake your hand first. There's no free lunch."

"Does Jean-Luc like to go on long car trips?"

he asked, his voice sounding casual. "Is there a twist tie for the peas?"

She raised her eyebrows. "No. I decided it was easier to just forget the twist ties and leave the bag open. I just reach in, snatch a handful, and slam the freezer door closed. They're not around long enough to get freezer burn. How long is a long car trip?"

"Bigger than a bread box. Jean-Luc, shake."

Jean-Luc, ever enthusiastic for frozen peas, if not for shaking hands, scrambled to a sitting position and held out his paw.

"Good boy," Ray said.

Jean-Luc slobbered noisily over the frozen pea.

"Hey, you do that very nicely," Sylvie praised him. "You ought to train dogs."

"Maybe someday I will. A long car trip would be, say, to New Jersey. Jean-Luc, shake. Good boy."

"What's in New Jersey?" Sylvie asked carefully. She pointed to a chair. "Sit," she said. He sat. Good guy. So did she.

Once again, his gaze reached out and took hold of her soul. "Helen and Phil, my foster parents. I'd like them to meet you. I'd like you to meet them."

"I think," she said softly, breathlessly, knowing that he'd given her a gift that was more precious than powdered unicorn's horn, more rare than a fertile dragon's egg, "that Jean-Luc would love a long car trip. And so would I."

* * *

After supper he went into the living room to put on the other CD.

"So do you think we should take their advice?" She had followed him.

"What advice?" he asked as he pressed the play button.

"To have a romantic evening."

Was it his imagination, or was the impish expression really replaced by something else? Something sensual, something private, something promising.

"I think it is excellent advice," he whispered as he reached out to smooth back her hair. Then he stepped closer to her, or maybe it was she who stepped closer to him. He wasn't sure. But now he was sure of the expression in her eyes, and in her face, and in her hands that were drawing them closer and closer together.

Her lips were as fine as he'd thought they'd be. Smooth and silky and soft, tasting slightly of lemonade. He could explore her mouth forever. Her hands were exploring his back. It felt good. His hands were slithering through her hair. That felt good, too. He liked the little sounds she made, little pleasure sounds. Then her mouth was gone from his. This was not good. In protest, he opened his eyes.

She was so far away from him, at least an inch. Her eyes had turned smoky and deep. Mysterious and untamed. When she smiled, it was the slow smile of an enchantress, of a magical creature.

"Ray," she murmured, her voice deep and soft.

"Hmm?" he answered lazily, entranced beyond all reason.

"Nice choice of music."

"I thought you might like it."

"Do you want to?" Her lips were against his. Her voice was deep and whispery and made him throb.

"Do I want to what?" But he knew exactly what he wanted to do.

"Seduce me."

"Yes, I do." And he did. And it was good.

"Are you going to turn me into a stamp?" he asked in the magical time after.

"I already did," she murmured, not quite sure she was awake. "Hey, there's a storm brewing," she mumbled.

"That's not a storm, that's your waterbed," he said as he stretched his long, warm length of leg against hers. "So, where is this stamp?" His lips were doing incredible things to the back of her neck. Delicious things. Delightful things. She shivered. "Where is it?" he asked again.

"Upstairs."

"Will you show it to me?"

Her eyes popped open. "Right now?" She thought men were supposed to go to sleep afterward.

"Yes," he answered in a slow sultry voice. "Do you have a problem with that?" He swirled his tongue around on a spot just below her ear. She tingled all over. He was toying with her, was he? Well, she'd show him.

"No," she said brightly. "No problem at all." She leapt up, grabbed his—her—bathrobe, slung it around her body and scampered giggling up the stairs to the sound of his frustrated groan. Silly man. Thought he could tease her.

Jean-Luc followed her up the stairs, then back down again. He was almost walking backward, trying to make eye contact with her, trying desperately to tell her something. "You want a cookie?" she guessed. She was right.

In a few minutes she was back, with him, next to Ray. But his—her—*the* bathrobe was on properly, and the knot pulled tight. She was on top of the comforter. Along with Jean-Luc, who was crunching a big cookie and dribbling crumbs. "Here it is," she said, holding out for him the drawing of the prince in pain. And with it, on another sheet of paper, a preliminary scene of the prince, with the succoring maiden, a hound at her side, the stamped crowd of onlookers peering curiously through the castle window.

"This is me?" he asked, reaching for the paper.

"This is just the drawing. I sent a copy of it away to be made into a matrix. That's the thing that . . . oh, forget it. When it comes back I'll show you. Anyway, when it comes back, I put it in Leonard with the sheet of rubber. I cook it for a set amount of time, and when it's done, voilà! We have rubber stamps." He didn't say anything for a long time. Well, it seemed like a long time to her. She glanced at him nervously. "Don't you like it?"

He was staring at the drawing, studying it, them, both of them, intently. "It's incredible," he whispered, not taking his eyes from the drawing. "Jessie said you were a talented artist, and I've seen some of your stamps," he continued. He shook his head in amazement. "The detail in the clothing . . . The expression on their faces. You are very good."

She cleared her throat. "Um, Ray?" she said nervously. She wasn't sure whether or not she should show this one to him. But, if they were going to be lovers—and they were already lovers—then he'd see it eventually, and if he was going to not like it, she'd rather know now instead of later, after she'd already turned it into rubber.

He looked up from the drawings.

She felt a blush start from somewhere deep and sweep over her neck and face. "Um. I did another drawing. I haven't sent it away yet, so if you would rather me not turn it into a stamp, I won't. I really don't know if I even will. It's sort of . . . um . . . well . . . you'll see." She handed him the third piece of paper.

There was a quick intake of breath when he

saw it. She didn't see his face, because she didn't want to look at him, not yet. She knew that drawing as if it had been embedded in her heart. For it was embedded in her heart.

The drawing was of a little boy, seen from the back, dejected, feeling totally and completely alone. He had curly dark hair. He was standing before a woman, soft and round, who was bending over to be on his level, her arms outstretched toward him, enough to make him feel welcome, yet still giving him room to turn away, as if she wasn't sure what his reaction would be. There was an expression of mother-love and compassion on her face, and something that said even if the little boy rejected her, she'd understand, and would be there when he was ready to come to her. Though both figures were dressed in the medieval peasant clothing of Delphine's world, it was a drawing of Ray and Helen. Or close enough.

Without a word, Ray reached out and gripped her hand, hard. He slowly drew her hand to his lips and pressed a kiss upon her fingers.

"Maybe, if I don't turn it into a stamp, I could clean it up a bit," she said quietly. "I could mat it, put it in a frame, and . . . um . . . maybe Helen would like it. When we go there. As a hostess gift, sort of." The silence stretched into forevers before he spoke.

"Helen will love it. And so do I."

* * *

Many hours later he spoke again. "We need to send them something," he said lazily. The waterbed sloshed as he stretched. Jean-Luc, disturbed from his short nap, raised his head and gave them a look of utter disgust. He clambered down from the waterbed and went to curl up on Sylvie's clothes, which were in a heap on the floor.

"Who them?" she asked just as lazily. She didn't want to send anyone anything right now. She wanted to stay here, with him, forever.

"Your wacky friends."

"Why?" And why did he insist on talking when there were so many other things they could do? And so many things they just had done. She liked the things they'd just done. She wanted to do those things again. She smiled to herself at the thought.

"To thank them for helping us with our romantic evening."

She punched a pillow into a head-propping shape. "Okay," she agreed, "we can send them something." Then a hint of suspicion hovered around in her mind. "What did you have in mind?"

He rolled over to face her, making the waterbed dance again. A glint of mischief danced in his eyes. "Can we send them pieces of cake?"

She considered. Cake was good. "Fake cake?"

"Yes," he answered, running the tip of one finger down the length of her leg.

"Pieces of plastic cake?"

"Yes," he told her as he trailed his fingers slowly up the inside of her thigh.

"Naked cake in the mail?"

"Yes." He dusted her shoulder and neck with billions and billions of tiny kisses.

She nodded. "Naked is good."

"Naked is very good," he murmured. And he showed her just how good naked could be.

IT'S A DOG'S LIFE ROMANCE

Stray Hearts by Annie Kimberlin. A busy veterinarian, Melissa is comfortable around her patients—but when it comes to men, too often her instincts have her barking up the wrong tree. So she's understandably wary when Peter Winthrop, who accidentally hits a Shetland sheepdog with his car, shows more than just a friendly interest in her. But as their relationship grows more intimate she finds herself hoping that he has room for one more lost soul in his home.
___52221-7 $5.50 US/$6.50 CAN

Rosamunda's Revenge by Emma Craig. At first, Tacita Grantham thinks that Jedediah Hardcastle is a big brute of a man with no manners whatsoever. But when she sees he'll do anything to protect her—even rescue her beloved Rosamunda—she knows his bark is worse than his bite. And when she first feels his kiss—she knows he is the only man who'll ever touch her heart.
___52213-6 $5.50 US/$6.50 CAN

Dorchester Publishing Co., Inc.
P.O. Box 6640
Wayne, PA 19087-8640

Please add $1.75 for shipping and handling for the first book and $.50 for each book thereafter. NY, NYC, and PA residents, please add appropriate sales tax. No cash, stamps, or C.O.D.s. All orders shipped within 6 weeks via postal service book rate.
Canadian orders require $2.00 extra postage and must be paid in U.S. dollars through a U.S. banking facility.

Name______________________________________
Address____________________________________
City_____________________State______Zip__________
I have enclosed $________ in payment for the checked book(s).
Payment must accompany all orders. ❑ Please send a free catalog.

Christmas means more than just puppy love.

"SHAKESPEARE AND THE THREE KINGS"
Victoria Alexander

Requiring a trainer for his three inherited dogs, Oliver Stanhope meets D. K. Lawrence, and is in for the Christmas surprise—and love—of his life.

"ATHENA'S CHRISTMAS TAIL" Nina Coombs

Mercy wants her marriage to be a match of the heart—and with the help of her very determined dog, Athena, she finds just the right magic of the holiday season.

"AWAY IN A SHELTER" Annie Kimberlin

A dedicated volunteer, Camille Campbell still doesn't want to be stuck in an animal shelter on Christmas Eve—especially with a handsome helper whose touch leaves her starry-eyed.

"MR. WRIGHT'S CHRISTMAS ANGEL"
Miriam Raftery

When Joy's daughter asks Santa for a father, she knows she's in trouble—until a trip to Alaska takes them on a journey into the arms of Nicholas Wright and his amazing dog.

___52235-7 $5.99 US/$6.99 CAN

Dorchester Publishing Co., Inc.
P.O. Box 6640
Wayne, PA 19087-8640

Please add $1.75 for shipping and handling for the first book and $.50 for each book thereafter. NY, NYC, and PA residents, please add appropriate sales tax. No cash, stamps, or C.O.D.s. All orders shipped within 6 weeks via postal service book rate.
Canadian orders require $2.00 extra postage and must be paid in U.S. dollars through a U.S. banking facility.

Name____
Address______________________________________
City____________________State________Zip________
I have enclosed $_________ in payment for the checked book(s).
Payment must accompany all orders. ❑ Please send a free catalog.

DON'T MISS *LOVE SPELL'S* WAGGING TALES OF LOVE!

Man's Best Friend by Nina Coombs. Fido senses his dark-haired mistress's heart is wrapped up in old loves gone astray–and it is up to him, her furry friend, to weave the warp and woof of fate into the fabric of paradise. Brad Ferris is perfect. But Jenny isn't an easy human to train, and swatting her with newspapers isn't an option. So Fido will have to rely on good old-fashioned dog sense to lead the two together. For Fido knows that only in Brad's arms will Jenny unleash feelings which have been caged for too long.

___52205-5 $5.50 US/$6.50 CAN

Molly in the Middle by Stobie Piel. Molly is a Scottish Border collie, and unless she finds some other means of livelihood for her lovely mistress, Miren, she'll be doomed to chase after stupid sheep forever. That's why she is tickled pink when handsome Nathan MacCullum comes into Miren's life, and she knows from Miren's pink cheeks and distracted gaze that his hot kisses are something special. Now she'll simply have to show the silly humans that true love–and a faithful house pet–are all they'll ever need.

___52193-8 $5.99 US/$6.99 CAN

Dorchester Publishing Co., Inc.
P.O. Box 6640
Wayne, PA 19087-8640

Please add $1.75 for shipping and handling for the first book and $.50 for each book thereafter. NY, NYC, and PA residents, please add appropriate sales tax. No cash, stamps, or C.O.D.s. All orders shipped within 6 weeks via postal service book rate.
Canadian orders require $2.00 extra postage and must be paid in U.S. dollars through a U.S. banking facility.

Name____
Address______________________________________
City__________________________State______Zip____________
I have enclosed $__________ in payment for the checked book(s).
Payment must accompany all orders. ☐ Please send a free catalog.

DON'T MISS OTHER STAR-STUDDED *LOVE SPELL* ROMANCES!

Sword of MacLeod by Karen Fox. When his daughter leaves their planet to find their family's legendary sword, Beckett MacLeod is forced to enlist the help of the best tracker in the galaxy—and the most beautiful woman he has ever laid eyes on. But Beckett has no patience for the free-spirited adventurer—until one star-studded evening she gives him a glimpse of the final frontier. Raven doesn't like working with anyone, but being in desperate need of funds, she agrees to help Beckett, thinking the assignment will be a piece of cake. Instead she finds herself thrown into peril with a man whose archaic ways are out of a history book—and whose tender kisses are something from her wildest dreams.

_52160-1 $4.99 US/$5.99 CAN

The Dawn Star by Stobie Piel. Seneca's sinewy strength and chiseled features touch a chord deep inside Nisa Calydon—reminding her of a love long gone, of the cruel betrayal of a foolish girl's naive faith. But she's all grown up now, and to avert a potentially disastrous war, she has kidnapped the virile off-worlder to fullfill her responsibility. But the more time she spends with the primitive warrior, the less sure she becomes of how she wants this assignment to end. For behind Seneca's brawn she finds a man of a surprisingly wise and compassionate nature, and in his arms she finds a passion like none she's ever known.

_52148-2 $5.50 US/$6.50 CAN

Dorchester Publishing Co., Inc.
P.O. Box 6640
Wayne, PA 19087-8640

Please add $1.75 for shipping and handling for the first book and $.50 for each book thereafter. NY, NYC, and PA residents, please add appropriate sales tax. No cash, stamps, or C.O.D.s. All orders shipped within 6 weeks via postal service book rate.
Canadian orders require $2.00 extra postage and must be paid in U.S. dollars through a U.S. banking facility.

Name______________________________________
Address____________________________________
City__________________State______Zip__________
I have enclosed $________ in payment for the checked book(s).
Payment must accompany all orders. ❑ Please send a free catalog.

MIRIAM RAFTERY

Taylor James's wrinkled Shar-Pei, Apollo, is always getting into trouble. But the young beauty never expects her mischievous puppy to lead her on the romantic adventure of a lifetime—from a dusty old Victorian attic to the strong arms of Nathaniel Stuart and his turn-of-the-century charm. One minute Taylor and Apollo are in modern-day San Francisco, and the next thing Taylor knows, a shift in the earth's crust, a wrinkle in time, and the lovely historian finds herself facing the terror of California's most infamous earthquake—and a love so monumental it threatens to shake the foundations of her world.

_52084-2 $4.99 US/$6.99 CAN

Dorchester Publishing Co., Inc.
P.O. Box 6640
Wayne, PA 19087-8640

Please add $1.75 for shipping and handling for the first book and $.50 for each book thereafter. NY, NYC, and PA residents, please add appropriate sales tax. No cash, stamps, or C.O.D.s. All orders shipped within 6 weeks via postal service book rate.
Canadian orders require $2.00 extra postage and must be paid in U.S. dollars through a U.S. banking facility.

Name____
Address______________________________________
City______________________State_______Zip__________
I have enclosed $__________ in payment for the checked book(s).
Payment must accompany all orders. ☐ Please send a free catalog.

Daughter of wealth and privilege, lovely Charlaine Kimball is known to Victorian society as the Ice Princess. But when a brash intruder dares to take a king's ransom in jewels from her private safe, indignation burns away her usual cool reserve. And when the handsome rogue presumes to steal a kiss from her untouched lips, forbidden longing sets her soul ablaze.

Illegitimate son of a penniless Frenchwoman, Devlin Rhodes is nothing but a lowly bounder to the British aristocrats who snub him. But his leapfrogging ambition engages him in a dangerous game. Now he will have to win Charlaine's hand in marriage–and have her begging for the kiss that will awaken his heart and transform him into the man he was always meant to be.

——52200-4 $5.99 US/$6.99 CAN

Dorchester Publishing Co., Inc.
P.O. Box 6640
Wayne, PA 19087-8640

Please add $1.75 for shipping and handling for the first book and $.50 for each book thereafter. NY, NYC, and PA residents, please add appropriate sales tax. No cash, stamps, or C.O.D.s. All orders shipped within 6 weeks via postal service book rate.
Canadian orders require $2.00 extra postage and must be paid in U.S. dollars through a U.S. banking facility.

Name____
Address______________________________________
City_____________________State________Zip____________
I have enclosed $__________in payment for the checked book(s).
Payment must accompany all orders. ☐ Please send a free catalog.

GIVE YOUR HEART TO THE GENTLE BEAST AND FOREVER SHARE LOVE'S SWEET FEAST

Raised amid a milieu of bountiful wealth and enlightened ideas, Callista Raleigh is more than a match for the radicals, rakes, and reprobates who rail against England's King George III. Then a sudden reversal of fortune brings into her life a veritable brute who craves revenge against her family almost as much as he hungers for her kiss. And even though her passionate foe conceals his face behind a hideous mask, Callista believes that he is merely a man, with a man's strengths and appetites. But when the love-starved stranger sweeps her away to his secret lair, Callista realizes that wits and reason aren't enough to conquer him—she'll need a desire both satisfying and true if beauty is to tame the beast.

_52143-1 $5.99 US/$6.99 CAN

Dorchester Publishing Co., Inc.
P.O. Box 6640
Wayne, PA 19087-8640

Please add $1.75 for shipping and handling for the first book and $.50 for each book thereafter. NY, NYC, and PA residents, please add appropriate sales tax. No cash, stamps, or C.O.D.s. All orders shipped within 6 weeks via postal service book rate.
Canadian orders require $2.00 extra postage and must be paid in U.S. dollars through a U.S. banking facility.

Name____
Address______________________________________
City_____________________State_______Zip________
I have enclosed $__________ in payment for the checked book(s).
Payment must accompany all orders. ☐ Please send a free catalog.

Midsummer Night's Magic

Four of Love Spell's hottest authors, four times the charm!

EMMA CRAIG

"MacBroom Sweeps Clean"

Stuck in an arranged marriage to a Scottish lord, Lily wonders if she'll ever find true love—until a wee Broonie decides to teach the couple a thing or two about Highland magic.

TESS MALLORY

"The Fairy Bride"

Visiting Ireland with her stuffy fiancé, Erin dreams she'll be swept into a handsome stranger's enchanted world—and soon long to be his fairy bride.

AMY ELIZABETH SAUNDERS

"Whatever You Wish"

A trip through time into the arms of an English lord might just be enough to convince Meredyth that maybe, just maybe, wishes do come true.

PAM McCUTCHEON

"The Trouble With Fairies"

Fun-loving Nick and straight-laced Kate have a marriage destined for trouble, until the fateful night Nick hires a family of Irish brownies to clean up his house—and his love life.

___52209-8 $5.50 US/$6.50 CAN

Dorchester Publishing Co., Inc.
P.O. Box 6640
Wayne, PA 19087-8640

Please add $1.75 for shipping and handling for the first book and $.50 for each book thereafter. NY, NYC, and PA residents, please add appropriate sales tax. No cash, stamps, or C.O.D.s. All orders shipped within 6 weeks via postal service book rate.
Canadian orders require $2.00 extra postage and must be paid in U.S. dollars through a U.S. banking facility.

Name______________________________
Address____________________________
City________________State______Zip________
I have enclosed $________ in payment for the checked book(s).
Payment must accompany all orders. ☐ Please send a free catalog.

ATTENTION ROMANCE CUSTOMERS!

SPECIAL TOLL-FREE NUMBER

1-800-481-9191

Call Monday through Friday

12 noon to 10 p.m.

Eastern Time

Get a free catalogue, join the Romance Book Club, and order books using your Visa, MasterCard, or Discover®

Leisure Books